EVIE

of the

DEEPTHORN

EVIE

of the

DEEPTHORN

ANDRÉ

BABYN

DUNDURN
TORONTO

Publisher: Scott Fraser | Acquiring editor: Rachel Spence | Editor: Shannon Whibbs
Cover design and illustration: Sophie Paas-Lang
Printer: Webcom, a division of Marquis Book Printing Inc.

Library and Archives Canada Cataloguing in Publication

Title: Evie of the Deepthorn / André Babyn
Names: Babyn, André, 1986- author.
Identifiers: Canadiana (print) 20190127201 | Canadiana (ebook) 2019012721X | ISBN
     9781459745575 (softcover) | ISBN 9781459745582 (PDF) | ISBN 9781459745599
     (EPUB)
Classification: LCC PS8603.A295 E95 2020 | DDC C813/.6—dc23

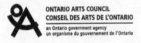 

We acknowledge the support of the Canada Council for the Arts and the Ontario Arts Council for our publishing program. We also acknowledge the financial support of the Government of Ontario, through the Ontario Book Publishing Tax Credit and Ontario Creates, and the Government of Canada.

Care has been taken to trace the ownership of copyright material used in this book. The author and the publisher welcome any information enabling them to rectify any references or credits in subsequent editions.

The publisher is not responsible for websites or their content unless they are owned by the publisher.

Printed and bound in Canada.

VISIT US AT

 dundurn.com | @dundurnpress | dundurnpress | dundurnpress

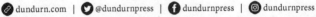

Dundurn
3 Church Street, Suite 500
Toronto, Ontario, Canada
M5E 1M2

For my parents, and their parents

Preface

I will begin by saying that I feel both as if I knew Kent very well and very little.

Sometimes we were like best friends who had been separated at a young age. Or like strangers sharing secret glances across a train. Two people trying to reach each other over an almost impossible distance. Contrary to some reports I've seen online, we were never lovers — only intimates drifting in and out of each other's lives.

Evie of the Deepthorn shares this ambiguity in many respects. Sometimes it felt like it was directed by an intelligence and order that was fully outside either's understanding, like we were keys working in the other's lock, moving Evie closer and closer to her final destination. When the final manuscript arrived at my door yesterday, after so many years of sitting in a drawer, I briefly entertained the fantasy that I was receiving a package from a world that was not quite my own, a world which neither of us had ever lived in or ever would.

Friends of mine who read the book long ago asked me, "Is this a ghost story?" And to that the only answer I had was "I don't know."

Maybe every story is.

There's a mystery at the heart of the novel, but the mystery is twofold. We could never quite figure out the influence that *Evie of the Deepthorn* had on us, the ways in which it seeped into our respective consciousnesses.

We could not quite agree on what it was, either.

The other mystery is the standard one: how to live. I'd be lying if I said I thought we came any closer to figuring that out.

Though *Evie* is a work of fiction, the events portrayed within are absolutely true, at least in the sense that they felt true to us. Sometimes that might seem hard to believe.

But there is rarely any ambiguity when it comes to the truth, or at least to how the truth feels, which is of course what is most important.

— Sarah Krause

One

Kent's Part

Then I had an idea and I started shouting at the top of my lungs, successively facing the four points of the compass. When my throat was absolutely paralyzed, I listened. A dog was howling, very far away.

— Guy de Maupassant, "On the Water"

It is not possible to step twice into the same river.

— Heraclitus

I

When I told Jeff that Lauren had said I should do my media class documentary on Durham, he told me it was a good idea. We were in the kitchen after school. He was making a peanut butter sandwich and I was still raiding the cupboards, looking for something better, without much hope of finding it.

It's weird, but some days it is difficult for me to remember Jeff's face or voice. I *know* what he looked like — there are pictures everywhere — and I *know* what his voice sounded like, but it's one thing to know something and another thing entirely to have that thing available to you, easily accessible, which you take for granted until it's gone.

But on this day, for whatever reason, it wasn't hard. He was right there in front of me, like he had never gone.

"It's not a good idea," I said. "Durham sucks."

Jeff agreed that Durham sucked, but he said there were lots of ways I could do it, anyway. For instance, I could just set up the camera on a tripod in the centre of town and leave it running for twenty minutes.

Last year the documentary only had to be a maximum of seven minutes (*maximum!*) and Mrs. Scala (now on maternity leave) baked cookies for the final presentations. If I could remember now who told me that media would be a cakewalk, I would egg their house.

"That sounds like it would be horrible," I said to Jeff.

He said that it would be "conceptual," and that I would seem "deep."

It was a good joke, but I knew that Wright would never buy it. He wanted something with a "traditional" narrative and at least four cuts. *At least*, he had said. *Bare minimum.* And music, too. (We were supposedly being tested on our editing skills, but I wondered if he had foreseen himself watching twenty twenty-minute documentaries of twenty intersections.)

I also had my potential audience to consider.

"I want my documentary to be good," I said. "I mean, at least okay."

"Why?"

"I don't know," I said.

"That's your problem," said Jeff.

Jeff stopped getting decent grades after middle school, even though he was probably the smartest kid I'd ever known. Or at least it sometimes seemed that way to me. His effort cratered after that. Or maybe it had never been very high to begin with, and it was just that school was asking more from him. He claimed that he didn't care. That it wasn't worth putting in the effort to do well, to be liked, to not to stick out. That he was fine with the way things were. Sometimes I believed him.

I'd heard Mom whispering to her friends on the phone that she thought he had "emotional problems," but I always thought he was just misunderstood. That he'd find his way in some other fashion, although not as radically as he hoped. It was too easy to say he had problems and to leave it at that. If he had a problem it was that he wanted to turn the world to do his bidding, to fold it in half in order to solve a geometry question that only required drawing a line from one point to another.

"Why don't you start with what you know?" he told me. "Isn't that what they always say? 'Start with what you know'?" He had a mouth full of peanut butter and Dempster's soft whole wheat and some of it flew out and landed on the counter. He reached his hand out past me, toward the sink, letting it hang mid-air, and I interpreted his motion and threw him the rag hanging around the faucet.

The problem was that I didn't know what I knew.

According to an article I read a while back in the *Durham Enterprise*, Durham is the fastest-growing small town within two hundred kilometres of the city of Toronto: "small town" being defined as containing less than twenty thousand people and "fastest-growing" determined via an aggregate score of year-to-year population growth, that population growth relative to the previous year's population, and relative growth of infrastructure.

After I showed the article to Jeff and told him that we finally had something to be proud of, he laughed and said that their criteria basically meant nothing. It was just a way to get people who live in Durham to feel like they're important. Which they're not, he said.

"Yeah," I said. "Duh."

But he looked at me like I was stupid and I knew then that I was, in a deep way, at my very core.

I was probably fourteen and I remember feeling that way all of the time.

It's been two years since he died and I miss him a lot, enough that sometimes I pretend he's with me, even to the point of making up conversations with him about what I have to do for school.

If Jeff were still around he probably wouldn't be at home anymore; he'd be working at some crap job and living on his own somewhere far away, or he'd have figured his shit out and be doing some kind of mathematics or science degree at a university downtown. Or in another province, or country, or on another planet.

We were different in a lot of ways, but we had a lot of things in common, too. He wanted to get out of Durham by any means necessary.

So do I.

* * *

Here are some facts about Durham.

Durham, the municipality, counts about fifteen thousand residents. We have an arena, a hospital, three strip malls, a bus system, multiple hamburger places, two cemeteries, a newspaper, a Tim Hortons, a Pete's Donuts, and a large chunk of real estate on Highway 89. We also have a single high school which is shared with all of the surrounding towns, including Saffronville, which is notable because students who live in Saffronville are often made fun of because it's one of the few towns that is an even bigger hole than Durham. We take a lot of pride in saying so. (Saffronville: half an intersection; one decrepit grocery store; an off-brand donut place; three sneering teenagers on the main drag at all times, in basketball shirts without sleeves; scary dogs barking somewhere; an old man heavy in a torn white T-shirt lying on someone's lawn, burping.)

In honour of our namesake, the late John George Lambton, first Earl of Durham, the high school is named Upper Canada Secondary School and the K–8 elementary school is Lower Canada Junior Middle School. Old Lord Durham was the one who drafted the report recommending the unification of the two Canadas (hardly rocket science) back in the heady days of BNA (British North America, for the uninitiated). The symbolism is idiotic. Not only because our great pride is in being accidentally named after a man who helped destroy French and Indigenous culture in the service of our British colonizers. The sports teams for both schools have the same name, the "Canadas," which, if you're following carefully, you know means that the full names of each team contains the semantically ridiculous repetition "Canada Canadas," as in "Upper Canada Canadas." No one actually says that, of course, because they'd sound like morons if they did (instead, they eliminate the first "Canada"), but it's there, lurking underneath the scores on the morning announcements, cheers on Spirit Day, and the sentimental *hoo-rahs* in the *Enterprise* ("Bobby Booby, son of David and Liz Booby of Booby Auto, north Saffronville, scored the lone goal in the Canadas' hard-working loss.")

Barring some miracle, the only teams our teams will ever play are teams from Canada, and so in that light, "Canada Canadas" becomes even more meaningless, both humiliating and demoralizing at once. At least if we were the Badgers or something we could claim exclusivity until we met another team from podunk-nowhere with the same spirit animal: at least a badger is fearsome, at least there is some menace in that name. And what if, say, the Lower Canada Canadas did ever make it to a national tournament and ended up playing a team from Quebec? The Upper Canada Lower Canada Canadas vs. the legitimately Lower Canada Kanata Canadiens —?

The problem with doing a documentary on Durham is that teachers don't usually like it when you're too negative, even if you're being realistic. I don't know why. Maybe they get nervous about the world they are about to throw us into, and they'd like to keep us insulated from all of the shit we're going to eat as soon as we get out.

But maybe it should be a documentary about how Durham is a hole and we are all trapped. Or about how I am going to get out

likely. Probably the latter. Since if the Leafs were playing you could count on at least their detractors to show up on purpose just to talk about how much the team sucked. It was stupid and it drove me crazy because I never, ever, cared about hockey, except for a six-month period in grade six when I became inexplicably infatuated with Mats Sundin (I created a narrative in which he was the polar opposite of Maple Leaf enforcer Tie Domi, predicated on the idea that Sundin somehow transformed Domi's hooliganism with his elegance and skill). (But now that I think about it, maybe Sundin wasn't even really elegant — just European.)

I was working with Michael and neither of us thought we could make the call on whether we could close early or not, even though we both knew it wouldn't have been a big deal to Joe either way. I had school the next day, of course, but I needed the hours, and Michael was older and needed the hours, too. I also sometimes had the impression that Michael liked taking time out from his girlfriend and his infant daughter. He was older than I was, but he wasn't *that much* older and he seemed exhausted and I thought he was probably upset, inside. I imagined he thought he had screwed up and was going to be a Durhamite for life.

He never said anything about that at all to me, and for all I know he loved Durham, loved going home, loved his girlfriend and his daughter and hoped to stay in town forever. That was just the impression I got from him or maybe something I invented based on how I thought I would feel in his situation. What's that called — projecting?

Anyway, it was dead quiet, but we stuck it out. There was always the off chance that we'd be greeted by a flurry of customers once the whistle blew on the final period — or whatever it was — and we might have told ourselves that we couldn't miss out on them, although I don't remember that happening and it wouldn't have mattered if it had.

We usually had something playing on the TV across from the cash registers, but when it was quiet we could turn up the volume and really focus our attention. It seems to me — although it couldn't have been true — that the lights were dimmer in the store that night, as if in preparation for what we were going to see. Maybe there wasn't a hockey game after all and we were just waiting out some monster storm that was flickering the overhead banks and blotting out the sky. But no, that can't be right, because that would mean that the television would be struggling, too, since they all ran on the same power. It's probably just that I got so wrapped up in the movie that it seems that way to me now, as if nothing else existed during that short, ninety-minute span.

Whatever the case, looking back it almost feels like the movie was waiting for me. Now I've seen it so many times that it's hard to believe there was ever a time I didn't know it, like when you look back and try to evaluate your impressions and prejudices when you were first introduced to your best friends, and how it's really hard to do that without bringing what you know about them back with you from the future.

Michael was a real movie buff, and *Evie* was one of his favourites, although I think he liked it for different reasons than I did, more because it was virtually unknown, especially outside of Canada, and for the weird bravado that allowed it to exist in the first place. At first I was struck by how obvious its premise seemed to me — I found it incredible that there weren't a hundred movies like it already. But then I started thinking deeply about why I'd never heard of it before and I inhaled sharply and realized that I was essentially alone in the world, my tastes far from universal.

Before Michael put the cassette in, he told me that the funding for the movie had come from a weird (long since closed) tax dodge, in which the Canadian government briefly, if unintentionally, allowed persons of means to obtain tax credits through indiscriminately funding arts projects (hoping to reap in a share of the — always nonexistent — profits). Predictably, this led to a lot of really bad, bizarre art, which is probably the necessary result when wealthy people toss money at artists who couldn't earn a living otherwise. If the rich knew anything about culture they wouldn't be rich, which is something that Mr. Wright likes to say.

Michael always told me that one day he would bring in the book which contained the record of all the weirdo paintings, photographs, poetry, music groups, films, and dramatic performances funded through the tax "loophole." (He also explained that after the Canadian government had caught wind of the project it had rescinded all credits and taken the accountants who had facilitated the arrangements to court, financially devastating everyone who had contributed.)

Of the projects, Michael said, *Evie* was by far the crown jewel. And he told me that it couldn't have otherwise existed in a thousand alternate universes.

It was true.

Michael never actually brought the book in. But it didn't matter. I was hooked before he even pressed play.

The story of *Evie* is basically cheap fantasy, the kind of thing you could find in any paperback in a used bookstore. But it is filmed with a restraint that elevates the material, imbuing the action with force and meaning. It is essentially a Western, set in a fantastic world, filmed in Northern Ontario. I'd recently discovered Sergio Leone (through Michael, of course) and I was crazy about Westerns, a genre that up until then I hadn't given any thought to at all, writing them off as vaguely capitalistic fantasies for American men who refused to grow up.

Which didn't mean that they weren't, but I liked to think that *Evie* was different, even if it wasn't, fundamentally.

I didn't really know, either way.

The movie opens with a long shot of a rickety cabin built on the edge of a forest clearing, ringed with squat jack pines and under-painted with pink tendrils of granite and red clusters of sumac. Which is a familiar scene to Canadian audiences. But, as Michael explained, the location was chosen because to foreigners it might more easily suggest a magical and alien world, one in which the fantasy might conceivably take place. But for those used to the landscapes of the Group of Seven, of the mythos of the North, the effect is jarring, as if an alternate dimension has been overlaid over your dreams.

It's early morning. No sound but the thrum of insects in late summer, the occasional bird call. The camera lingers on the scene, setting a leisurely pace, only broken later by short bursts of action. Despite the obviously poor quality of the cameras themselves, which Michael says were at least a decade old at the time of filming, the framing and editing is, frankly, incredible: it's the first project from the director of photography who would later go on to work on *The Apprenticeship of Duddy Kravitz* and *Wake in Fright* (Michael talked about those movies all the time, but I never got to see either before Joe's shut down).

The silence is finally broken by the voice of a little girl inside the cabin. She's humming to herself, playing by the fire with a little doll. She's unspeakably dirty and her dress is torn. This is Evie. Her parents are behind her, sitting down at a table, as if for breakfast. Evie says something to the doll, and the doll replies, in Evie's tiny voice. Then Evie does something quickly, and the doll rips. She drops the doll on the floor and leaves the shot.

"Wake up!" we hear her say. "Wake up! *Wake up!*"

Finally, crying. Evie, obviously.

Shot of the mother, then the father. Both are dead. Their deaths were obviously violent, and they've been dead for a while.

Flies buzz around both corpses. There's no telling how long Evie has been taking care of herself alone in the house. But it's time to go. Somehow the spell is finally broken.

She gathers her things and sets off into the forest — the Deepthorn, vast and primeval, "a continent unto itself," according to text that runs on the screen following her departure. I don't know why, but it chokes me up: something about the way that her little body disappears into the woods, stumbling through the underbrush, slipping and falling in the stream. Sometimes I'll pause the tape there and get out of my seat, look out the back window or get something from the kitchen, maybe, because I find that part so affecting, I don't know why. That first night, Evie dreams about a bear who speaks to her in a deep, booming voice, rendered clumsily but to great effect through an uncanny editing technique. Over the course of several nights, the bear teaches her how to survive and tells her, in a final dream, that it is her destiny to kill Llor, the ice queen. Llor's troops have overrun the Deepthorn, and it's she who is ultimately responsible for the death of Evie's parents. This dream upsets Evie and she is shown moaning and turning in her makeshift bed. But in the morning she finds food outside her shelter, a cache of berries and root vegetables, and she accepts the gift, and with it, her destiny. The bear's voice echoes as she gathers up the food.

Ten years later Evie emerges from the Deepthorn leading her horse, Excalibur, whom she ties to a post beside her parents' wrecked cabin, overgrown with greenery and collapsed in on itself. Evie has come to pay her last respects before embarking on the journey that will finally lead her to Llor.

There's a lot of buildup for that final action, and in lesser hands, in a lesser movie, it's very possible that it could all have come undone. It's a blessing in disguise that the film had such a low budget: instead of elaborate costumes and effects, which would have undoubtedly looked cheap with time, instead of dragging out the final action unnecessarily, Evie just stabs an old woman in an ice-grey dress. An old woman who commands an army but who spends her nights alone. Who stands up from her bowl of porridge when Evie walks into her tent. With a book open beside her on the table.

Evie has to pass through a camp of guards to get at Llor, quietly, quickly, and the simple and abrupt climax works in the movie's favour, highlighting the irrevocable nature of action and the desolation that follows it. It even seems, for a second or two, that some flash of recognition occurs between the two players, wherein each understands and simultaneously rejects their role. I read that in a cult movie magazine that Michael brought in one day, but I think it's true. Evie has killed before, but regardless you can see that she wants — even for a brief moment — to undo the thrust. And Llor, maybe, wants to undo everything, for her life to be the book and the porridge and the table, nothing more. To not have to be responsible for whatever she has done to Evie, not to escape her fate, but to free her killer from hers. At least that's how it seems to me.

When Evie leaves the tent, limping, and stands before the guards waiting outside, it's impossible not to reflect on the fact that every action has its consequence, and that the consequences of all actions are necessarily dire, because they bring us one step closer to where we are all going. That's super dark, I know, but I think it's true. Somehow it is immediately clear to the guards what has happened, as if Llor was a sense that they lost after she died. Evie just stands there, and they just look at her, and no one has any idea what to do. Evie's lost a lot, and maybe she has even found a kind of glory, but it's unclear what that glory means. Maybe she's going to die. Maybe she'll claim a reward. It doesn't matter. The price has already been paid, and I don't mean Llor's death. It's more complicated than it seems, and it gets more complicated with each viewing.

I love *Evie* not just because it shouldn't exist but does, not just because no one knows about it, not just because it feels so *Canadian*, awkward and so earnest at times that it verges on sentimental despite how much it tries to come off as cold. I love *Evie* primarily because the movie is about growing up. It is about being abandoned by those you love and being forced to fend for yourself.

When I watch *Evie* I feel like my brain is expanding, like I am ready to be dispersed into space and to become part of all of the possibility that I see before me. I wanted to put *that* feeling into my documentary. I wanted to create a work of art that would raise myself and all my peers together into a kind of holy ecstasy. But I didn't know how to do that. And whenever I sat down and thought about it I got scared, really scared, like I was a scrap of paper about to blow away in the wind.

2

We found out how long our documentaries were supposed to be on the day we handed in our communications essays. The subject of my essay was "net speak," specifically as employed on MSN Messenger, and how it wasn't "degrading" language (as I'd heard a lot of — *mostly older* — people claim) but adding "an additional register," aping the language of an article I had read in the paper several weeks prior. I thought I'd made some good points, even if the essay was a bit rushed, and I had been hoping for an A. Walid finished writing his in the library at lunch. He said his essay was "hot garbage," but that so was Wright. I liked Wright, but I agreed with Walid because it was more fun to continue the joke than it was to shut it down. I liked imagining hot garbage walking the streets in the shape of a man, shadowed by a squadron of hungry seagulls.

But anyway, I felt good about my essay, for once, and I wanted to get a head start on the next project, so when I got home from school that day I headed straight to the attic. There, in a box marked APRT: Msc was a dusty JVC camcorder. From the late eighties, I think. The tapes were about the size of a pack of cards and they fit into an included master tape (which was also inserted, weirdly, inside the device) that fit into any VCR. The camera itself was about the same size as half a cheese wheel, maybe twice as heavy, was just as conspicuous raised to my shoulder, and probably got about as good a picture, all things considered.

Jeff and I found the camera six summers ago, when for twenty bucks each we cleaned out all of the junk in the attic, swept a bit, and put everything else into some kind of rudimentary order. We found a bunch of things we hadn't expected, including a stack of old letters from my parents that we were too afraid to read, though I think we both read them, anyway, in secret, or at least I did, as much as I could stomach. There was also a stack of old film cartridges buried in an adjacent box.

Most of the tapes contained a weird and uncanny vision of a trip my parents took to Nova Scotia sometime after Jeff was born. Before me. I'd heard about it only because my grandfather was living in a place out there when they did the drive, and it was one of the last times my mom saw him alive. On the tapes, younger, thinner versions of my parents addressed each other, in turn, following shaky-cam monologues and extreme long shots of waves breaking on the ocean (as seen from the window of their inn). It was weird because even though I'd seen photographs of him, older and more recent, I didn't really have a great image of my dad in my head. In the video there he was, reclining on chairs, on couches, in front of the en suite television, my mother popping into mirrors holding the camera, which proved that she hadn't always disliked it as much as she now claimed (maybe only because it was tied to him). Most of the video was a montage of shots of the drive, terrain becoming progressively rockier, tired parents eating at road stops, hope, teased hair, signs in English, French, English, and the same procession again, but in reverse order, at the end of the tapes, on their way back (fewer shots of the countryside, subdued tone, mournful even, talk of picking Jeff up from Aunt Wanda's, WELCOME TO ONTARIO, my father cursing at the wheel, a near miss, black car rapidly passing through the frame, camera switched off in the midst of a violent outburst, Mom telling him to calm down, hyperventilating herself).

A brief shot of my grandfather, which Jeff and I rewound and played back multiple times, saying, with his slight accent, "What is that stupid thing?" before the camera was turned off again. Then a sneaky five-minute cut of him working in his garden, shot through a window. We told Mom about it and she watched it with us once, asking herself how she could have forgotten. Then it cut back to Dad and her and she said, "Oh, yes," and went back to whatever she'd been doing, making sure to let us know that she wanted us to give the tapes to her when we were done so she could put them somewhere safe.

There was a blank in the box, too. Jeff and I spent a few weeks using it to make movies with old action figures, movies about the neighbourhood, its fictional underbelly, movies that used that old stop-camera trick, movies about falling down in one place and getting up in another, movies about disappearing in the blink of an eye (following a moment of anticipation, a tension, as we froze in place, waiting while the ancient camera ground to a stop). Something was always threatening to revoke itself in our movies. We screened them, at most, once or twice, and only for ourselves, sometimes for Mom, then we rewound back to the beginning and started again, callously destroying all of our hard work in the name of future production, just to save the cost of a new blank. Our rationale was, I guess, that each new video contained the seed of the previous ones, so that if we wanted to look backward we only needed to look at what we'd just done to see everything that had come before it. We must have thought that we would keep making those videos forever.

But, of course, we didn't. We kept on rewinding and recording until one day the little tape exploded, shooting out little black threads that got tangled so badly in the stupid master tape that they had to be cut out. Then we put the camera back in the attic and no one's touched it since.

I wish I had that tape now, that it hadn't exploded, so I could watch the Jeff caught there and remember him in greater detail. Instead just the camera, filled only with his traces.

*   *   *

I see Jeff everywhere. It's hard not to. Even when I close my eyes. There are pictures of him all over the living room and kitchen downstairs, so maybe I am exaggerating when I say that I don't remember what he looked like. Or that it is hard to. But looking at them only makes his absence larger, since they don't really show who he was, just his physical characteristics. If that makes any sense. It's him, but without *him* the images feel like so much less.

Mom still hasn't done anything with his room. I'm not sure she'll do anything until after I move out. Or when she does. She vacuums it out every once in a while, but that's basically it. The door stands half-ajar, inviting, as if he were home and felt like talking or as if the room itself was waiting for him to come back. Sometimes I will walk to the bathroom in the partial darkness and see him in the mirror before I turn on the light. Nothing spooky — just my own face, our resemblances, which evaporate without darkness to smooth over our differences. I'm a lot smaller than him, my face is thinner.

I'm alive.

A while back I started leaving the house in order to get away from his ghost, and now I do that just to be alone. There is a place I like to go in the forest near where we live. A spot that is quiet and lonely and where only I am allowed: moss and needle carpet;

ceiling of low cedar limbs; fifty yards away, downslope, the soft trickle of a brook. And me. That's it. It looks like a long time ago the clearing belonged to someone else — when I first found the place there was a folding chair sitting by itself in the centre of the clearing, plastic worn and tattered. Like it had been waiting thirty years for someone to fill its place.

Maybe it's stupid, but I feel something like Evie when I sit there. Evie in the moments before she embarked on her quest to do away with Llor. Evie preparing for her journey. Taking in the quiet like a potion. Using it like a whetstone on her sword. I feel like I'm preparing myself for something, too, except what I'm preparing myself for isn't a battle or a long journey.

It's just life.

*   *   *

Maybe I'm preparing myself to talk about how Jeff died.

Maybe not.

Lauren asked me about that once. Long after we got to know each other. Why I never talk about him. Or about it.

We were sitting in the cafeteria. It was during a free period, after an assembly or something. We both had time to kill. Everyone else we'd been hanging out with had left, I can't remember why. But they rose in a huge flock, leaving their napkins and cans of pop or whatever behind. Then we just looked at each other, really looked, like we were seeing each other for the first time, and she asked me that question.

I didn't know how to respond. I felt slow, and stuffed up, and for a moment — though I didn't, I didn't — I felt like I was going to break down. Which is weird. Because people do ask me about him sometimes and I don't feel that way. I just ignore it — or I respond to them, but I go somewhere in my head and it *feels* like I'm ignoring it.

I know I should talk about how he died. I know that. And I don't know why I don't want to. But I don't. And I can't explain why.

I just don't want to.

And that's all.

The week after we found out the documentary requirements
Lauren took me out in her car again, and we bombed around on
all of the side roads outside of town. In some ways Lauren seems
like she is so much older and wiser than me, even though we are
the same age, but she drives like someone unhinged. She goes fast
and sometimes goes over the shoulder — and my heart starts racing and sometimes she laughs, surprised, before getting back on
the road — but we have hit nothing yet. Though her little blue
Pontiac is already pretty dinged up. We missed a merge sign on
the highway and when the lane began to cut down to nothing she
gunned her car until it growled hoarse and throaty to catch and
pass the car that was threatening to nose us off the road. We could
have waited, I guess, but that's not Lauren's style.

"Holy shit!" she said. "I didn't think we'd make it."

Not a reassuring thing for a passenger to hear. But she spoke
with all of the weight gone out of her, surprised and light, in a
way that made it okay somehow.

I wanted to impress her badly, so I grabbed her bare arm.
With anyone else, I would never. With her, it's an extension of
the game.

"My hands are sweaty!" I said. "Feel that. You almost killed us."

"Ah!" The car lurched. She gave me a scolding look, but I could tell she was delighted. "*Jesus* — you made me jump."

At Wok-In she went up to the counter to pay and for a minute I was able to fantasize that when she turned around again, with our noodles, our bean curd, our beef and vegetables, our soy sauce packets, and our individually wrapped fortune cookies, I would put an arm around her and we would leave together. I mean, we left together, anyway, but I mean *together*, entwined. When she got the food and raised it to me triumphantly, I said something ironic back to her, I don't remember what now, but nothing of what was actually on my mind. She has a boyfriend and I don't like him and I don't need to I guess, yet she is with me, driving me around, and I don't know whether that means anything, or if it should.

I've never been such good friends with a girl before, and I don't always know what that means or what to do.

She drove us to a distant park she knew of, in Orangeville, maybe one that she used to go to as a kid. Cracked asphalt parking lot with weeds poking through. We lapped up noodles in the darkness but were otherwise mostly silent. I was thinking of what everything meant and I guess she had something on her mind, too.

On the way back to Durham I watched as the hills and fields rose and fell beside us, feeling the power of the earth as the car moved across it, and how small we were on the road between everything, wondering how big mountains must be and thinking about the space between the hills and the air underneath birds and the low grey of clouds, rolling and cracking, passing over and surrendering the moon high above.

I enjoyed the silence and when she pulled her car in front of my house I got the feeling that we both had. Still, there were questions running through my head as we sat in the shade of the maple glistening in the soft, blue light. Are we just friends or are we more than that? Should I make a move? Is anybody watching? Why has it become so still, so quiet? What's she thinking? Her body was turned away from mine and she was fiddling with the little knob that controlled the car's side mirrors.

I put my hand on her armrest and hesitated. She didn't notice. Or if she did notice she didn't make a sign. Tension in the air elevated. But it was almost imperceptible.

It might have only been in me.

"I gotta go," I said, removing my hand.

She looked back at me and turned the car back on.

Relieved, I popped the door open.

"See you in bio," I said.

"Yeah. See ya."

She pulled away and she was smiling, I think, but it was hard to tell, because when I looked back at her again she seemed as hard as asphalt, concentrating on the road.

*　　*　　*

For a long time Lauren was one of those people I always heard about but never met, for whatever reason, like she ran in a circle whose circumference almost touched mine at every point, but never, somehow, overlapped. Maybe that's easy to explain — maybe it just means one circle was bigger than the other. Maybe hers was a little bit bigger than mine. I had the basic information: Dark, curly hair, short. Sort of preppy, but not really. Maybe more of a skater? But a subtle kind if she was one. A smallish head — not in a weird way, everyone quickly explained. Just kind of smallish, like an elf, but a pretty one. Walid told me she was hot, but in a grudging way that confused my idea of her. Like she would be angry or have a third hand. (They don't get along.)

I didn't know what to expect, not that I felt like I should expect anything. Not that I was waiting to meet her. I was probably more afraid than anything, which is pretty consistent with my general fear and apprehension of meeting new people.

But when you hear about a person as much as I heard about Lauren, you eventually meet them. And then it seems like the most obvious thing in the world. I met Lauren in biology class, the first period of the new school year. She was sitting about a foot away from me, and Mr. Salazar made a really stupid joke about the transfer of energy in an ecosystem. I don't remember it at all. I just muttered, "Cemeteries," under my breath and Lauren laughed sharply but quietly and said, "What?" and I was surprised because it had been a joke just for me and I didn't think anyone would hear me, let alone laugh. I just said "Cemeteries" again, but seriously this time, and she nodded very sagely and crossed out her last note and just wrote down *cemeteries*, on the handout in front of her, and I nodded like she'd done the most obvious thing in the world.

So, the first time we ever hung out after school was at a cemetery, of course, the old one on Main with the huge stone gates and all of the graves from important people who had lived in the town in the last hundred and fifty years. The place closed at five normally, but we parked on a side road and hiked around back. Lauren said the caretaker was only there from ten until three and I asked her how she could know something like that. "Are you goth?" I said. "Are you a secret goth? Do you come here all the time?" and she said no, she wasn't goth, her grandfather had just been the caretaker after he retired.

I asked her if that meant she knew all of the cemetery's secrets.

"What secrets?" she said.

"Like, where the famous people are buried," I said. "And who rises up from their graves on the full moon?"

She told me that I was an idiot and that her grandfather had been a not extremely nice man who never would have told her anything even if he did know. And that he was dead, anyway.

"But knowing Durham, if there are secrets," she said, "they would be ridiculous secrets. The kinds of secrets you would be embarrassed to know."

That was a funny thing to say and I thought about it for a minute.

"I don't know what that would be," I said.

"I don't either, really," she said.

Then she got distant and for some reason I felt sort of embarrassed and I wondered whether meeting me at the cemetery was an embarrassing secret for her. Because, and I know this is stupid, I was a different sort of person than the kind of guys she usually hung out with. I didn't think that's what she had meant, but the longer she was quiet the more I wondered that. It was in the silence, too, that I remembered that Jeff was buried across town, and that I shouldn't joke so much about cemeteries and death, because, I don't know, it made me a dumb and callous fucked up idiot, I guess. It was just that sometimes I didn't make the connection. Because I still didn't always want to connect the general to the personal and I thought that if I didn't do that maybe Jeff would still be around, somehow.

"Hey," I finally said. "I have one."

"Have what?"

"A ridiculous secret."

"Okay," she said. "Let's hear it."

"Knowing who the Saddest Man is."

She laughed. "What?"

"Knowing who the saddest person is who regularly visits the cemetery."

"Hmm," she said.

For some reason I started wondering if she had been thinking about Jeff, too. Did she even know about him? I was sure I'd never mentioned him to her before. There had been an announcement in school and there had been a page in the yearbook, but it seemed like the kind of thing that would be easy to overlook if you didn't know him, especially because he was a few years older than us. I definitely didn't talk about him in class.

Obviously, I guess.

What I wondered was this: Did she think I was secretly sad? Had I just admitted that?

"Does it have to be a man?" she asked.

"I guess not," I said. "I just like imagining a guy in a top hat. He's not even visiting anyone. He just walks around. Very formal. And very sad."

She thought about that for a moment.

"Okay. That's pretty funny. But is that really a secret?"

"No," I said. "I guess not."

Soon we walked back to the car and drove around for a little while with the windows down and her stereo turned up. Until we got tired of that and she drove me home. Mom was asleep so when I got inside I quietly walked up to my room and got under the sheets.

I closed my eyes and tried relaxing, but I couldn't fall asleep. Instead, I debated whether I was an idiot or a moron. I wasn't quite clear about the lexical differences between the two but I eventually decided "moron." It seemed important to distinguish between them even though I knew I was definitely one of the two. "Idiot" seemed more incidental and "moron" seemed more internal, inherent. I thought I'd been boring and fucked everything up. That she would never want to talk to me again, not even as a friend. But the next day in bio, nothing had changed.

Definitely a moron, I thought to myself.

*   *   *

Mom had been coming home later than usual. They were short-handed at the real estate office because a few of the brokers had retired and their other full-time administrator had suddenly quit. Mom had taken a course in real estate sales and she was hoping to become a broker herself, so they had her filling in for a few clients while doing everything she normally did and covering for the new hire while they were being trained. I'd started fixing dinner on the nights she knew she was going to be late. Really simple stuff: rice and ground beef, frozen lasagnas, spaghetti with canned sauce and frozen meatballs. Some days she came in so late that I'd already be in bed, and I'd come down the stairs in the morning only to find her asleep on the couch with the television on at a low volume. One morning I found her standing at the sink in her work clothes from the night before, staring out the window that looked out onto our neighbours' brick wall.

"Good morning," I said, cautiously walking around her and grabbing a box of cereal. She just looked at me and winced.

"I don't want to talk about it," she said.

I poured myself a healthy-size bowl and grabbed a spoon.

"Did you sleep on the couch again?" I asked.

"Yes," she said, without turning around.

"*Yes*," she said again.

I was worried about her. I wondered if she should step away from some of her responsibilities, at least until the other administrator was up to speed. Maybe even wait until the summer to take on her new duties, since the office typically hired on a student assistant. But she told me that she had been waiting a long time for the opportunity that she had now and that she wasn't going to jeopardize it by stepping down.

"What about your health?" I asked.

"What do I care about my health?" she said.

"I'm serious."

She didn't say anything for a while.

"You know, last night I dreamed that you were a jungle," she said, finally. "Like, a person, but also somehow a jungle. And you kept sending me packages that I didn't want to open. The living room was filled with them."

I was offended. If I was sending her packages I assumed they were important.

"Why wouldn't you open them?"

She looked at me.

"Because I was worried that you and your dumb-ass friend Walid were playing some kind of a trick on me. All of the packages were addressed 'From Jeff,'" she said.

"Oh," I said, quietly. "I wouldn't do that."

"I know," she said. "And then I started worrying that they actually *were* from Jeff and that they were time-sensitive or something — like he was in trouble and he was sending me clues. But they went missing and I had the idea that you stole them."

"Jesus," I said. I wished she hadn't told me that.

It was like a light went on in her.

"Oh my god, I'm sorry," she said. "I know you wouldn't. I'm just — I don't know." Then she was silent for a long while. After I finished my cereal I got up to put the bowl in the sink and I saw that her eyes were closed. I was worried she was crying, but I couldn't find any evidence that she was. I watched her for a long time before I put my bowl and spoon in the sink. For a minute I wondered if she'd actually fallen asleep standing up.

She opened her eyes as my dishes clattered.

"I better get ready for work," she said, heading upstairs. Then, calling from the hallway: "Believe it or not, I made you a lunch. It's in the fridge." Lunch was three slices of cheese between two slices of bread. A banana sat on top of the Ziploc bag.

I guess I couldn't complain.

4

Instead of comments on my communications paper, Mr. Wright had written a note on the bottom of the page: "I'd like to meet with you after class. I have a free third and fifth period. If that doesn't work, please see me after school." For a moment I felt a flush of pride — did Wright think I'd plagiarized something? That had always been my secret desire, to write something so polished that my teacher would think it couldn't be mine.

But I checked the mark — only a seventy-eight. Ruled that out.

Walid got a seventy-four, and on his paper it said: "Good effort, but you need to spend more time refining your ideas." Walid made a big show of cramming his paper into the nearest waste bin as soon as we got out of class. All through high school he had maintained a ninety-something average in all of the maths and sciences, but the story wasn't the same for the liberal arts. For some reason he thought media would be different.

"What do I need this class for, anyway?" he wondered aloud.

"For watching CNN?"

He told me I should make sure to leave the door open a crack when I go to see Wright, to not let him get between me and the hallway, and to relax my throat when I have his cock in my mouth.

"I only got four percent higher than you," I said.

"That's because you didn't relax your throat last time."

After I finished eating lunch I went upstairs to find Wright's office. There's no such thing as a "media" department, and the class itself occupies a weird grey zone between the social sciences (which at Upper Canada is pretty much just geography), English, and art (somehow even less of a department than social sciences, just Ms. Reisley and Mr. Winn, in this little closet off of the shop hall, with one desk shared between both of them, crammed with binders and stacks of papers; a boxed slide projector in the corner; piles of old art assignments, their pages stiff with paint; boxes of pencil crayons and pastels; paintbrushes fanning out in every direction; crumbling clay and acrylic "sculpture"; some joker's weird snowflake ornament dangling from the ceiling, held in precariously by a taped-in-place paperclip, ornament itself looking worse every year; a beaten-up computer that beeps and hums like a droid from *Star Wars*; coats; spare pairs of shoes; like eight tightly wrapped umbrellas; and, somehow, behind it all, faded Monet and Van Gogh prints from really old AGO exhibitions tacked up on the walls).

I took art every year from grades nine to eleven, although I was never very serious about it. Media was the nearest thing available for seniors. Mr. Wright, however, is English — straight English, except for media, now. According to the staff photos tacked up in the main hall, he's been at Upper Canada for about fifteen years; it looks like since he graduated from teacher's college, though he does sometimes allude mysteriously to time spent teaching at a school in East Toronto somewhere, those years being training or post-graduation, I'm not sure which. Years when, he tells us, he appeared in a few plays: Fringe-y stuff, he says, "nothing serious," in a tone of voice meant to suggest more than he is letting on. Frequent searches of Google have, as of yet, not been able to confirm or deny. We're hoping for a compromising cast photo or for a scene or two from a really old recording to appear on YouTube.

Wright is distinguished as the only male teacher at Upper Canada who isn't at least thirty or forty pounds overweight. He also tends to wear many layers of clothing, so that rarely an inch of his skin shows between his wrists and below his neck, even when summer is at its absolute hottest (the air conditioning at Upper Canada being pretty much a rumour, a slow banging of pipes that the maintenance guy is always attending to but never resolving). Wright had on what looked like at least four cardigans, two button-up shirts, his boots, jeans, and two plastic pastel Livestrong bracelets to go along with his oversized, and never securely fastened, watch. He got up from his computer and waved me in, and I sat there for a few moments while he finished up whatever he was doing.

"You want something to drink? Tea, maybe?" he asked, waving to an electric kettle in the corner.

"No, I'm fine, thanks," I responded, a little leery.

"I suppose you're wondering why I asked you to meet me here."

"I thought you might have thought my essay was plagiarized?"

"Ha! — no." He stood up, turning his chair around and reseating himself to face me: a move so fluid, yet also measured, that I associated it, for some reason, with the motion an aspiring actor might make coming to rest before his instructor in a studio. Not that that at all reflected our relationship. He took a swig from an opened water bottle by his computer.

"But I did want to talk about your paper," he said, putting the bottle down.

"Okay," I said.

"Did you spend a lot of time on it? You can tell the truth, I won't be offended."

I looked at him for a while. He seemed sincere.

I shook my head. "No, not really."

Wright smiled. "I thought so."

He began rummaging in a drawer behind him, and pulled out a sheet of paper — it looked like a brochure — and laid it on his lap.

"Why do you think that is? Did you not like the topic?"

"No, I found it interesting."

"I thought that was obvious, too. So what else could it be?"

"Maybe I'm overworked."

Wright smiled. "You have a job right now? A girlfriend?" My response was negative. "A boyfriend?" Again, negative. Double negative. "An unreasonable amount of other homework?" No.

Okay, so maybe I wasn't overworked.

"So, what?"

I looked him in the eye. "My brother died."

We spent a few moments sitting in the silence that rippled out from that statement. Finally, Wright sighed and shifted his position, re-crossing his legs and moving the sheet of paper from his lap to the desk.

"Yes, I know. I'm sorry about that. I taught Jeff. He was a good kid, mostly."

I nodded. I knew what he meant.

"But I don't think that's what it is."

"What?"

"I don't think that's what it is." He re-crossed his legs. Almost petulantly, I thought.

"What?" I said again. Was he allowed to say that?

My chest started heaving. Maybe too quickly. I was ready to storm out, or to punch him, I wasn't sure which. I didn't, of course. I wouldn't. And something about that feeling made me suspicious of myself.

He continued. "I'm not wrong."

"You don't know —"

He cut me off. "I don't. But I think it's obvious that you're not being stimulated. And maybe there are other issues, too."

I didn't respond.

"I'm sure you're still upset about your brother's death. But I think it's more than that. You did an okay job, but the paper didn't ask for very much of you, and that was all you were willing to give. No more. Even though it seems like — I get the sense you want to do well."

I nodded.

"I'll be the first to admit, it wasn't a very challenging topic." He tapped his fingers on the desk. "Of course, your colleagues are thinking about university ..."

I didn't say anything, keeping my eyes on the floor.

"What are you thinking of doing after high school?"

"I want to get out of here." Meaning Durham.

"Okay, but where?" Wright asked.

"University. I want to move to Toronto. Or somewhere else."

"That's what I thought. You know, every few years I get a student like you. Someone with obvious ability, but who doesn't see it, or doesn't know how to use it. Or who has friends who are holding them back."

"What are you saying?"

"Nothing. I can't pretend to know how others are influencing you. But it does seem sometimes that you and Walid aren't a good match."

"What?"

"I'm sorry. Just an observation. But I'm not the first teacher to have noticed."

Who was he talking to?

"Walid isn't the reason I'm not doing well."

"I didn't say that," he said.

What did that mean?

Wright sighed. "Okay, I'm sorry. Maybe you weren't ready to hear that. Or maybe I'm wrong. I forget sometimes what it's like to be a teenager."

"Yeah," I said. Not really knowing why.

"So what do you think the reason is?" he asked, re-crossing his legs for the third or fourth time. The conversation was getting uncomfortable, and I was beginning to wonder why Wright had singled me out. There must have been tons of underachieving students in that class. I mean, that's high school. Walid, for example. Why wasn't he talking to him?

"I'm sorry?" I asked, to buy time.

"Why do you think you aren't doing well?"

"I don't know," I said.

Wright stood up. "You don't know," he repeated, as he began fiddling with something on his desk. It was a plastic pencil sharpener. He was still holding the brochure in his other hand.

"That's right, I don't. Can I leave?"

Usually I don't realize that I'm feeling weird or emotional until I say something, and then it comes out in my voice, beyond my control. It's really annoying. When I asked to go, something in my voice quavered, which caused Wright to turn back to me. Then he shook his head — as if dislodging something — and sat down again.

"I'm sorry for taking up so much of your time. But we haven't quite got to the reason that I called you in here."

I nodded, afraid to speak.

"I want you to think of the documentary project as your opportunity to do something really exceptional. The CBC is holding a contest for video shorts. If you enter, you could win a pretty big scholarship, and your video would play at a film festival downtown. That's one of the reasons I changed the requirements this year. I'm not saying you're guaranteed to win, and you're not the only one that I'm telling about this — in fact, I'm going to announce it to the whole class. I just don't want it to wash over you when I say it. I want you to really think about it. I think you have potential."

Potential to be what?

"Thanks," I said, a little unsteadily.

"I also want you to know — that if you ever want to talk, about whatever, that this office is always open to you."

I didn't know why he was making that offer or what we would talk about.

"Okay," I said.

I got up to go.

"Wait," said Wright. "Take this, too."

I took the paper he'd been holding. On top, in big, bold letters, it read: STAYING TRUE TO YOURSELF.

"Oh," I said.

I started inching out the door.

"I know high school can be tough. That it seems like what you are here will carry over into the rest of your life. But that's really not the case. You're going to change a lot."

"Okay," I said, from the hallway.

I threw the flyer into the first trash bin I found. As I did so I happened to glance up at my reflection cast into the glass of the fire extinguisher case. Then I quickly ducked into the nearest washroom. Luckily, it was empty.

When had I started crying?

*   *   *

I stayed later than usual at school that day, reluctant to leave. I watched football practice with Kyle for a little bit, then hung around with some of the guys in the caf until I was practically the only one left. When Jackie's dad pulled into the front parking lot to pick her up it was almost six o'clock. They offered me a ride, but I decided not to take it. I wanted to delay going home as long as possible. On my walk I kept thinking about Jeff — Jeff and the contest, like they were ône and the same. Like winning the contest would bring him back to me somehow, like I could use the camera to trace his outline and summon him home. It didn't make any sense. I tried to straighten them out in my head, separate them.

They weren't related at all.

Evening was already setting in by the time I walked up the front steps to the empty house. I put my bag down in the foyer and stood there in the stillness before turning on the hall lights. "Jeff?" I called, into the darkness. "Jeff? Jeff?" Each time a little louder. Then I listened as carefully as I could, not even sure what I was waiting for. A footstep overhead. A closing door. A cool breeze sweeping the hallway. But if there was any response I couldn't tell: it was just me, standing in the hallway with my ears ringing and goosebumps rising on my neck.

I turned on the lights as fast as I could, then ran to the living room, the ground floor bathroom, the kitchen, and turned them on there, too. There were leftovers in the fridge, meatloaf, soggy vegetables, and cold pasta, but I wasn't hungry. Or maybe I was, a little bit, but I didn't want to eat. Instead I grabbed the phone off the wall and dialed Lauren's home number. It rang for a long time before anyone picked up, and then it was Lauren, sounding very far away, like she was at the bottom of the ocean. "Hello?"

she said. Somehow I could tell she was home alone, too, like her voice was echoing off an absence.

We talked for a long time. I walked back and forth through the house, turning on more lights, opening and closing windows and curtains, but sticking to the ground floor. I told her about Wright and our conversation, the contest, and what he had said about Walid. "It was weird," I said. "No one has ever talked to me that way before."

There was a long silence. I pushed a curtain aside in the front room and stared out the window, into the street. There was no one out there, just a few abandoned cars and lights on in some of the houses.

"Why *do* you hang out with that guy?"

I was confused. "Mr. Wright?"

"No, Walid. I don't get it. He seems like a dick."

"I don't know," I said, unsure what to say. "I mean, he's not so bad."

"Really?"

"Yeah. He can be pretty funny sometimes."

"I guess," she said.

"It's different once you get to know him."

"I'll take your word for it," she said.

We kept talking. She talked about her dad, about her boyfriend, who had been distant lately, and about her mom, who seemed a bit like a menace, to be honest. But we talked about a lot of nothing, too. Eventually I felt like all of the lights were starting to bore into my skull, so I turned off the ones in the kitchen and lay down on the floor, staring up into the emptiness. That was how Mom found me, eyes closed, with the cordless lying on my chest, long after we had hung up.

5

For a brief, stupid moment I decided that I was going to do my documentary on *The Catcher in the Rye*, by J.D. Salinger.

Until the previous summer I had consciously avoided reading it, I guess because it was so admired by the annoying, pretentious types at school, the ones whose parents encouraged and recognized their individual talents and tried to foster their growth and development by introducing them to art and literature tailored to their specific interests.

I always had a sinking feeling that those kids were cooler than me, even if they weren't. And not only cooler, but that they would do better in life overall. With less struggling, less pain. Ironic, maybe, that a book that was supposed to be a badge of alienation could instead signify that you belonged, that your parents loved you, or at least that some other member of your family did.

Or maybe you were like me, and you came across the book purely by chance. I found *The Catcher* in the attic, its beaten-up corpse buried beneath the collected dust of centuries of what I can only assume was spider shit. With it were other books first boxed roughly two and a half decades ago when my parents made the first of many transitional moves. We'd missed them in the purge years earlier, probably because we didn't feel qualified to judge their contents. But this time I chucked most of them. They were wrecked and rotten and I had never heard of any of the authors before. But I took *The Catcher* down, and after beating it on the brick and the sidewalk outside, hung it from a string and let it air out in my room. It was something of an experiment. After a few days it didn't smell quite so much like musk anymore and its spore count had dropped to levels where I didn't sneeze whenever a draught from that corner came upon me as I lay awake in bed. The spider shit tanned to roughly the same colour as the thin board that bound its pages and so I could pretend that its new blotchy design was just part of the original cover design.

Someone once told me that Holden was the biggest phony of all the characters in the novel, because he never aired his reservations. I had never read *The Catcher in the Rye* when this person, whom I forget now, told me this, but because the afore-mentioned annoying kids in my university English class had, the interpretation stuck. It seemed damning. I thought they were all phonies, too. Which of course they were, but in a different way than I thought.

One of them, Christian (he hates it when we call him "Chris") Heslop, asked me to proofread an essay of his once — perhaps sensing from my classroom discourse that I was something of a thinker, though maybe not a future pseudo-intellect like him — and when I took it in my hands I had to push down the sense of intimidation just to register the first few sentences. But those sentences, and the ones that followed, hardly registered even then. They were gibberish. When I finished I looked at him and blinked for a full seven seconds. Then I explained that his essay was really good, and it didn't need any changes.

Christian is so wealthy that it wouldn't have mattered whatever I said. I don't know for sure what his father does, but I've heard that he invented some simple form of plastic used in an ubiquitous product, like, say, the lid on your Coke bottle. When Christian turned sixteen he pulled up in a brand-new car. When Christian first met me, on second period lunch in grade ten, he took me aside, and sensing either a kindredness in us — or maybe just the fact that I was a willing listener — told me about how awesome things kept happening to him, like how some of his older sister's friends had told him out of nowhere they'd like to sleep with him, or give him a blow job, and how during the first week of grade nine he and Luna Scapey made out in the stairwells within ten minutes of knowing each other. He spent the whole lunch telling me these things, things so removed from my own experience that he might have been describing the landscape of an alien planet. I still don't understand why he felt compelled to let me in on all of that stuff, but it was the beginning of what you could call our friendship.

In the past year or so Hess has started affecting a pair of academic-looking glasses which somehow only serve to highlight the fact that he doesn't know as much as he claims to and that he will never have to. There's a kind of gap between his eyes and the frame, like he's admiring a spot of grease on the lens. I told him I was doing my documentary on "local responses to the influential novel by J.D. Salinger, *The Catcher in the Rye*." Before lunch I lined Hess up in one of the hallways and pointed the camera at him. Once I asked Christian if he rode horses himself. He said no, but that his mother owned a few at a local barn and went riding most days. I knew that already, but I humoured him.

"So who's the horse?" I asked.

"You're hilarious."

I didn't end up asking Hess anything really good about *The Catcher*. Just when he first read it, how he'd felt, that kind of thing. What other books he likes. Had he read any more of Salinger. Who told him to read it. The thing I discovered when I finally read *The Catcher* is that it really is pretty good. Holden is a complete basket case, and it's true that he's a phony. But we're all phonies. That criticism has no legs because the book's about something else. Holden's kind of like a holy idiot somehow in that he believes in the ideal of a world where we're all on the level. But he can't even be on the level with himself. Which is fine because no one is. The book is about the human condition, I guess.

Hess said his favourite part of *The Catcher* is when Holden is dancing with the three women from Seattle in the hotel night-club. Specifically when Holden tells one of them that he saw Gary Cooper, and even though it's a lie she tells the others she caught a glimpse of GC just as he was leaving the nightclub.

He likes the trick.

I can think of better parts than that.

On camera I asked Hess whether he was really doing the documentary on his father. He told me that had been a joke. He doesn't know what he's going to do the documentary on. He thought he might do it on Toronto.

"Oh, fuck you," I said, still filming.

I tried to get my leg kicking him into the shot.

Hess can drive into Toronto pretty much whenever he wants.

* * *

After interviewing Hess I set up the camera in the hallway to capture the flood of students clearing their lockers after the final bell. Then I got a shot of Walid, Kyle, and some of the other guys talking by the doors. Lauren waving goodbye from her car. I also got lucky, because the Christian club — that's a club for Christians who study the Bible, not a club for fans/admirers of Christian Heslop — had organized a prayer circle in the island in the centre of the parking lot, holding hands around the Canadian flag. If I wanted to include it in the movie I knew I'd have to make sure to edit out Kyle's comments in post.

After Kyle had gone, and I had my camera bag packed up, just heading back to my locker, I heard shouting from down the hall. A crowd was blocking the hallway to the Athletic Hall. Kids were pushing back and forth against one another and some idiots on the far side were chanting "Fight!" I went to the edge and saw two figures sparring. Without thinking, I reached into my bag and fumbled with my camera, slipping my hand into the strap and turning the device on. Bringing it up over the edge of the crowd I spent a second working the focus until the camera finally found one of the two figures.

Red-faced Pat Hudson, standing with his legs wide apart, clumsily spaced. A black-and-yellow Batman T-shirt riding wrinkled up above Huddy's fat belly, spilling over his jeans. I wanted him to tuck the shirt in — not for my sake, but for his. I guess it didn't seem to matter to him. His glasses were a bit crooked, but his glare was hard and focused. Across from him was Dave Pullman. A guy I knew, but never really liked, but who Walid was sort of friends with because they shared a lot of the same classes. Dave was moving back and forth, pretending he was juking, trying to fake Huddy out and make him look stupid. He didn't have to work too hard. You could see a complete hopelessness in Huddy, a weird determination that meant that he kept charging clumsily past Dave, like a bull tripping through a china shop. And, in the rare moments when he wasn't moving, he stood absolutely still, as if nothing could have fazed him, as if nothing, not even kindness, could penetrate his exterior, and watched as Dave made him look really, really stupid, jabbing him in the stomach, slapping him on the face.

Huddy was a total mess. Which was basically par for the course.

I moved the camera from fighter to fighter, trying to keep it above the crowd.

"What happened?"

Arty Walls turned to look into the camera.

"Dave took something of Huddy's. I didn't see what. Um — should you be filming this?"

Kristina Dupont, next to him, also turned.

"Uh, hello. Dave took Pat's hat when Pat wasn't looking. He was wearing it around like it was his."

Kristina started to pop her eyes and blink into the lens.

"Cut that out," I said. "This is serious. It's for a documentary."

She stuck her tongue out at me.

Behind Kristina and Arty, Huddy had gone into a wild flurry, but Dave, who was breathing hard now, picked him up in a wrestling hold and slammed him onto the floor. Those idiots who were chanting before were laughing. Mostly Dave's friends. Huddy lay on the ground, dazed.

The fight was over. Dave dropped Huddy's hat on him, and Huddy snatched at it wildly.

The crowd began to disperse.

"Just a minute —"

The voice of Johnson, our VP.

"What's going on here?"

My back was turned to him, but I quickly turned the camera off and put it in my bag. He came up and kneeled down to Huddy, beckoning Dave and others closer, demanding to know what had happened.

I felt bad that I had turned the camera on. And lucky that he hadn't seen. Because of my guilt I started to walk away. "Slink" is more like it, like one of Sash's dogs after doing something it knew was bad, like stealing a hot dog off a picnic table.

Someone must have pointed me out.

Johnson didn't know my name. He just called down the hallway. It was only on his third or fourth "Excuse me!" when I realized who he was speaking to. Some kid tapped me on the shoulder and pointed for my benefit, but I would have turned, anyway, because his last "Excuse me!" had been so loud.

"What's your name?" he asked, when I reached them. He was mad.

I told him.

"Were you filming this?"

I said that I was.

"What happened?"

I looked from Dave to Huddy and back to Johnson again, though I was having trouble looking Johnson in the eye.

I said that I didn't know.

"What do you have on camera?"

I said that I had come after the fight had started.

Johnson asked me to take the camera out of the bag. "Show me," he said.

I flicked the camera into the appropriate mode and started to rewind.

"Do you know the school policy on video cameras?"

No, I said. I told him that I needed it for a documentary I was shooting.

"On fighting?"

No. For media. Mr. Wright.

"Did you know that a fight was going to occur here?"

I said that I didn't. The tape stopped at the appropriate location. I told him that it was ready.

"Could I look at it?"

I turned the sound up and handed it to him, pointing to the "Play" button.

"Fuck," said Dave.

"Quiet. And stay where you are," said Johnson, without taking his eyes off my camera.

He watched the fight through the viewfinder until his own words came out of the tinny little speakers and it cut out.

"Do you need this tape?"

I said yes, because it had Hess's interview on it, and the prayer meeting, and the stuff I'd filmed in the hallway, and because I hadn't brought another tape. And because tapes are expensive.

"Okay." He looked down at the image of Huddy lying on the floor in front of all those people, Dave suspended in the air above him at a forty-five degree angle, on his way up again. He handed the camera back to me. "I want you to erase this," he said. "I don't care what your motives were. I don't think Mr. Wright would like to know what you were filming here. If I catch you doing something like this in these halls again, I am going to confiscate your tape and the camera with it. If I find out that you did not erase it, you are going to be in an equal amount of trouble."

I said okay. I said I would erase it as soon as possible.

"Start erasing it right now."

I fumbled with the camera a bit, then I hit record. I showed him what was happening.

"Good," he said. And he let me go.

I hate getting into trouble.

* * *

The next day I set up my camera on the edge of the table adjacent to where Huddy regularly ate lunch. I expected more of the gang to wander over and ask me what I was up to, but just Walid and Sam appeared, and I quickly shooed them away.

On the walk back home the day before I had realized that poor, pink-faced Huddy was Upper Canada Secondary's version of Holden Caulfield. There were a few obvious differences — for example, I couldn't imagine Huddy taking any girl out, let alone double-dating with jocks, or dancing confidently with older women at a club in New York. He wasn't any good at school, either — teachers would ask him things in class only to have their questions bounce right off of him, like he was vibrating at another frequency that made him impervious to inquiries from our universe. It was heartbreaking watching teachers like Ms. Ambrose gradually lose their faith in him as the year progressed, their kindness calcifying into a cold mask. And, unlike Caulfield, I was pretty sure that Huddy's family was poor — which meant no private schools or sprawling Manhattan apartments.

But those were all superficial differences. Huddy's essence was Caulfield. I understood perfectly well, from his smouldering glare — *even when he wasn't looking at anything in particular* — that there was an intense inner monologue running in his head, calling all of us out for being the phonies that we were. But unlike Caulfield, Huddy can't be a phony because he doesn't aspire to be *anything*: he's just himself, like moss or trees or a prayerful hermit banished to the deep woods. Strip away all of the pretension from Caulfield and you get *Huddy*, anger blistering, silent, and righteous.

He reminded me a bit of Jeff, to be honest. Jeff when he finally decided he wanted more but didn't know how to get it. But Huddy was even more removed than that, and, as a consequence, I think more pure. There was nothing compromising about Huddy because of his complete indifference to arbitrary social mores.

It was in making the comparison to Caulfield that I started thinking of Huddy as a subject for the documentary. I thought there was a lot that I could learn from him.

I decided to approach him in the style of Jane Goodall: spend a few days (weeks, if necessary) observing his habitat, then gradually introduce myself into his environment, then — eventually — contact. I'd proceed the same way in conversation, working around his anger, skirting it like it was an army encampment, stalking through the treeline, until I found the right entrance to make.

If I played my cards right, Huddy's words, his real words — if he saw fit to utter any, I mean, for my benefit — would give my documentary the force of a thousand Holden Caulfields, thanks to all those years of repressed wisdom he had buried deep inside.

* * *

A kink in my plan, made immediately apparent: because of the heft of the camera, and its limited zoom — 5x optical, no digital — I was about as inconspicuous as a fireworks display. Huddy had already looked at the camera directly twice. I noticed his forehead reddening, and watched the sprouting of an extra crease or two. He moved a few seats down — not enough to make himself obvious to anyone else, but enough that I had to spend a few seconds dismantling and reassembling my makeshift tripod (consisting of three textbooks: history, biology, and a rebound school copy of *The Great Gatsby*).

I debated with myself over whether I should attempt my planned "as it happens" behind-the-camera narrative of his actions or if I should just take notes and add all that stuff in post (although I was still unclear how I was going to do that, exactly). I thought it made more sense to put the narration in later — on the National Geographic channel they don't whisper about hyenas in real time as a baby zebra gets torn apart. That would be tasteless, more like a boxing match than a documentary.

I had only a couple of observations scribbled down. Looking at them I briefly panicked, wondering if Huddy would yield sufficient material to justify inserting a narrative of any kind, even after long-term study. What if this was pretty much it? Huddy slowly chewing, looking annoyed. Then I would have to go with ambient noise, to count on his silence in the face of the deafening cafeteria to construct my narrative wordlessly.

Walid bent over the camera before I noticed he was there and said that the camera operator was jerking his skinny cock underneath the table. I tried to punch him in the stomach, but he was already scampering back to the other guys before I turned around.

The first note I took was about Huddy's sandwich: what looked like soft whole wheat, tuna-fish insides without fixings, and a five-hundred-millilitre water bottle filled with what I hoped was apple juice. Point of similarity? Could that be my emphasis? Today I had a few slices of cheese on the same cardboard-y bread, no butter (we were out), my drink a few quarters that I'd yet to insert into a machine.

Actually, maybe Huds was a little bit ahead of me there.

Walid came back and said something about Huddy's "butter tits." I turned around and queried him re: his current obsession with the male body, making sure to speak loud enough for the camera to pick it up.

"I'm just hot for you and Huds," he said, rubbing a nipple through his T-shirt. It wasn't worth moving the camera for.

Second note: "huds tick when nerv." For about two minutes before Huddy finally decided to look straight at the camera for the first time he did this interesting sort of twitchy thing where his body spasmed every thirty seconds or so, kind of like a horse's muscles when you run a brush over its body — not that I'd ever seen this operation anywhere but on TV. I wrote: "interesting mark of his self-consciousness/interesting connection between mind and body?"

Third note: "past the tic stage — progress? / <u>Fuck Walid</u>."

* * *

In media, during a free period meant to be used for storyboarding (no one was doing this; like me, maybe, not yet with any clear idea, except for Bobby Booby, sweetly bent over his paper and pencils, sketching frame after frame of himself scoring goals), I was loudly sounding off about the genius project I had embarked upon, playing it up a bit, knowing my audience — speaking to Huddy's patheticness more than his righteousness, suggesting a case study of sloth more than purity, Walid catching on and getting even more carried away than I was — when I was interrupted by Lauren, sitting a table over, her brown eyes flashing, bangs mussed from the quick snap of her head.

"I think your video idea is really disgusting, just so you know."

"It's not like that," I said.

"Oh, really?" said Lauren, clearly unconvinced.

Walid barked some retort, but I hardly noticed. I had been halted dead in my tracks. Lauren's eyes haunted me all through leisure sports (her disapproval making a soft *thwack*-y sound, like the squash ball bouncing against the wall of the court at the Durham Sports Complex). I lost three games in a row, a new record. She followed me in my transit through the hallway from the athletic corridor, to lunch, so cowed and reluctant that I was still at my locker, staring into space, when the second bell rang and startled me into nearly dropping my camera, camera bag, and second measly lunch in a row (one Ziploc of half-destroyed crackers — we'd run out of bread that morning — and another containing a few slices of marble cheddar slick with sweat).

More bells were ringing, this time warnings, as I set up the camera's makeshift tripod in its place across from Hud, who was, I'm sure, not relieved to see me (maybe he'd hoped I'd given up?), taking in a bit of a wider angle so as to account for his possibly moving again, scanning the cafeteria for Lauren — sweat running down my neck — until I realized that she didn't even have my lunch (she was day one, second period).

Huddy'd already finished eating by the time I set up, but he was still working on his apple juice (or whatever), staring sullenly down at the table in front of him. Few notes to take: I drew a butterfly instead. I think Huddy'd resigned himself to my presence, except to occasionally lower his eyes and mutter in my general direction.

Walid popped in again, trailed by Kyle, Walid slapping me reassuringly on my back and telling me how proud he was of me for sticking it to Lauren and demonstrating real commitment to my art. I just kept nodding my head and wishing he would go away.

"Yeah," I said.

I wondered what I was doing. I hoped she would talk to me again.

By Huddy's sixth or seventh bout of muttering, impossible to pick up, but probably angry and directed at me, I finally realized that Lauren was right. If I hadn't already. Morally and artistically my position was essentially bankrupt. Huddy wasn't an animal. He was a human being who couldn't be tricked into association. And he wasn't doing anything and I was wasting my time and disrupting his, demeaning the both of us. Is it a rule of quantum physics or just a general scientific principle that observation alters both its object and subject?

I turned the camera off and sat there for a few moments, making sure to place it on its side so it was clear that I was done. I took a few deep breaths. Eventually I started to put the camera away, slowly and methodically, with the hope that Huddy wasn't paying me too much attention.

I mouthed "I'm sorry, I'm sorry," on the off chance he did decide to look over.

I'm sure he didn't.

Finally I zipped up the camera case and slid the biology and history textbooks back into my bag. I was sort of afraid of vacating my spot entirely — I don't know why, I thought if I made it seem like it was my intention to sit there all along it might appear like I'd just been filming emptiness, the scene before me, rather than a specific person (despite all evidence to the contrary — I'm not saying it wasn't stupid). So I picked up *Gatsby* and opened it for the first time.

I read a few sentences about the narrator's adherence to his father's good advice. I wasn't in the mood, exactly, to follow most of what was being said, but kept returning to the father's precept: "Remember that not everyone's had the same advantages you have," which rang in my head over and over.

What were Huddy's advantages? Did he have *any*? I'd made his silence into one, but that wasn't the same thing.

Maybe the difference between Huddy and me wasn't a matter of purity. Maybe it was that no one, in his entire life, had ever left him alone.

The least I could do was ask him if he even wanted to be filmed.

And if he said no, that was it.

* * *

Huddy didn't acknowledge me until I put my things down heavily beside him.

"I think we got off on the wrong foot," I said.

Huddy snorted and took another sip from his drink — I could see that it was instant iced tea, not apple juice as I had thought, based on the familiar spidery residue of powdered mix at the bottom of the bottle.

I pulled up a chair. Huddy turned his head a few degrees in my direction to look at me in his peripheral vision.

"I'm making a video for media," I said. "A documentary. I thought …"

He turned and looked through me.

I could see there was a hole in his T-shirt, just below the left armpit. Not at the crease of the fabric, but below, extending to his back. Loose black threads bridged the gap.

"Have you ever read *The Catcher in the Rye?*" I asked.

He made a farting noise with his mouth.

"Uh ... I just wanted to get to know you better, because I think you could offer a lot to my documentary. I bet you have a really interesting perspective."

"Beep-beep," he said, looking forward.

Like the Roadrunner.

Things were going really well.

"But I think I went about it the wrong way. I'm sorry for filming you without your permission ... that was wrong."

Huddy stared at the table while I sat there fingering the strap of my backpack. I looked up just in time to see Walid sneaking up behind Huddy. He draped his arms on Huddy's shoulders and sat down next to him on the bench.

"How's our movie star doing?" he said, looking me in the eye, like it was a private joke we shared.

I guess it was.

Huddy stiffened. Walid took his arms off Huddy's shoulders and started massaging his back instead.

"You know you're going to be a big star when this comes out, right?"

"Hey," I said. Meaning *stop.*

Huddy's face was turning red.

"You think he doesn't like it?" asked Walid. "What's the matter, big guy?"

Walid was giving me ironic looks, as if he could push the joke far enough that I'd eventually be okay with it. I didn't know what to do.

"You should leave him alone, man."

"I think Huddy just needs to relax," said Walid, pinching harder into Huddy's flesh.

Huddy slapped away Walid's hand and turned toward him, snorting loudly, his chest heaving up and down.

"Don't touch me," he said, firmly and slowly.

People were starting to notice.

"That's probably a good idea, Walid."

Walid ignored me and held his hand up in front of Huddy's face. Finger pointing, threatening. Like he was talking to a dog.

"*Don't* tell me what to do," he said to Huddy.

Huddy kept trying to grab Walid's hand, but Walid used his other hand to bat him away.

"*Don't* tell me what to do," Walid said, again.

"Jesus," I said. "What the fuck, man?"

Huddy finally caught Walid's hand and started squeezing it. Huddy looks strong, and he's much bigger than Walid, but his grip was so frantic that it didn't seem like he could be causing Walid any pain. And summers spent hauling bricks for his uncle's construction company meant that Walid was stronger, despite the considerable size difference.

I think Huddy mostly sits around and talks to himself.

Walid grabbed Huddy's arms and pulled them behind him, pinning him to the table. It must have hurt, because Huddy was shouting now.

"Get off me! Get off! Cocksucker! Get off!"

I stood up from the table. I could see the nearest teacher on lunchroom duty, Mrs. Baker, with her back turned, talking to someone, not far away. It was loud in the cafeteria, but not *that* loud. It was only a matter of time before she noticed what was going on. I tried to get Walid to stop, but it didn't seem like he could hear me, and Huddy just kept yelling for him to get off.

"Hey!"

That was Mrs. Baker. I froze. Walid jumped away from Huddy, who slowly picked himself off the table.

"What's going on here?" she asked.

"Nothing," said Walid.

"He was hurting me," said Huddy, rubbing his arms.

"Is that true?"

"No," said Walid.

"No? That's not what it looked like to me."

"Okay, maybe?"

"Maybe?" asked Baker.

"I didn't realize I was hurting him," said Walid.

"You didn't realize?"

"No," he said, suppressing a smile.

"That's smart. What about you?" she said, turning to me.

I shrugged.

"I don't know," I said. It seemed impossible to explain.

"You don't know?"

"He hurt me, too," said Huddy.

"What the fuck?" said Walid. "He didn't do anything."

"*Excuse me?*"

"He didn't do anything," said Walid, cowed.

Mrs. Baker asked us all our names.

"I want all three of you to come with me."

"Are you serious?" asked Walid, knowing already that she was.

* * *

"Kent," said Vice-Principal Johnson, as I sat down across from him. "How quickly we've become acquainted. This is the second time I've had to deal with an altercation between you and Mr. Hudson. I'm beginning to see a pattern." Walid and Huddy were waiting in the office reception. They'd both already spoken to him.

"There wasn't an altercation between us," I said.

Johnson's eyebrow rose — he could do the Spock thing, just one.

"I don't know," I said. "I was just trying to talk to him. Then Walid came up, and ..."

"And what?"

"They had a disagreement."

"About what?"

I shrugged. "I don't know. Nothing, really."

"That sounds about right to me," said Johnson. "But would you say it would be more accurate to suggest that your friend Walid started the disagreement?"

I didn't answer. I didn't want to throw Walid under the bus, but he had also made that pretty fucking hard to not do.

"That's what I thought," said Johnson.

I guess it was pretty clear.

He gestured to my bag. "Is your camera in there?" he asked.

I nodded.

"Is there anything you need to show me?"

I felt heavy. Obviously I couldn't let Johnson see the footage or hear anything that Walid had said while I was filming. I felt like an idiot for shooting it in the first place. Lauren was so, so right.

"No," I said. "I just don't like keeping it in my locker."

Johnson looked at me for a long time. He was calm and his calm was giving me a migraine. Adults. Time moves faster for them. I tried to look as innocent as possible.

"Okay," he finally said. "I believe you, but only because I've already heard Walid and Patrick's versions of events. I will accept that you were just in the wrong place at the wrong time. But in case you weren't aware, and I don't understand how you couldn't not be, Patrick is not having a good time right now. It is our duty, as decent human beings, to be as understanding of that as possible. If I catch you bothering him again I won't go so easy on you."

"Yes," I said. "Of course."

"This is a warning. You are not completely exonerated. The slate has not been wiped clean. Remember that. I won't forget." He stared at me, hard.

I nodded.

"Okay. You're free to go."

Astounded, I blinked for a few moments, then mumbled my thanks and left. Johnson called both Huddy and Walid in after me. Walid gave me a confused look, as if it was my fault that he was going back in. Huddy looked like he'd been crying. I completely understood. I felt like I'd been crying, too. I hated being talked to like that.

Especially when I deserved it.

I had to get a note from the secretary excusing my absence because the second bell had rung long ago and I was late.

I learned afterward that Huddy had burst into tears when he and Walid were called in together, and that Johnson had threatened Walid with suspension. Instead, somehow, Walid argued him down to a couple weeks' detention, with much more serious consequences to come if he ever bothered Huddy again. I thought Walid was smart enough to know not to ever fuck with Huddy in the future. The only reason he escaped suspension, as far as I understand it, was his grades. And his eloquence, I guess.

His parents would have completely flipped if he'd been sent home.

"Fucking Huddy," said Walid, after he'd finished telling me the story. "It didn't have to be such a big deal."

I didn't say anything, because something had dawned on me after I'd left Johnson's office, during my long walk back to

English: Huddy hadn't told Johnson anything about the camera or the two days I'd spent filming him.

When I got home that night I tried to call Lauren at her house, but no one picked up. I sent her an MSN message later, but there was no response. I was going to have a lot of explaining to do the next day in bio, if she'd even talk to me. I felt like the worst person in the world. Or at least a pretty bad one.

6

What does it mean when someone dies?

I was thinking about that a lot.

Sometimes I thought about Mom and me, about how we were all that we had left. And how I felt guilty about that without really knowing why. And also that I was afraid, somehow, that whatever it was that Jeff had felt, I would feel it, too. Like it was contagious. And then I thought back to the beginning of *Evie*, Evie entering the Deepthorn, lost, alone. Only it wasn't Evie disappearing into the trees, it was Jeff. And that gave me a glimmer of hope. Like he could come back.

I wanted him to come back.

But I was worried that if I went after him, I'd get lost, too.

Sometimes I'd go down to the creek and imagine that it wasn't a creek, but a river or a lake. And that off in the distance I could see tiny lights blinking. And I imagined that there was something else out there, an apartment building or a neighbourhood or a whole city, where everyone is different, just slightly. Like, it's not easier or better there, it's just different. And in that world Jeff is like me, confused and maybe struggling, but still alive. And then I think, maybe I'll write a novel and it will be the life that I want Jeff to live. And it won't be a perfect life. Just a life. But as if I could change it. As if representation was more than fantasy. And then I think, is that why it's so difficult to figure out what I'm doing with this documentary? Is that why it means so much to me?

* * *

On Saturdays or on Mom's days off during the summer, when we were kids, she used to take us to this park on the edge of town. Just a swing set and a jungle gym and some benches, but it felt special because the park was near a creek and little forest. The forest has recently been cleared, now it's just sand and piles of dirt, ready to accept the housing development that they're building next year, which, I'm told, will surround the park in concentric rings of crescents and cul-de-sacs and detours and long, leaning lanes cutting across from Fourth to the highway.

Behind the park there was a path that led over a stream and into the forest, where it meandered and criss-crossed over itself before coming out of another exit about a hundred metres away. But you could also follow the creek deeper and deeper into the bush on a separate trajectory. If you followed it that way, the creek walls got higher and higher, like a sort of trench, and you'd have to make the decision to walk along the top, which was sometimes difficult, depending on how thick the forest was, or right alongside the creek itself, which was the more dramatic route, but didn't always offer a dry place for you to set down your feet, although if you were really careful you could pick your way across some of the less shallow areas, or, since the creek was pretty narrow at times, wedge yourself across the banks.

By the time Jeff was thirteen, he would usually just wander off to the creek as soon as we got there, leaving me to play by myself. I would have rather gone off with him, but I felt like with him gone someone had to entertain Mom, so I usually played on the swings while she watched. Maybe that's weird. But the way Mom always announced that we were going to the "*good* jungle gym," even though it wasn't much different than any of the others in town, made me feel that it meant something to her, like she was doing something special for us. Even though we'd probably dubbed the park "good" arbitrarily one morning when we were feeling bratty and she was dragging us somewhere else.

The last day I can remember all of us going there together, I had been feeling so generous that I had even allowed Mom to push me on the swings. I was ten by then, and old enough to find that a little bit humiliating, but Jeff had been a dick in the car and I wanted to make up for it. I don't remember what he'd said exactly, but he was pretty snipey then. Often the smallest comment would set him off. Even just asking questions about what he'd done at school could cause a mega fight, because Mom would keep pressing and pressing even though it was clear that he didn't want to talk about it at all. And instead of giving in and telling her about his day he snapped and turned it back on her. I always felt like it was my responsibility to smooth things over, like my being good would somehow reassure Mom that Jeff was okay and that she could leave him alone. Or that Jeff would see that there was a way to get along with Mom without causing things to escalate so quickly. But I know that Mom didn't feel like Jeff was okay, that he had surprised her or astonished her somehow, so that now she was always ready for him to explode, even when he was just minding his own business, like he was a psychopath or a killer that had snuck into our home.

After a while, Mom went to sit down on a park bench somewhere and I kept swinging. I was finally able to go as high as I wanted. But I started thinking about Jeff and wondering what he was up to.

The forest was usually abandoned, and even the park itself was pretty quiet on that particular June afternoon. I don't think it even occurred to Mom to be worried. Durham is sleepy, and even if it's hard not to notice that there are plenty of sketch people around, when you really start to look for them, it's also easy enough to pretend that they don't exist if that's what you'd prefer.

Maybe she should have been more worried, though.

It wasn't much of a forest, or at least that's what I'd always thought, but I'd always gone in with Jeff, and when I was with Jeff I felt brave, like nothing could hurt me. Which was maybe stupid since he was only three years older than me and he was just a kid, too. And if I went in with him there was at least one thing that could hurt me, and that was him, and he often did, turning and whaling on me out of nowhere or running off and pretending like he had abandoned me. I always knew when he'd run off that it was just a game, but that didn't stop me from playing my part and crying like it wasn't.

Once I got farther up from the park, and I could no longer hear the cars passing on the road, or see the field or the swings, once I realized that Jeff was going to be harder to find than I'd thought, I started to get scared. I called his name and hoped that would dispel my fear, but when he didn't appear and there was no answer, not from him or from the forest itself, it just made things worse. It felt like the birds and the plants and the insects were holding their breath, as stupid as that sounds, like they were waiting for something to descend on me, waiting for me to screw up so that they could catch me when my guard was down and tear me to shreds. It also wasn't out of the question that it was Jeff waiting, that he was just behind a bush and he was going to jump out at any moment and make me shit my pants, which was comforting, in a way. But not really comforting. Only more comforting than the alternative.

I tried to keep cool as I kept looking for him, fighting the panic that threatened to overtake me at any moment, as I imagined all kinds of dangers, from the relatively benign — but much more probable — lurking animals, to crazed child-killers, to supernatural horrors that were completely undefined in my imagination, but which somehow terrified me the most, filling up all of the negative space with a kind of profound and focused malevolence that I had somehow deeply offended or betrayed. I imagined for a minute that I wasn't looking for Jeff, but for myself, like it was my own body that was lying somewhere among the ferns. And not to say that I was looking for a body, although the thought had crossed my mind that whatever was waiting for me in the forest had gotten Jeff, too. In any case I was ready to panic and run screaming at any moment, and it took everything I had to stop that from happening.

Jeff would have seen that I was falling apart. He could smell my weakness. He knew when I was ready to cave, usually, well before I did. He had it down to a science: my psychic pressure points were ingrained in his DNA. You get that when you're an older brother, I think. So even if he hadn't planned on surprising me, it would have been impossible for Jeff to resist if he was spying. The fact that he hadn't jumped out yet was disconcerting, either because I was walking into a really exceptional trap or because something was actually wrong.

I don't know what I was imagining, but I also didn't want to clarify that too much for myself either, because to think about the horrors waiting for me was, to a certain extent, to bring them into being.

There was a place in the forest he liked to go, along the creek bed, where the banks were steep, and the vines — raspberry bushes, I think — thick overhead. The creek was narrower there and there was a little room to move around. Not far away enough that he wouldn't have been able to hear me calling for him, but I headed there, anyway.

Where Jeff liked to go. I didn't, not especially. But I could see the appeal. The place seemed enclosed, like a fort or a home, but it also seemed menacing to me, like it belonged to someone else and they could come home at any moment. It was hard to get there, at least without getting wet or falling on your ass. At times the creek went right to either bank and the only way to cross was to inch across slippery tree trunks or to nimbly skip across the tops of the least-submerged rocks.

The first time we'd gone that way had been weird, too. It was midsummer, and we'd spent all of this time navigating the creek bed, which seemed private and secret and almost magical because we were discovering it for the first time, and then we heard voices, hushed voices, speaking intimately, like we were waiting outside someone's kitchen or bedroom, and we stopped. I must have been seven or eight, and the idea of meeting anyone in the forest terrified me, but Jeff wanted to keep going. After watching him push forward for a while I reluctantly followed him, because the alternative — missing out or being alone in the forest or being called gay or a pussy, later — was much worse.

There were three teenagers where the creek narrowed, two men and one woman. A couple and another man. Maybe I should say two boys and a girl, but they seemed like men and women to me then, although more dangerous because men and women didn't seem capable of the same kinds of things that I knew teenagers were. One boy was leaning against the creek wall and the other two were sitting on a log pushed up against the bank. All of them were smoking, the couple sharing a single cigarette and the boy with his own and sparking a lighter in his hands.

"Look, Paul," said the boy standing by himself, when we rounded the final bend.

"How did you guys get here?" asked Paul.

We just stared at them quietly. Jeff gestured behind us.

The girl laughed. "They look so confused."

I wanted to leave immediately, but I could see that Jeff was in awe, either of the little space and how it expanded out and felt secret, or of the teenagers themselves and what they stood for: death, sex, secret knowledge.

The first boy barked and Jeff flinched.

"We own this forest," said Paul.

"No you don't," said Jeff, quietly, as if he couldn't be sure.

"You aren't allowed here," said Paul.

"That's not true," said Jeff.

He wanted so badly to belong, even when he had no business belonging. I thought I saw tears forming in his eyes.

"Guys," said the girl. "Come on. Be nice."

"This is nice," said Paul.

"Fuck you," said the boy, to us.

"See?" said Paul.

"Go home," said the boy.

"We don't want to," said Jeff, picking up a stick and, for a second, holding it in a vaguely threatening way. Then thinking better of it and whacking it idly against the creek bed instead.

"What's your name?" Paul asked me.

I just looked at him.

"His name is Kent," said Jeff.

"Can he talk?"

"Yeah," said Jeff.

"What?"

"I said '*Yeah*.'"

"You can talk?" asked Paul, looking at me.

I nodded.

"He probably shouldn't be here," said the boy.

"Yeah," said Paul. "We're bad."

"Maybe you can stay, though," said the boy, looking at Jeff.

"Jesus," said the girl, rolling her eyes.

"Don't mind her," said Paul.

"Yeah," said the boy. "She's on her period."

"You asshole," said the girl.

"What's your name?" asked the boy.

"Jeff."

"You seem cool," he said.

Jeff shrugged. He knew he didn't seem cool.

I could tell we were losing.

"Smoking is bad for you," I said.

"Is that right?" said Paul, taking an exaggerated drag.

"We know it's bad for us," said the girl.

"Are you going to tell?" asked the boy.

There was a moment of silence, as if Jeff was actually considering the boy's words. Was he going to tell on them or not? And, if so, to whom?

"Hey," said Paul. "Come over here."

Somehow, without our noticing, Paul had put his hand up the girl's shirt. It looked like a surprise to her, too, and she was trying to squirm out of his reach, but he was holding her close with his other hand.

"Do you want to feel?" asked Paul, looking at Jeff.

"Stop it," said the girl. "Come on." She tried to hit him away, but he adjusted his grip so that he was holding back one arm with his far hand and the other one back with his shoulder. That arm was pinned between them and she tried to manoeuvre it out.

"C'mon," said Paul. "They feel pretty good."

"Can I feel?" asked the boy.

"No," said the girl, finally ripping Paul's hand out from under her shirt and pulling the material back down to her waist. She got up and walked to the other end of the clearing. But first she grabbed the cigarette out of Paul's mouth and threw it into the water.

"Fucking asshole!" she said.

Paul shrugged.

"Look at him, he's so scared," said the boy.

Jeff was really scared, I could see that. He was still staring at Paul.

"How old are you?" asked the boy.

Instead of answering, Jeff turned and ran. I looked at them for a minute longer, unsure what had just happened. I think they were surprised, too.

Finally, the boy laughed. "That was so fucked up, Paul."

"I know," he said.

Somehow they'd forgotten all about me.

"That kid is going to have a wet dream tonight," said the boy.

The girl just looked at Paul.

"That wasn't okay," she said.

"Ugh," said the boy.

"He wasn't going to do it," said Paul.

"You're right he wasn't," she said.

The two boys laughed. Paul was lighting another cigarette.

"Like. What the fuck," she said.

"It was a joke," said Paul.

"It wasn't very fucking funny."

"I thought it was funny," said the boy.

"See?" said Paul.

She gave him the finger.

"*Like, what the fuck,*" said the boy, in an idiot voice.

"Fuck off," said the girl.

67

There was a moment of silence. My heart was pounding. I wanted Jeff to come back, to show them up, to prove that he was better than they thought he was. That he was better than they were. But I knew that he wasn't coming back. And that it was an impossible dream.

"Don't say 'fuck,'" I said, instead.

The girl jumped a little when she noticed me.

"I thought he was gone," said Paul.

"Don't say 'fuck,'" I said again.

For a minute it was quiet. Then the boy grinned. Paul started to laugh.

And then I ran back the way we came, just like Jeff had.

* * *

Then I'd been scared, too, going back down the creek on my own, so scared that I hadn't been watching my feet while crossing over a log and slipped and soaked myself. And made things much worse digging out one of my shoes from the muck in the creek bottom. Jeff got in trouble for that, of course, when I came back, stoically limping in my dripping clothes, because he was supposed to be watching over me, and Mom and him got in a huge fight and he ran out of the car when we pulled into the driveway, and didn't come back until later that night, well after dinner, which Mom said she wouldn't have let him eat, anyway, when we were at the table without him. Although when he came in the door she told him about the Tupperware full of lasagna in the fridge and he put some on a plate and ate it cold in the dark kitchen (he didn't bother turning on the lights), working slowly, I could tell, while Mom and I watched *Law & Order* in the living room, dropping his plate in the sink with a crash when he was done, which got Mom on her feet. He whispered sorry loudly from the kitchen, but everyone knew it wasn't a mistake, and Mom told him to go

to bed, and me to go bed, which I did immediately, not even hes-
itating, and which he did only after muttering something which
my mom asked him to repeat and which turned out to be, when
he finally said it, "I *was* going to bed."

We'd been back to the creek lots of times afterward and
though I always thought the teens would be back, not without
some hesitation, we hadn't seen them once. Not even from a distance. Though Jeff wouldn't admit it, I think they were why he
insisted on going there week after week. He wanted to see them
again. I don't know why. Or what he was trying to prove.

I made my way up the creek slowly, occasionally calling his
name. My fear was different than it had been back then. I was alone
and something was wrong, but I didn't know what. I was afraid that
he wouldn't be there and I wouldn't know what to do. I couldn't
search the whole forest by myself. I'd have to get Mom, and then
even if we did find him it would be a huge deal and he'd probably
run off again.

Eventually I started to hear a low sort of mewling coming
from down the creek. Little breathy squeaks that sounded like
they were coming from a hundred miles away. Which obviously
couldn't have been possible, it was just the way that the sound
dispersed into the air. It reminded me of this time I had been
mowing the lawn and noticed only when it was too late — just
as the lawn mower passed over — that the movement between
the blades of grass I had assumed was the wind wasn't the wind
at all, but a baby bird straining to be fed. I turned off the lawn
mower and went inside, afraid to move it forward or backward,
afraid to disturb the site of the massacre, until Mom came home
from work and yelled at me for leaving the lawn unfinished, the
mower out on the front lawn. When I reluctantly went back to
the mower and moved it off its little square, I couldn't find any
traces of the little bird at all, which felt like a miracle, even though

I was certain that the bird was dead. Even though I hadn't been able to hear the bird at the time, because of the lawn mower noise, obviously, the mewling that I heard now sounded like what I imagined the bird must have sounded like, the sound which I had heard over and over in my dreams. If there was a baby bird on the ground, maybe I could manoeuvre it back into its nest somehow, with sticks or leaves or something, without the mother bird noticing. Small atonement. I forgot about Jeff for a minute and began scanning the ground.

But when I rounded the bend in the creek it was Jeff I discovered, lying on his side, half his body in the creek, his head on the far bank. He was staring into a middle distance and he was the one mewling. His head was bleeding, and the blood was running down his neck and staining his shirt.

I didn't want to touch him because I was afraid I might make things worse. Also because I was afraid to touch him. Because he was bleeding and I was scared and I didn't know what to do. He didn't look real to me. It was like he had crawled out of my imagination. I thought maybe if I closed my eyes and told myself he wasn't real that he would go away, like a bad dream, and I'd find him farther down the creek bend, waiting where he always was, and he'd call me a loser for getting so afraid over nothing, just a walk in the woods.

He somehow managed to look at me but he was only able to make more of that mewling sound, infinitely more disturbing than from the bird in my dreams.

7

I ran back to get Mom, and she ran into the forest with me to see what she could do. Someone at the park volunteered to call an ambulance from home. I led Mom to Jeff and then ran back to the forest entrance to wait for the paramedics.

It looked like Jeff hit his head on a boulder lying near the creek bed. It was lucky that he hadn't face-planted into the water. He could have drowned.

I mean, I led her most of the way, pointing her down the final bend of the creek. I was too afraid to see him again. I didn't even look in his direction when they carried him out of the forest.

Mom camped out in the ICU overnight and I stayed over with Aunt Wanda. Mom was upset, but also angry, angry at Jeff for injuring himself, and angry at herself for fighting with him on the way to the park. I think she wondered, too, if she had driven him to it, like it wasn't an accident at all, but a weird form of revenge. I mean, it seemed to me like she thought that but she never articulated it that clearly, probably because she knew to suggest that would be seriously crazy. He was just a kid. He slipped.

The next morning they said his condition had stabilized and they took him out of intensive care. I went to visit him with Aunt Wanda around ten o'clock. He was sleeping and the whole right side of his head was swollen, a gross purple blotch. There was a bandage wrapped around his head, and some of his hair was shaved. He had to get the whole thing shaved later to even it out, and it didn't grow back in properly until the first week of school, at least not according to his complaints.

I was afraid that if he woke up he might start mewling again, and eyed him cautiously from across the room. Mom smiled wearily from the chair next to his bed when Wanda handed her a Thermos of coffee and a muffin that she'd picked up on the way over.

"I'd strangle him if I wasn't so happy he was okay," she said.

Wanda laughed.

Jeff opened his eyes slowly, as if he hadn't been sleeping, only play-acting.

"Hey," he said.

"Look who's up," said Mom.

"I was trying to sleep, but I couldn't," said Jeff.

He looked at me.

"Hey," he said.

"Hey," I said.

"I saw those kids again," he said. Obviously I knew exactly what he meant, even though we hadn't talked about them in a while.

"What kids?" asked my mom, suddenly concerned.

"No, you didn't," I said. In his dreams, maybe.

"What kids are you talking about?" Mom asked.

"You're right," he said to me. "I didn't."

"You sounded like a bird," I said. I was already warming up to him. When he spoke I was somehow able to look past the purple blotch and see through to his real face. But only when he was animated. Otherwise he was unreadable, an abomination that I didn't want to confront.

"I know, Mom told me. Although she said I sounded like a mouse."

"Kent, what kids?" asked my mom.

"That was a joke," said Jeff.

"Yeah," I said.

"What do you mean, a joke? Kent, were there any other kids out there?"

"No," I said, feeling worried.

She lowered herself to my level. "Are you sure?"

"Trish," said Wanda.

"Wanda, will you stay out of this?"

She turned back to me and grabbed my arm.

"*Mom*," said Jeff, "*I was joking.*" He sat up a little bit and then winced in pain and lay back down.

"Why would you joke about a thing like that?"

"I don't know!"

"I think he's telling the truth," said Wanda, looking very confused.

"What if someone hurt him?" asked my mom.

"No one hurt him," I said.

"What? Who did?" said my mom, snapping her attention back to me.

"*No one did,*" I said, bursting into tears. "*No one hurt him.*"

Somehow I'd broken the spell. Mom suddenly softened, pulling me close and putting her arms around me. I hid my face in her shirt, embarrassed because Jeff and Aunt Wanda were there.

"No one hurt him," I repeated.

"I'm so sorry, baby, I'm so sorry," she said, running a hand through my hair.

"It was just me, Mom," said Jeff.

"I know that, Jeff."

"Maybe you should get some rest," said Wanda, cautiously.

"You're right," said Mom, standing up again, very slowly. "I'm exhausted." She looked down at me. "How are you doing, buddy?"

"I'm okay," I said, wiping tears from my eyes.

Wanda patted Jeff's arm.

"I think the real question is, how are *you* doing?" she asked.

"My head hurts," he said.

"I'll bet it does," said Wanda.

Mom laughed and kissed Jeff on the forehead.

"I'm so glad you're okay," she said.

Jeff tried not to smile.

*   *   *

Jeff didn't change after the accident, but I sometimes thought of him that way, as if there was a before and after that could be separated into two distinct periods. But in reality maybe that process had already begun long before then.

He outstripped puberty, growing larger — in every direction — weight piling on his frame, lumbering from the kitchen to the couch like a bear stumbling home after gorging himself on turned berries, his eyes intent on whatever was playing on the screen. Not that I didn't have the same rounds — we both ate constantly, when we were home, but somehow it stuck to him and not to me. Maybe I got out of the house more, or ate a little less, or watched less TV, or maybe I was just lucky.

He still fought with Mom. But the fights changed — it took less, a lot less, for him to get angry — though that anger didn't always show itself immediately. His anger was always on the surface, but it often manifested itself in quieter ways. In silence. In brooding. In comments that hid their aggression, but were aggressive nonetheless. But it could lead to real violence, too — once he utterly annihilated a Super Nintendo and ten-inch television that he'd set up in his room. When I asked him what had happened he told me that it was the fault of whichever fucking asshole had designed Donkey Kong Country. I was angry that he had wrecked a thing that belonged to both of us but it seemed pointless to get upset about it in the face of his anger. All I could do was shrug.

Mom told him that he was lazy, that it was his fault that he was unhappy, that he needed to get a job, to do better at school, that he had an anger problem, that it would help him to have more friends, that he was going to grow up miserable. I'm ashamed to say now that I usually agreed with her. I wanted him to be happy so there could be peace at home.

He never really came out of his shell, but when Wizard Palace comic book shop opened and he got into Magic: the Gathering, he at least started leaving the house more. He made friends that he spent time with outside of school. This was when he was in either grade nine or ten, I don't remember. Before, he would do his best to ignore Mom whenever she asked him who his friends at school were or whether he wanted to invite any of them home. After Wizard Palace, he could at least name them. First, kids his age, Spink and Ted Linnean. Later, Watt and JC, Watt in my grade and JC two years above. There were other players, too, on the periphery, guys in their twenties and kids in middle school, whom they occasionally talked about but who were never officially part of their group.

Wizard Palace ran casual games at a table in the back, and he usually went there after school, coming home first and dropping his things off in the mud room, eating a snack and maybe watching an episode or two of *The Simpsons*, then heading back out again, eschewing homework most nights, and only picking at dinner at nine o'clock, after the Palace had closed and he'd already filled up on Doritos and Mountain Dew. He got his spending money from a job that he held in the summer, and sometimes on the weekends, sautering simple circuit boards in the garage of our neighbour, Mr. O'Shaunessy.

Jeff built me a deck out of his cast-off cards so we could play, and he was always trying to encourage me to purchase my own, so that the games between us could become more heated. When we played I had brief flashes of insight that caused me to get more involved, that made me rush to my pile of extras and trade cards in and out of my deck, brief thrills when I managed to pull off something that Jeff hadn't anticipated (because he hadn't thought I was capable of it), flashes where I could see what drew him and his friends to the game. It was the feeling of control, of dominance, of mastery, of creativity made into a corporeal force that could inflict itself on your opponent. But those moments were fleeting, and whatever gains I made were always paid back double in the next match, when Jeff — eager to compete — would totally adapt to my strategy and blow me out of the water. Eventually Jeff had to beg me to play, which took the fun out of it for both of us.

But there were other things that threatened to draw me to the game: the little fantasy portraits and scenes on each card almost always showed something in motion — between two actions, making it impossible not to speculate on the before and after, on the context that established the rules of our encounter. The cards were little pieces of another world thrust into ours, and their mannered presentations raised questions in my mind. But I made sure not to become too intrigued. I was happy for Jeff, but careful not to get too wrapped up in that world. Watt, JC, Linnean, even Spink, though everybody loved him, they were all just a rung or two higher than Huddy, and maybe only because of their ability to blend in, to remain out of sight, to seem innocuous and mundane by comparison.

Maybe something I had been trying to do with my documentary was discover what separated Huddy from them, to trace their respective outlines, to see him through that lens, inhabit the terror that Jeff must have felt even if he didn't cop to it, what they all must have felt, the worry, constant, that it was possible they could slip even lower.

8

Lauren ignored me the whole next week in bio, making a point of sitting a couple seats away. I watched her all through that first class, confused and unsure how to make things better. I approached her after the bell rang and asked if we could talk, but she told me that she didn't talk to bullies. I said that she didn't understand and she told me that she always understood and abruptly stalked off. At lunch Walid told me that it was better that she wasn't talking to me, because she was a bitch and uptight and I was spending so much time with her that I was killing any chances I had of "getting any" with anyone else, but I told him that Lauren was probably the least uptight person I knew, and that I liked hanging out with her and it wasn't like that even though it sort of was, and that she had principles and that I even agreed with her. He asked me if I was on my period or if I was feeling sick or faint and I asked him if he was bleeding out of his penis because his logic sucked and (the implication was) he was a dickhead getting soft and losing focus. He told me that was lame or a reach and I had to agree, it was a reach, and that was the end of that, things were fine, mostly, and I got up to buy a chocolate milk.

"I need to change my tampon," I said, joking. Walid and Kyle laughed and Alex said, "Gross, man," and Devon said, "You wear *tampons?*" like he had caught me in something and it was *his* fucking joke. He could be a total moron sometimes. I wasn't sure if he was just playing along or being an idiot, but I didn't care either way. When I was standing in line I told myself that reality didn't matter to me and that I could make any joke I liked. That I could make anything into anything else. That was a strange thought for me to have but I was getting sick of the guys, I guess, and their sometimes — I thought — limited repertoire. I can't wait until I'm out of here for good, I thought, or for forever, whichever comes first.

For good or forever.

I felt stupid.

All of a sudden, a wave of feeling.

I was lost.

I was so deep in my thoughts that I didn't notice Watt standing in front of me. He kept looking back, like he wanted to say something, and I only realized what he was doing when it was too late. I didn't want to talk to him — more than any of Jeff's friends, Watt was weird: tall and gangly, always choking back his words, even then saying the wrong thing, constantly directing conversation my way, asking more of me than I could ever hope to give, because I was kind to him, just kind, because he had been my brother's friend, and for no other reason. I was too polite to tell him that it wasn't okay, but it really got on my nerves. And he'd only gotten weirder with time, as the others graduated and moved on with their lives.

Finally, after we'd both gone through cash, he stopped me. It took him a moment to come out with what he was struggling to say. I braced myself, but even then I wasn't prepared for what came next.

"Do you still have any of Jeff's cards?" he asked.

My face must have told him everything he needed to know, because he took an alarmed step backward.

"What?" I said.

Was he serious? What the fuck did he want with Jeff's cards?

"I just —"

"Fuck you," I said.

"That's —"

"Get lost."

But I didn't give him the opportunity to, because I left him standing by the registers. I heard him calling after me, but weakly, like a mouse pulled into a hurricane. Not even worth turning around. When I sat down Devon asked me if I'd put my tampon in wrong and I asked him what the fuck was wrong with him. If he'd ever had an original thought in his whole fucking life. He shrugged. Walid asked me what the hell was up with me and I told him that Watt was a creep and that he wanted some of my brother's things and Walid said, "Jesus," and I said, "Yeah."

I didn't even blame Watt, weirdly, because I knew that whatever he was after he didn't know any better, but I was still pissed off. There was nothing that Jeff put more of himself into than his cards. Every one of them bore his fingerprints. Each one told a small part of his story. Together they combined to form the most accurate picture of him that remained.

When I got home later that day I headed straight upstairs, in a hurry, but afraid to run. I was afraid that when I made it to his room everything would be changed somehow — his things suddenly boxed, or swept away, or gone. And that if it wasn't like that, that hurrying would make it so. When I crossed the threshold I realized that I hadn't entered his room since the night before he left for the tournament, when I went in to wish him a hesitant but sincere "good luck." To take another look at his cards and

determine whether they were good enough to do what he wanted
or needed them to.

The cards I am now careful not to touch.

* * *

I sent Lauren a long email, explaining that I had gotten carried
away in class and that my intention wasn't to make fun of Huddy,
but to understand him, that I had misrepresented myself, but that
I agreed with her, anyway, that the project was stupid and maybe
I was a bully and I wasn't doing it anymore. And that I had made
this decision before my encounter with Johnson, though I told
her about that, too, and how I knew I was lucky not to have got
in worse shit. For some reason I didn't mention what Walid had
done. It seemed like it wasn't important.

I sent the email to her on Saturday afternoon and two days
later she still hadn't responded. I was nervous, because the two first
semester grade twelve English classes were going on a field trip
that Monday and she would be on the bus. I didn't want things
to be awkward between us. I mean, to continue to be awkward.

We were going to see *As You Like It* at a theatre in Brampton.
Our class hadn't read the book yet, but the other form had. I
was kind of nervous about seeing the play, both because I wasn't
sure I would understand it and because it had such a stupid
title. Mrs. Wilson seemed really excited, too, which was a huge
point against.

On Monday I deliberately dragged my feet in the parking lot
to avoid an awkward encounter with Lauren, sitting out on one
of the benches in front of the school, getting carried away talking
to Chris and Nick, neither of whom had English that term, but
who did have a free first period. I saw that people were lining up
to go, but by the time I got to the bus the doors were clear and
the engine was rumbling.

I mumbled an apology to Mrs. Wilson and hurried down the aisle, looking for a spot. Walid was sitting next to Samantha, Kyle with Alex. Even Mrs. Wilson had a partner, Karly Gladkis, who had taken the opportunity to discuss her ISU project in more detail. The only seat remaining was next to Watt. I had to take it, trying not to make eye contact with him when I did.

My only consolation was that Lauren had gotten on the other bus.

I was only a couple seats away from the others, so I perched on the edge and tried to lean over to hear what they were talking about. But it seemed like everyone else was wrapped up in their partner. And with the windows open anyway and the sound of all the other kids it was impossible to hear what they were saying. I was stuck, for at least the next hour.

About halfway through the drive, which I had spent watching hills undulate through the window across the aisle, I noticed that Watt was getting restless. He wanted to say something, I was sure of it. I tried to absorb myself even more in the view outside, which was hard because people I loved were between me and the far windows and I wanted to talk to them but their heads were bowed together, cloistered, oblivious.

"Hey," Watt said finally, touching me on the arm (I guess giving up on ever making incidental eye contact).

I turned, reluctantly.

"*What?*" I said.

He looked at me for a moment, his eyes watery.

"Oh, sorry," he said.

And was quiet. I waited.

"Before, I didn't mean to ..." he started.

"Jesus," I said, turning away from him.

A few minutes later he touched my shoulder again.

"I'm sorry for ... the other day ..."

I just looked at him. In response he banged his head softly against the window, and remained with his head pushed up against the pane for the rest of the ride.

He tried talking to me again when we were pulling in. I was already standing in the aisle, and I only heard him the second time he raised his voice.

"*I said*, I didn't want the cards for myself. The other day."

"Good for you," I said.

The line moved.

*   *   *

I guess I could have been nicer to him. But maybe I didn't care. Watt was a creep but he should have known better. There are some things you just don't ask for.

Ever.

Walid turned to me as we were walking into the lobby, briefly separated from the others. "So — an hour with Watt, eh? You two looked like you were having fun."

He made a jerking-off motion with his hand. Right. Sometimes he was the stupidest person in the whole fucking world.

"Go to hell," I said. "Thanks for saving me a seat."

Walid looked around, and seeing that Samantha was momentarily distracted, gave me a knowing look before dragging his index finger under his nose and sniffing audibly.

"*Butterscotch*," he said.

It was a line from a movie I had never seen. But I knew what he meant.

"You did not," I said. I tried to remember their posture on the bus. They'd just been talking. I was looking their way almost the whole ride, and I hadn't noticed anything unusual.

I looked at Sam. Would she actually let Walid do that? On the bus?

For that matter, would Walid really do it? In front of everyone? "Believe whatever you want, man," he said, shrugging.

It couldn't be true. Could it?

I felt backward, like I was a lamb or a holy innocent taking their first, hesitant steps into the world. I hated that feeling, but it came over me all the time. I wouldn't have cared that I was a virgin except for that. I wanted to know what everyone was talking about, not just to experience it for myself, but so I could stop feeling so left out.

*   *   *

Theatre seems really dumb until the lights go down and the curtains open. But as soon as the lights *do* go down, something changes. There's a hush, and you realize that everyone else is immersed in what's happening on the stage, and it's impossible not to be caught in that charge. Mrs. Wilson spent a lot of time talking about "suspension of disbelief" when she was talking about the play and about our coming trip. But I wondered if it couldn't be looked at from the other way around. Not that reality was being suspended, but changed — creating an entirely new reality, dreaming the characters into existence.

I'm sure I'm not the only person who's ever thought that before. But that's exactly how I felt sitting in the theatre, watching Orlando as he walked out of the wings, bearing the weight of his tyrannical older brother.

Orlando is supposed to be young. But the guy they had playing Orlando was not young, except in comparison with some of the other actors in the play. They'd shaved his face clean, but by the middle of the second act I swear I already saw a five o'clock shadow. And his heavy gut and puffing face weren't exactly a testament to his youth, either. But something about the way he walked and spoke made me buy it. Maybe I was just ready to.

The day before our trip, Mrs. Wilson went on and on in class about that speech of Jacques's — the famous one, which begins "All the world's a stage" — and about how that speech was a kind of comment on the device of the play. As if that's all it was. As if the play couldn't escape its bounds and impose itself on the world of the reader, as I had imagined it was doing. I like to think Shakespeare wasn't just speaking playfully about the relationship between his play and the Globe Theatre, he was saying something terrifying about the nature of the world. That no one is anything so much as the role they've been forced to play. That underneath they are nothing else. Bound by time and by our pasts and the parts that we play in other people's lives — and that all of these things together don't really form a true identity. That we can be undone at any moment. That the play changes and takes us with it.

It makes me feel so sad and alone.

*   *   *

I didn't get all of that then. I went home and read *As You Like It* that night, staying up 'til two in the morning, pushing past whole stanzas I didn't understand, using what I had *felt* in the theatre for reference.

When Orlando outwrestled Charles, saving himself from the gruesome fate Oliver had intended for him, I don't know why, but I just broke down crying. It was the stupidest thing. I still had so far to go. I pulled my pillow close and just heaved into it — I mean, I really wept. For a good ten minutes, which is a modern record for me. Then I lay back on the bed and stared up at the ceiling, trying to figure out what the heck had just happened. I had no idea. I made it through to the end of the first act before Mom called me down for dinner.

I washed my face in the mirror and tried to restore my appearance before I walked downstairs. Mom kept squinting at me and asking what I had been doing up there. I think she was joking or that she wanted to get me talk about the book. I just kept saying "reading," trying not to meet her eyes.

Finally I got so mad that I pushed myself away from the table. "What does it matter what I'm doing?" I said. "What's it matter?"

I wouldn't say that I'm proud of doing that. I ran upstairs and slammed my bedroom door shut behind me. Then I pulled my dresser in front of the door. Then I unscrewed the doorknob and took out the pin that made it work, since I don't actually have a lock.

I heard my mom downstairs. She wasn't happy. But there was no one for her to talk to except herself. I lay in bed a long time, half-heartedly trying to go to sleep, and then I picked up the book again and read until two in the morning.

*   *   *

After the play was finished Lauren leaned over and tapped me on the shoulder, asking if I wanted to go for a walk. "I got your email," she said. Walid was busy talking to Samantha, and we slipped down the opposite end of the aisle without them even noticing. We had an hour to kill for lunch. Lauren said she knew a place and I followed her up three flights of stairs and to an unlocked door marked STAFF.

"Is this okay?" I said, meaning "Are we going to get in trouble?"

"It's not a big deal," she said.

"How do you know?"

"I used to do theatre when I was a kid," she explained. "When I lived here. We used to go out here all the time."

I didn't know she used to live in Brampton. I knew about Orangeville, but not Brampton.

We found ourselves on the lobby's gravel roof, with the brick of the theatre proper behind us. I could hear people on the sidewalk, but couldn't see them. I walked out to the edge, once, caught a glimpse of the crowd, and then I hurried back.

From where we stood we could see the buses camped out in the parking lot, a few drivers standing in a clump before one with its engine running. The theatre's asphalt parking lot spread out before us like an ocean, hundreds of yards, the traffic on Bovaird like waves breaking in the distance. A few gulls swooped down and strutted haughtily on the roof. I thought I could make out, above the general thrum of conversation, Walid's discordant "caw" — he sometimes liked to tease birds — and the sound of someone's laughter.

"I'm glad that you aren't doing that documentary anymore," she said.

"Yeah," I said. "It was a stupid idea."

"I don't think Wright would have liked it," she said.

"I don't know what I was thinking."

There was a pause in the conversation, and then Lauren told me that she'd just broken up with her boyfriend.

"Wow," I said. "That's big." I tried to imagine what he looked like, to picture him sad, I guess. But realized I couldn't. I'd only met him a couple of times. He seemed obnoxious to me, some dumb skater in the grade above us, with a condescending smile. But, then, I hadn't ever really given him much of a chance. I mean, Lauren must have liked him for a reason.

"How do you feel about that?" I asked.

"Good," she said. "I think. Also not good."

We continued talking. I took an apple out of my bag and when I was done I threw the core down the roof for the birds to fight over.

As we were talking, I picked out a few cars in the distance that — probably just because they were so far away — sort of looked like hers. Like I was waiting on my porch for her to pick me up. It was an old habit that was especially stupid when I was sitting right next to her.

When we saw our buses emerge from the others, identifiable by our school's crest posted on neon paper in the windows, we reluctantly stood up and started brushing ourselves off.

Leaning against the door inside, spooking when we pulled it out from under him, was Watt.

"Jesus!" screamed Lauren. She quickly apologized when she realized what had happened. And then she grew suspicious.

"Were you spying on us?"

"No …" said Watt, in his soft, slow-gathering way. "I didn't know you were out there."

"Right," said Lauren. "Well, I hope you got what you came for."

Watt looked at me for support. I didn't think he was lying. I felt sorry for him, because I was pretty sure Watt went up there so he could be as inconspicuous as possible, to be alone and to not get in anyone's way. But Lauren was already way ahead of us. So I shrugged and ran down the stairs.

The bus was almost full, but, miraculously, Walid and Samantha had saved a space for each of us. Watt was the last one on, and he had to sit up front with Mrs. Wilson.

9

Jeff had told me there was going to be a huge Magic tournament in Toronto that February, held at the Metro Toronto Convention Centre over three days. Winner and runner-up earned automatic qualifications and airfare to the Worlds in Berlin, plus prize money, and anyone who finished in the top eight was guaranteed at least qualifications. Jeff won most of the bimonthly tournaments at the Palace, a degree of consistency that was impressive regardless of the generally low level of competition. But he had another trick up his sleeve. The deck he was working on, he told me, was nothing like the rotation of five or six decks currently considered competitive. He let me see it once in action, moving quickly to demolish Linnean at our kitchen table, taking the match in something outrageous, like four turns. Linnean was the only one allowed to see it because even though he planned on going to Toronto with everyone else, he hadn't registered for the tournament. He was just going to offer his support. He'd also signed a flimsy-looking non-disclosure agreement that Jeff had drafted and printed off of our ancient Compaq. Jeff tried to make me sign one, too, but I just laughed at him. He didn't want word to get out in advance of the

Toronto contest, although I don't know how far he could have expected the news to travel. Even though you can do the trip in just a couple of hours, it's a long way down 10, longer than it seems.

High-level Magic play, Jeff explained to me, is something like a complex game of rock-paper-scissors, with chance to level the playing field. After the first few tournaments for a particular set, a number of decks appear which are considered viable, and these decks all have their own particular strengths and weaknesses, which a knowledgeable opponent will know how to identify and exploit. Creating a viable deck that was outside this rotation — looking at cards in the format, determining which underused cards had potential, and then developing a unique engine or variant — could therefore create a huge advantage against an opponent. All decks changed as the season progressed, and so the aim was to create something entirely new, to not just keep up with the new developments, but to get a step or two ahead of everyone else and blow them out of the water.

Fifteen thousand dollars was on the line, not to mention the trip to Berlin the following August. Jeff told me that if he won the tournament he was going to drop out of school. Lots of professional Magic players did, he said.

"Yeah, but high school?"

"What's the difference? School is school. You don't need it to play."

But he only had a few months to go. We were in his room, and he was shuffling through his cards and laying them out in piles. He had just paid the eighty-dollar entrance fee. Things weren't going well, he said. Even if he finished out the term he'd still have to come back for another full semester.

I was incredulous.

"What are you talking about?" I said. "You're already doing an extra year."

"That's what I mean," he said, looking at his cards.

"You have to finish. Just, I don't know, buckle down."

"I'll just get my GED."

"That's stupid."

"No," he said, separating a stack of cards into small piles, "it's smart. You're stupid."

He was always saying that the education system was a scam, that you could learn more reading on your own. He'd read that on the internet somewhere. I'd already known he wasn't going to university, but this was still a huge surprise.

I mean, high school is free. That's what I said. It's free.

He just shrugged. "There are other costs," he said, ominously.

School was generally a subject that we never addressed because I knew it embarrassed him and in a way it embarrassed me, too, even though I didn't like to think of it that way. Because it wasn't his fault. Not really.

"Is this just because, like, people make fun of you?"

I could hear something rising in his voice, either anger or another feeling I couldn't identify. A messier feeling.

"Who does?" he said.

I was afraid to answer, at first.

"I don't know … people." I shrugged.

He looked at me, in the eyes, once, then lowered them to the floor.

"You aren't exactly popular," I continued.

"I don't care about being popular," he said, turning back to his desk and reshuffling the cards.

"I know. I was just saying."

I felt like I'd gone too far, even though I hadn't said anything that either of us didn't already know. It still seemed like a violation whenever it came up in conversation. But him dropping out was an extreme enough situation to warrant crossing that boundary.

"You should forget about the other kids and just focus on finishing."

"I'm doing that. Just in another way."

"But —"

"*Listen*," he said, rounding on me. "I don't need your advice, okay? I've thought a lot about this. It's a good idea. Mom thinks so, too."

"She does not."

"If you don't believe me, ask her yourself."

I didn't believe him. I thought he must have exaggerated or deliberately misinterpreted something else she had said.

I was on the point of leaving, but I decided to watch him some more. I needed to calm down and I didn't want to storm out. I wanted it to seem like I wasn't that upset, like it wasn't a big deal, or like it was a big deal, but it was his problem, not mine.

I wanted to reassure myself, too. Even then I wanted to know that the world wasn't as flimsy as he made it seem.

That it wouldn't be, for me.

After a while I noticed that he wasn't really doing anything, just moving cards around in a way that seemed to soothe him. He built up piles and tore them down without any purpose that was apparent.

I started to find it soothing, too.

But one thing was bothering me. I mean, more than one thing was bothering me. But I wanted to ask him another question.

"What if you don't win?"

"Huh?"

"What if you don't win the tournament? Or come in second. Or finish in the top eight. What if you don't even qualify for Worlds?"

He thought about that for a bit.

"I'm still dropping out. Maybe I'll write a book."

It was the dumbest thing I've ever heard anyone say in my entire life. I punched him in the shoulder and walked out. He seemed surprised. I was lucky that he wasn't in the mood to chase me down and give it back — he had at least fifty pounds on me, and he could really go at it if given half a chance.

I asked Mom about it later. Maybe the next Saturday. We were in the car. She was running errands, and I had tagged along. That was usually the best time to talk. I had spent the entire trip thinking of ways to bring it up. I guess I was acting strange because she asked me if I was feeling okay.

"Do you have a fever?" she asked.

"No," I said.

"Are you sure?"

I nodded.

She put her hand on my forehead. "You feel clammy. Maybe it was something you ate. What did you have for breakfast?"

"Just cereal," I said, weakly, afraid to give away any more.

I put my seat belt on and stared out the window, watching the hydro poles and imagining that the passenger-side mirror was a buzz saw that cut down every single one.

I blurted it out, finally, as we were pulling onto the highway on our way back.

"Did you know that Jeff wants to drop out of school?"

Mom didn't look at me. I wondered if she hadn't heard — the heat was on and so was the radio. I lowered the volume and repeated myself, but louder.

"I heard you the first time," she said, not taking her eyes off the road.

"Oh," I said.

"I don't think it's a good idea."

"That's what I thought! He said —"

"But it might be the best idea," she said. "For Jeff."

I was stunned.

"I just don't have time to deal with this. Right now."

"What?" I said, finally.

She didn't answer.

"Deal with what?"

She gave me a look that said *I mean it*.

So I resigned myself to looking back out the window. Eventually Mom turned the radio up, and the rest of the way home we listened to a story about how Greenland was losing its ice cover in the face of global warming, and what that meant for the Inuit people who still made their living there.

"It's a changing world," said the announcer.

*   *   *

"Another reason I'm dropping out," Jeff told me, later, "is that I just don't feel compatible with any of my friends."

"What?" I said. I felt like I'd been saying that a lot lately. Like I was a bird and that was the only noise I could make: Whaaaat? WhaAAT? Like instead of asking for bread crumbs I was strutting up and down sidewalks asking fundamental questions about the decisions people I loved were making. I had only just recently sort of accepted the fact that he wasn't going to finish high school, which was made a little bit easier by the fact that he'd made a nonsensical pact with Mom to finish out the term (he was still going to fail most of his classes).

We were leaning on the wall outside Mac's, eating Klondike bars. The one thing I'd always envied about Jeff, even if he wasn't doing great, even if people made fun of him, was that he had his group of friends, and they shared a lot of common interests, hanging out after school all the time. They seemed tight — like there were no ambiguities between them. Like they were part of a team. But maybe I didn't really know anything about that. I guess I didn't.

He shrugged.

We watched the cars go by. Someone honked, either at another car or at us. The driver might have been a friend or an enemy, I wasn't sure. They looked young, but in Durham that meant they could have been twenty-five or seventeen. Or thirty-six. It was difficult to tell.

"I don't know," Jeff said, finally, shielding his eyes from the late-afternoon sun. "I just ... I don't belong here," he said.

"I don't belong here, either," I said, trying to hide my relief.

"But you belong here more than me."

Why did I have to explain to my older brother that "belonging" was constructed and that if you didn't want to belong you didn't put in the effort and if you wanted to belong you did? Hadn't he sort of taught me that?

"I thought you didn't care," I said.

"I don't."

"Okay ..."

"It's like, look." He reached into his pocket. "See this card?"

It was a Magic card, of course.

"Yes," I said. He just had it in his pocket? It was pretty beat-up, I guess partially from being carried around, but it also looked pretty old. Like it was from an older set. On its face there was an angel, painted in a vague Renaissance style, but wearing battle armour and looking up to the heavens. Behind the angel, gross combinations of machines and flesh ("Phyrexians," Jeff had told me), were battling knights in (literally) shining armour.

"Don't tell me that you're the angel," I said.

"Why not?" he asked.

"And the knights are your friends?"

He nodded.

"You're letting them fight alone."

"I'm asking for help from God. Or a god. I'm not actually sure how that works in the Magic universe. I don't read the books. But, anyway, she's praying for favour — see? The card prevents damage to up to three targets. It's a decent card, though maybe a little bit expensive. But that's not the point. The point is," he continued, "that the angel is painted differently than everyone else. A higher level of detail. She's different. Everyone in the background runs together — there's nothing that really distinguishes the knights from the Phyrexians, or any of the combatants from the battlefield itself, or the sky, or from the birds scattering in the distance. At that resolution. I mean, there is, but there isn't."

"They only have, like, three inches to fit in an entire painting," I said.

"That's true," said Jeff, shrugging. "Never mind. You don't understand."

"Everything in that picture is paint. It's all paint," I said. "The angel *is* the same as everyone fighting in the background. She's the same because she could be them and they could be her. Every inch of that canvas carries the potential to be anything else. You can't just ... separate an object from itself like that. They're all constructed together. One allows the other to exist, even if it seems like they don't fit together or they exist on different planes.... The background gives the angel definition, context. It's all an illusion. That's all painting is."

"You really don't understand," said Jeff, putting the card back into his pocket, annoyed.

I don't think he knew what he was talking about.

*　　*　　*

I thought about what Jeff had said that day, so long ago now, as I walked around town with my video camera stuffed in my bag, looking for something to film for the documentary, but too shy to carry the camcorder at the ready on my shoulder. I thought about the angel in the painting and how she was different just because the artist had painted her with highlights, because of an accident of orientation that put the angel in the foreground and the others in the back.

I thought about what I had said about the paint, too, about how you can't separate yourself from your environment, not entirely, and I wondered whether I could use that in my documentary. Even though I hated Durham and desperately wanted to leave, I was also a product of it, probably in a lot of ways that I didn't understand, that I wouldn't even begin to see until I had finally put Durham behind me for good.

I only had so much tape left — I had wasted a lot on Huddy, and wasn't quite ready to erase it, even though I knew I'd have to eventually to finish the documentary — and I wanted to think about what I was going to put in next, really consider it. Or at least that's what I told myself when I made the decision to keep the camera off my shoulder. Actually, I think I felt afraid of taking my documentary in any one direction, afraid that it would be wrong and that I would be wasting my time. And since that was the case, it was better to delay. The only way to get there was to think deeply about it. That's how it seemed to me. But I wasn't making any progress, and all of a sudden, even though I'd started so well, or at least I thought I had, I looked up at the calendar and realized that I only had two weeks left. That meant that I didn't have time to think at all, that for my own sake I had better start frantically shooting, but the problem was that I was still stuck.

I walked around town for a little while, absently dismissing everything I passed as a potential subject for my movie. The fish and chips spot, the donair place, the gas stations, the convenience stores, the main strip, the highway, the real estate office, the cemetery on the edge of town, and the park. None of them seemed like worthy subjects for one reason or another. Finally, I sat down on a bench and watched some elementary-school kids run circles around a jungle gym while a five-year-old, younger than the rest, stood at its highest point and shouted frantically, over and over, while pointing his finger down at them with damning purpose. I'm not really sure what his deal was. I looked around for a parent and didn't see any. The other kids didn't notice, or care, what he was doing. They seemed concentrated on their game, which seemed like tag to me, but with more complicated rules. A variant I'd never played before or one they'd made up themselves.

I thought about taking the camera out for a minute, but decided against it. In general it doesn't seem like good practice to film young children at the park when you are older and male and sitting alone. After a while the kids got tired and either stopped or finished the game, and one of the girls climbed up the jungle gym and tried to pick up the little guy up top. He was obviously too heavy for her, but she managed it, anyway, holding him at chest level, his legs dangling close to the ground. He'd long ago given up his weird crusade and had instead sat down on the platform and looked to be deeply investigating the wooden planks that made up the structure. He might have been reading the graffiti that I'm sure was scratched up there, or trying to, or maybe he made up his own game, in his head, with imaginary players. Instead of letting himself get lifted up by the girl, who was probably his sister, he wriggled away and ran down the stairs and then off the jungle gym and away, forcing his sister to chase after him. He started running faster and faster and tripped and fell in the grass. He didn't seem too bothered by it and his sister jumped on him and pretended to attack him. He squealed at first with what sounded like pleasure and then with a kind of forced ill humour.

Like he was having fun but he thought it would be better if he wasn't. While I was watching that action most of the other kids had sort of wandered away, and I thought that it was probably time for me to head off, too, so I walked over to Walid's house and knocked on his front door. When he answered he said it was perfect timing because he had just called me at home. He wanted to work on his documentary and asked if I could help. I said yes because I had long ago given up any hope of doing anything productive for myself that day.

I walked into Walid's house and said hello to his dad, who responded by barely acknowledging me. Maybe he nodded, I don't know. He was sitting in a chair in the living room and staring off into space. It looked like he had a couple of medical articles or something on his lap. He was an MRI technician at the hospital down in Orangeville and Walid said that it was his mom's opinion that the research he did was basically professionally unnecessary, but that his father liked to do it because it gave him an excuse to zone out.

Walid told me not to take it personally, and I didn't, because it wasn't the first time I had walked into the Khan household and felt like I was a ghost.

"I've been working on my storyboard all day," said Walid, as he led me to his room. "I think I'm going to blow this documentary out of the water."

"Oh yeah?" I said. I tried to remember what Walid was doing his documentary on. We talked about it a lot, somehow, without ever getting into specifics. I think it changed from day to day, and the only thing that remained constant was his expectation that it was going to be great.

"Yeah," he said, handing me a bag to carry. "It's a new idea. It's going to be so good."

"What is it?"

"I'll tell you later. I had a bolt of inspiration last night." He reached into the refrigerator and pulled out a Gatorade. "Want one?" he asked.

"Sure," I said. He handed me an orange bottle. I took a swig and then carefully resealed it and put it in my bag.

"Okay, Dad. I'm heading out," Walid called from the foyer. His dad grunted in acknowledgement, but called us back when we were at the door, putting our shoes on.

"Where are you going?" he asked.

"We're going to shoot a video. It's school work."

Then his dad said something in Urdu and Walid responded. There was a little back and forth. I couldn't tell what they were saying, but his dad seemed angry, or at least annoyed.

"*Okay*, we're going now," said Walid, finally, bringing me back into the frame in order to cut the argument short. "Bye, Dad. C'mon," he said, gesturing to me.

"What did he say?" I asked, after a little while.

"Nothing," said Walid. "He just doesn't like it when I go out without telling him."

"But you told him," I said.

"Yeah, but I didn't, like, submit any formal documents. He usually tells me that I should be studying — not like he cares — so I think he was a little bit pissed that we're going to go do something for school."

I nodded. Walid could be punished for really random things.

"He told me I should have picked different courses," he said. "More serious ones."

"But you're taking all the sciences. And calculus."

"Like I said. He doesn't really care. It's stupid. And it doesn't matter," said Walid.

The day was bright and clear and there was a crisp wind blowing. The streets were empty, and we saw only the occasional

car. In some of the houses we passed I could see through the front
windows to entire families sitting in front of radiant televisions.
We walked a little farther, finally turning into a little crescent,
where Walid set his things down in the grass near a fire hydrant.
"Anyway," he said, "this is it."

The houses looked familiar. Probably because I walked past
their clones all the time, but I also wondered if it was possible that
I knew someone who lived on this street. Or knew someone who
knew someone.

"What's 'it'?" I asked. "Are you doing your doc on Durham,
too?"

"No," he said. "Fuck, no. But I did get the idea from you."

I felt a sudden sinking feeling in my stomach.

"What do you mean?" I asked.

Walid was digging into the bag I had carried for him, pulling
out parts and setting up a tripod.

"Guess who lives here," he said. "In this crescent. You'll never
guess."

"Walid, are you sure ..."

"*Watt.*"

For a moment I was stunned, and even a little relieved,
because I had expected him to say Huddy. I had been worried that
Huddy was going to turn the corner at any moment. Huddy, or
Vice-Principal Johnson and Huddy linking arms. Or Huddy and
a police officer. Or Huddy and an axe from his garage. I didn't
know what he was capable of outside of school.

"What? Since when do you care about Watt?" I asked.

"Since last night. I saw him duck into this street and I tailed
him to his house." He had his camera open and was watching the
screen boot.

"Yeah, but — what's the hook? You're just going to film his
house?"

"No, man," he said, putting his hand on my shoulder. "I'm going to, like, do a kind of exposé on him. Find out why he's so messed up. You said it yourself — he's a creep. I'm going to find out why."

"Yeah," I said, "he's creepy, but …"

I stared across the street, at the house Walid had singled out, while Walid made himself busy, happily flitting from his notes to the camera, to a microphone he was unwrapping from its cord and preparing to slot into the top of his camera. I noticed that he was already recording.

"This is insane," I said.

"Sure," he said, through a huge grin.

"But, like — Wright's going to destroy you."

Walid stopped what he was doing.

"No, he isn't," he said. "I'm going to do this like how you were planning on shooting Huddy. Like he was a mystery or something."

"You think that's why I was filming Huddy? To make fun of him?"

"Wasn't it?" he said.

"No," I said, sitting down.

"Hey, can you grab the camera for me? I think we should be closer to the house. I want you to knock on the door later."

I just looked at him.

"Okay," he said, picking up the camera. "Then can you grab those bags?"

He came back a minute later and picked up the bags himself. "Are you going to help me at all?"

I shook my head. "No," I said.

"What do you mean?"

"This isn't a good idea."

"Oh, Jesus. Come on."

"Watt might be creepy, but he doesn't deserve this."

Walid laughed. "What! Are you kidding? Yes, he does."

For some reason I imagined Watt as a giant papier-mâché doll, with huge spider limbs that let him move quickly through the streets as he was chased off by attackers.

Creepy and weird, but delicate, too. I was sorry that Walid had discovered where he lived.

"I'm going home," I said, picking up my backpack and walking away.

"Really?" Walid said, after a minute. Just loud enough so I could hear him.

I didn't turn around.

"Fuck you!" he screamed, suddenly, at the top of his lungs.

I turned around.

"What?"

"Fuck you!" he yelled again. "You think you're better than me?"

I shook my head. "No," I said.

"Good! Because you're not better than me. Just because you're quiet doesn't mean that you aren't a piece of shit, too."

He was genuinely angry, really angry, and I didn't know what to do.

"I'm not a piece of shit," I said.

The last time I'd gotten into a shouting match with anyone who wasn't in my family was in grade five, during lunch break, when some kids from the other class wrecked our soccer ball. That was before I'd met Walid. I'd spent the whole rest of the day crying.

I thought it would be best if I left.

"Turn around!" Walid yelled. "I'm not done!"

I kept walking.

"You start hanging out with Lauren, and all of a sudden you're better than me?"

I shook my head, but I didn't turn around.

God, he was so wrong.

He ran up and pushed me from behind.

"Hey!" he said.

"What?" I said. My face was hot. I was angry, but I felt like crying more than anything. I was afraid of breaking down in front of him, like I had broken down in Wright's office. I knew that he would never let it go if I did.

He pushed me again.

"Fuck you," I said, and I pushed him back. It was much easier than I thought it would be.

"Do that again," said Walid, with menace in his voice.

I did.

10

It was Spink who told me about what happened at the tournament. I knew it hadn't gone well, because if it had gone well Jeff would have told me about it himself. Instead, when JC's dad dropped him off, early Sunday afternoon, Jeff stole into the house quietly, dropping his coat on his shoes and creeping upstairs. His footsteps were heavy, like it took all of his strength not only to climb each step, but to stop himself from sinking into the floor.

The tournament was supposed to be for the full three days. The winner wouldn't be declared until seven or eight o'clock that night.

"How'd it go?" I asked, later. At his door.

He just looked at me.

"What do you think?" he said.

"Are you still going to quit school?"

"I haven't decided," he said, getting up and looking at something on his shelf. Turning his big, dumb back to me. Mom didn't come home until much later that night. When she saw his stuff in the foyer she came into the living room and asked me how it went. I told her that I had no idea.

"Not good, I think."

She sighed and shook her head. "Well," she said, "that's too bad." Then she laughed, like she was letting go of something. Like she'd thrown her wallet off a bridge. "That's just too bad," she said, again.

Jeff stayed pretty quiet from then on. I'd knock on the door to his room and he wouldn't answer. Sometimes he would tell me to go away. Once or twice I opened the door and peeked inside to say hello and he got angry and told me to shut it. I never did, not right away, and so he kept yelling. Once he rushed me and knocked the door so hard back in my direction that it cut my lip.

"You asshole," I said, tasting blood.

"Stay out of my room."

He missed a tournament at Wizard Palace and stopped going to the weeknight hangs. I was worried about him, mostly because I knew what he was doing in there. He hadn't given up. He was still working on his deck, trying to refine it and to figure out what had gone wrong. But it seemed obvious to me that it didn't matter anymore. He'd missed his chance. Not because he'd failed, but because of what he let that failure do to him.

How badly had he missed his chance? I wasn't sure why it even mattered to me. Why the specifics of it mattered.

But I had to know.

I found Spink sitting by the windows, his bright canvas sneakers propped up on a chair next to him while a girl I didn't know tossed microwave popcorn into his mouth from across the table. "You're missing me deliberately," he said, after the fifth kernel bounced off his cheek. She laughed. I'd already finished eating with the guys. Spink's jeans were covered in marker drawings and safety pins, pretty much a daily look for him.

He told me that Jeff had won the first two matches, which surprised me because it was already much better than I expected. "He actually did better than most of us," Spink said, shaking his head. Jeff's first victory seemed to go exactly according to plan. Jeff's opponent was playing a known variant, but wasn't particularly skilled. The second game was against a totally unique five-colour deck that managed to keep Jeff off balance for most of their three matches. "Jeff won by the skin of his teeth," said Spink. "I mean, he was really sweating." Then Jeff and Spink got separated. "I heard he'd split against his next two opponents," he said. "I'd only won one of my first four matches. I was pretty envious." But Jeff's victory had been against an opponent he had planned for, and it had been really close. "He was having trouble getting his mana out," Spink said. "Or he maybe thought he had too much. It was one or the other."

Linnean leaned over from the other side of the table.

"Are you talking about Jeff?" he asked.

We both nodded.

"He thought it would be easy. That he could just roll over the competition. But it's not easy. Not everyone plays as bad as me."

"Of course," said Spink.

Linnean tried to hit him from across the table.

"But anyway, he thought he didn't have enough mana. So he traded some in from his sideboard. And then he lost the next two matches."

"The next four, really," said Spink.

"He didn't win any more?" I said.

"But he took the mana out again after the next two losses. And then he tried putting more in again. And then tweaking other things. But he didn't win again," said Linnean. "I couldn't stay with him for the last two matches. I kept an eye on him, but not very closely. You could tell he was really upset. I mean, Jeff would never say it."

"No," said Spink.

"But he was practically on the verge of tears —"

"I don't know if Jeff would cry," said Spink.

"Maybe that's true," said Linnean, thinking about it.

"More like a nervous breakdown," said Spink. "Like he might start flipping tables."

"Yeah," Linnean and I said simultaneously.

"Anyway," continued Linnean, "I was surprised he even finished those matches. He wasn't playing like he normally did. He'd draw a card and the look on his face —"

"I saw the last match," Spink said. "Or the last fifteen minutes of the last match. I'd drawn my last opponent. It was a quick game — I think we both were relieved to be able to pad our standings a little bit. I finished at two-four-two. Not bad. But obviously the tournament was over for me."

"It was over for Jeff, too," said Linnean. "After his third loss? I think? No chance of getting into the top eight."

"Right — but it wasn't over for him. The look on his face. When he drew a card — as I was saying — good or bad, he always looked crushed. It didn't matter what he got," said Spink. "It was like his cards had been infected somehow."

"He didn't go out with us that night," said Linnean.

"What, really?" I asked.

"Not even for dinner. He stayed at the hotel," said Linnean. "Said he was practising. Which was crazy. He wasn't practising. Or, at least, I don't think he was. I offered to stay with him, but he told me no. Said I should go out with the others."

"He wasn't there when we got back," said Spink.

"Where did he go?"

"That's the thing," said Linnean. "We have no idea."

"He didn't tell you?" asked Spink.

"He hasn't told me anything," I said.

"He didn't get back until late the next morning. We had to lie to JC's dad so that he wouldn't freak out," said Spink.

"But we were pretty worried," said Linnean.

"Has he ever done that sort of thing before?" asked Spink.

"I guess," I said. "But not in a strange place."

"It was so messed up," said Spink.

"Why didn't you guys tell me any of this?" I said.

They both shrugged.

Where could Jeff have gone?

* * *

I wanted to ask Jeff where he'd been when I got home, but when I went upstairs I saw that his door was open and his room was empty. On the days he didn't go to school it was often a long time before he came home. I used to think he was at a friend's, or at Wizard Palace, or maybe at the coffee shop, but I wasn't so sure about that anymore. I wondered, for some reason, whether he wasn't in the forest on the edge of town, the one we used to go to when we were kids. And the one we hadn't really been back to after the accident.

I decided to walk out along the highway to find him, and I left a note for Mom to let her know. I didn't say where I was going, only that I was out and probably wouldn't be back until dinner, if that. I hoped she would save me some.

We were in the middle of a freak warm spell. A few days with the temperature at five or six degrees Celsius. Which maybe wasn't so freakish for March, but it felt that way, because the winter had been long and that was our first relief. I put on my coat and my boots and a hat and I left my coat unzipped and took my gloves, but stuffed them in my pockets because I didn't expect to use them.

Jeff could be a mystery sometimes, since it was so rare for him to talk about what was on his mind. Or for him to respond directly to what he would consider personal questions. He was always lobbing them back to you, forcing you to respond to something else entirely. Even with me. I guess I was kind of hoping that if I caught him he would finally break down and open up.

I imagined Jeff playing his last few matches. Feeling like the cards were conspiring against him, melting into each other, turning diseased and spreading the disease to him. Like the angel, dragged into incoherence by the knights and the Phyrexians, losing her detail, becoming just a smudge of paint. Evacuating the foreground, leaving only a ray of light, a call from God that was left unanswered. I could see it. And it scared me because I hadn't thought he would take it that seriously and I didn't know what he would do.

Why hadn't he just stopped playing? I wish he had put down his cards and gotten up from the table and walked back to the hotel room. As soon as he realized he wasn't going to win the tournament. I wish he'd gone out that night with his friends and had fun and gone to the second day of the tournament just to take it all in, as they'd planned, and told me all about it and then gone back to school again on Monday. Like normal. And put the game behind him, at least for a little while.

The park was almost deserted. There was a small child playing in the snow with their mother near the fenceline, a sled on the snow behind them. The kid so deep in their purple snowsuit that I couldn't tell if they were a boy or a girl. A tiny pink backpack lay abandoned by the jungle gym, sitting on the frozen gravel. It was half-unzipped, and a crumby Ziploc bag peeked out from the hole.

I felt a peculiar kind of sadness looking at it.

I don't know what I was expecting — I thought that by the time I got out to the park it would be eight or nine o'clock at night and I'd have to brave the forest in pitch-black darkness to find Jeff. Which was absurd, it was barely four. It was getting darker, but the sun wouldn't set for at least another couple hours. I had imagined a ghostly scene, with the threat of animals patrolling the park's border. For some reason it didn't reassure me to see the park so differently, bathed in white, in the daylight, in its mundanity. I didn't want to think that it could be indifferent to the crisis that I thought was on its way.

Without leaves to define the space, to conceal its limits, the forest seemed much smaller than it had when I was younger. Maybe part of that was that I was bigger, too. Or knowing that there wasn't much living in there that would be likely to hurt me. The forest was nothing like it was in the movies — like Evie's, in other words: no bears or goblins or snakes or dragons. At most, a few foxes or coyotes resplendent with mange.

There were more footprints than I would have thought at the entrance, splitting off in every direction. Human footprints, I mean. The creek was half-unfrozen and it didn't seem safe to follow it along the bed, so I took the high route, which was easier going in the winter, anyway, without as much underbrush and with full body cover to protect myself against thorns. Along with several sets of boot prints, one of which I thought might have belonged to Jeff, a deer's dainty hoofprints followed the creek for a hundred metres or so before branching off deeper into the woods. Or the prints of several deer, as I've heard they walk in the steps of their partners to conceal their numbers.

The farther I walked along the creek the more absurd it seemed to me that I would find Jeff there. I knew that what I was chasing wasn't in Jeff, but in myself, like I could turn back time, go back to his accident and erase it, like it was his accident that had changed him, like what was different about him wasn't something that had been always waiting inside him and would have come out no matter what. I almost turned back, but I kept going, reasoning that since I had come so far I might as well find out for sure whether he was there.

A set of footprints diverged suddenly from the group following along the ridge and dipped toward the creek. You could see from the way the snow was depressed, from the chunks of exposed brown clay, that whoever it was had fallen as much as climbed down. My heart skipped a beat, but I took a few breaths and closed my eyes, and when I opened them again I was careful to note that the ice hadn't broken and there was no body lying in the creek. Or anywhere.

"Thank Jesus," I said.

Even though I wasn't religious I immediately regretted saying that. It seemed needlessly blasphemous to bring Jesus into the picture when things were so tense.

I followed the new set of footprints from the height of the creek bank, watching it meander across logs and over the places where the ice was heaviest.

As best as I could see, the footprints stopped at the old clearing. The raspberry bushes were thick up on the ridge, and the thorns kept catching on my clothing, so I climbed down, carefully holding on to the base of a sturdy-looking maple. The ice looked solid enough, and the creek was narrower there, anyway. Where the footprints ended was a flattened area where it looked like someone had sat down right in the snow. It was difficult to judge the size of the person who had been sitting down because the impression wasn't clear — whoever it was had been there for a while and moved around a lot. I put a naked hand over the print and thought for a second that I could feel the departed person's body heat, but I realized that was impossible, that there was no way the snow was going to keep that kind of information.

The footprints left the impression and went up the other side of the creek, where they headed back in the direction of the path. I studied them for a little while and then I turned around.

When I got home I found Jeff in the kitchen, eating soup directly out of a can. Mom wasn't home yet.

"You aren't even going to heat it up?"

Jeff shook his head and kept eating.

"Why weren't you at school today?" I asked.

"I felt sick," he said, between sips. "I've been home all day."

I just nodded.

I looked at the counter and discovered my note was gone.

"Are you feeling better now?" I asked.

He shrugged and lifted another spoonful of soup to his mouth.

*   *   *

Some days I think back to that moment and instead of just accepting what he said without question I wish I had grabbed him by the shoulder, tried to jerk him out of his unreality, brought him back to the present, back to me. Even if that meant conflict. Even if he retaliated. Even if it made things worse.

It couldn't have made things worse.

Why didn't I reach out to him? Why didn't I think he was worth fighting for? Didn't I love him? Wasn't I going to miss him?

Why was I so afraid?

11

I came home angry and panicked after the fight with Walid. And hurting, but I cared less about that. I had calmed down a little bit on the walk home, but somehow crossing the threshold caused a lot of the feelings that had dissipated to rise up again, choking me off.

I kneeled on the scuffed linoleum just past the entrance, to my relief just managing to close the door behind me. My breath came in rough, heaving gasps. I wanted to cry, but I wasn't going to, because I didn't want to admit what had happened and also because I didn't want to own up to the fact that Walid had hurt my stupid fucking feelings.

I limped into the bathroom and turned on the light. There was blood caked over the right side of my face, my lip was fat, and my left cheek was swollen. My right eye was starting to bruise, too. I ran my tongue around my mouth and spit into the sink, and my spit was bright crimson against the porcelain. But at least I hadn't lost a tooth. I was pretty sure.

I looked a little bit better once I washed my face. I thought I was lucky that the cut over my brow wasn't so deep that it would need stitches, or at least it seemed that way — it had mostly closed up on its own by the time I got home.

I wish I could say that at least I'd gotten my share of hits in, but I'd only landed a few desperate punches before he really started returning fire. Walid is a lot stronger than I am, and he's been in real fights before. I only really connected solidly once, with his chin. I could see that it had shocked him, but his next few punches were that much harder.

I went to the kitchen and took out a container of leftover pasta from the fridge. Then I put it back after staring at it with the lid off for a few minutes. I hadn't had anything to eat since breakfast, but I wasn't really hungry, and I wasn't sure whether I should eat, anyway, because my jaw was so sore. I didn't want to make things worse, or bite off a piece of my tongue or something. Instead I poured myself a glass of milk and took it up to my room. It was early still, not even five o'clock, but I didn't want to see Mom before I went to sleep, because I didn't want to talk about what had happened, although I knew I'd have to see her eventually and that she would figure out pretty quickly that I'd been in a fight. I didn't think I could lie to her.

Not well enough.

The camera, at least, was okay. I'd had the good sense to put my bag down before I rushed him. Because Walid was such a dumb asshole there was a moment when I was lying in the grass where he threatened to kick my bag or throw it in the street, but the look on my face, I think, told him what was inside. If he had fucked up my camera I would have gone to his parents without hesitation, and he would have got in real shit.

I knew that Walid could be a dick, that he was angry, but I'd always played it down, making excuses for him in my head. I also thought that I was protected, somehow, because we were friends. Because we had been friends for so long. But I guess that protection only went so far. Or maybe there was no such thing as protection. From anything.

I didn't want to think about what I would do on Monday at school.

After wallowing for a while I got up and tried to call Lauren. Her mom answered and said that she was out. She didn't say with whom or where she had gone. Lauren had a cellphone but I didn't want to bother her so I just got back into bed. A little while later I heard my mom come in downstairs, but I buried my head in my pillow when she called up. Not too long after that I heard my door opening.

"Kent?" she said.

I lay absolutely still, with my head facing away from the door. When I didn't answer her she turned the lights out in my room and shut the door.

I don't know when I fell asleep. I didn't intend to. When I woke up the house was eerily quiet. My clock radio said it was three in the morning. I stripped off my sweaty clothes and thought about getting under the covers, but put on new clothes instead. There was no way I was going to be able to get back to sleep.

The swelling in my lip had gone down, and my jaw didn't hurt as much as it had before. I was able to eat a couple slices of toast. I put the dishes in the sink and went outside to sit on the front steps. It was cold, and so I put on my full winter gear. Most of the leaves were still up and I liked the way they looked in the street lights: their silence and their stillness. In the distance I could see cars passing on Highway 89, their lights twisting away in the dark.

My dream the night before had been crazy. I was climbing the stairs in an old hotel. I knew it was haunted and I wanted to get out of there, but for some reason I kept pressing upward, trying to escape a dull, thudding sound coming from below, like my heartbeat but louder by an order of magnitude. Coming from above or below. Actually I hadn't been sure, unclear whether I was moving away from the noise or heading straight for it, like I thought I could pierce it with a javelin and get the noise to stop. The more I thought about it the more unsure I was. The hotel gave me an uncanny feeling: I imagined that behind each door I'd find a different future. Or past. I wasn't sure. But each one distinct from its neighbours. In any case the hotel was at the centre of time, at its nexus. Jeff was in the dream, too, although he wasn't a central figure, and I had to work hard to remember he was there. *Jeff*, I thought. Whenever I needed to remember. In the dream he had been waiting for me somewhere, but I couldn't remember why or where or even how that knowledge had been communicated.

I sat out on the front steps for a little bit longer, watching the night lift, although sunrise was still a long way away. I started to think about my documentary, wondering what I was going to do, how all of my plans had fallen apart so spectacularly, how I was left with less than nothing even though I had already put more work into it than I thought most people would.

I watched the street and thought about how funny it was that I was up that early. That what I was seeing could only be seen just then, in that particular moment.

It was as I was sitting there watching the quiet when something clicked in my head. I realized I was trying to force myself into creating something obviously larger than I could handle. Why was I starting so big? It was *true* that I had put more work into the documentary than other people would.

It was stupid. Why not just shoot the Durham that I knew?

Just shoot it and see what happened.

I put on a pot of coffee and sat down at the kitchen table with a pad of legal paper and started writing out a script. By the time

Mom got up I had already storyboarded some scenes. I was so deep into my work that when Mom asked me what had happened to me I almost told her about my dream until I realized that she was asking about my face.

* * *

I spent the next two weeks in the editing room, after school and over lunch, recording my voiceovers and putting the documentary together piece by piece. I got Lauren to show me how most of the equipment worked. She had experience with the machines because she sometimes made videos for drama class. When other people had the room booked I went in anyway, both because I could count on them sometimes not showing up, and because it was a relief to get away from the guys and the cafeteria. If someone else was in there I helped them out on the equipment or with their own editing, learning a lot in the process. No one seemed to mind.

Things were weird between me and Walid. For the first few days I started coming to school later, so that I wouldn't have to spend any time hanging out before school, avoiding the hallway where we all stood, but after I got tired of rushing to my locker and then to my first class I'd find Lauren or Sash or Kyle or Christian in the caf. I discovered that it felt good to disrupt my habits like that, to realize that I had more friends — a wider circle — than I had thought. At first I was a little shy about changing my routine, but I realized after a while that nobody cared about what had happened, if they even knew, and that if they cared they probably felt sorry for me, because it was obvious that Walid had kicked my ass and not the other way around. And because most people thought he was kind of an asshole. When people asked me what had happened I told them that I'd gotten into a fight with a rhinoceros or that I'd been in a helicopter crash, and they laughed, and I could usually keep it at that.

When Mr. Wright was taking attendance that first Monday after the fight, he stopped what he was doing when he noticed that Walid and I were sitting far away from each other and asked out loud whether anything was wrong. "Trouble in paradise?" he said. He had meant it ironically, but the fact that neither of us responded told him everything he needed to know. He might have even made the connection to the bruises on my face, which I had explained coming into the class that I had picked up in a squash court, trying out a new manoeuvre.

The truth is, though, I felt better not hanging out with Walid. I don't know if I could say that I felt happy, but I felt free, which made me realize that I hadn't felt free before. Which was a weird thing to realize. I wondered how much of it was an illusion and how much of it was real.

* * *

I was still nervous the day of the documentary presentation, despite how much time I had put into the video. I was worried that too much of myself had gone into the project. That morning on the way to school I was overcome by the sudden urge to burn it and piece together something light and easy and safe — above all, something that didn't have any part of me in the frame. Or only the most superficial parts. But it was too late for that.

Somehow Wright got us out of our other classes. Drama wasn't running that semester, and so he had the drama room booked for the entire day. It was nice, with wall-to-wall carpets and a little stage on the far end. A huge black television had been wheeled into the middle of the room. It was only something like thirty-two inches, but it was the nicest TV I had ever seen on the premises of any school in Durham. It was huge and boxy and had a tremendous weight, sucking in all of the available light in the room.

"I grabbed this out of the staff lounge," Wright explained.

"Chalmers must be pissed," someone said.

There were twenty of us in all, and we'd watch eight videos in the morning and eight in the afternoon. The other four we would watch over the next two days, in our regular class. I was in the afternoon. We had a forty-minute mongrel lunch in the cafeteria, catching the tail end of period two and the first half of period three. Walid stopped me in the hallway as we were coming back from lunch.

"What," I said.

"You aren't going to believe what my camera picked up, man," said Walid.

"Okay," I said, pushing past him. I wanted to say something else, too, like that I didn't care, like he could go fuck himself, but I didn't want to go that far. I didn't want a repeat of before. Maybe it was a good sign that he had wanted to talk to me and maybe that meant that things were going to quiet down between us, even though they could never go back to where they were. I didn't want them to, either.

I was also too nervous to give Walid any more of my attention than I already had. I'd spent most of lunch sitting with Lauren and her friends, trying to keep up, but too distracted by what I was going to show later that afternoon.

Most of the other videos were about achievements, hobbies, favourite bands, sports teams, actors, after-school jobs, revered elderly family members, topics I'd overlooked or hadn't been able to think of a way to execute. I was rubbing my head after every presentation, getting more and more nervous, upper lip sweating, hands trembling, fever in my head, tangled fibrous knot forming in the pit of my stomach.

Bobby Booby's video was a shakily rendered compilation of hockey highlights he had already sent to a selection of NCAA colleges. Except for a living-room interview that he conducted by getting up from his seat and stopping the camera on its tripod to change angles between his place on the couch and his mother in an easy chair, it was obvious that his father had shot the entire video, the elder Booby grunting "Yeah," "Look at that," "Marge, *Marge!*" and "Go, Bobby" underneath the soundtrack, Smash Mouth's "All Star" on repeat (even playing at a low volume throughout the entire interview with his mother, which felt like a step or two too far, but was probably just because he couldn't figure out a way to turn it off while he was editing).

The class erupted in cheers at the video's culmination, half-ironic, half-sincere, when Bobby scored a soft third goal to complete a hat trick, and, after pumping his fist, found his dad with the camera in the stands and, pointing his stick right down the lens, did a deep knee-bend flourish, while his teammates skated around him, confused and waiting for the theatrics to end so they could pat him on the back.

Bobby got up from where he was sitting on the carpet and did a couple of bows in front of the class before he ejected his video. "Thank you, thank you," he said. He was totally sincere. He came by it honestly, probably from staring too hard and too often at the hockey posters above his bed, through too many repeated viewings of Don Cherry's *Rock 'Em Sock 'Em* videos.

Wright called my name. I was next. Lauren patted me on the back and I stood up, stiffly making my way to the front of the room. I put the video into the VCR, but didn't push it in all the way.

"Okay, uh, so I decided to do a documentary about Durham," I said. "Because I didn't know what else to do."

I looked at Mr. Wright. I couldn't read his expression, which made me even more nervous.

"Okay," I said. "I'll just start it now."

* * *

"Durham. Town of 'X'-thousand (the number's too small to matter). Located one and a half hours out of Toronto, in the exact centre of nowhere. The centre's centre? Not by accident, it's the precise location where Principal Chalmers parks his 1999 'Woodland Pearl' Toyota Camry on the Upper Canada Secondary parking lot."

Some laughs.

"Like a zen koan, the question inevitably repeats itself: 'What can anyone say about Durham?' Is it possible to film a documentary on the nothing that this town is? What, if anything, is being filmed?… Durham wasn't my first, or even my second, choice for the topic of this documentary. In fact, if I'd made a comprehensive list of all the things I wanted to produce a documentary on, Durham would be right at the very end, footnote to triple-z omega, double-bracketed, point-six font. But, like everyone who ends up in Durham, I ran out of options, and was stuck with the one topic I couldn't escape. Durham: sinkhole, vortex, labyrinth, perpetual eye of the hurricane, leaking storm shelter, closed harbour, mirror world, fallback option, no one's first choice — *ever*, emptiness, tabula rasa, sound of one hand clapping, home."

My documentary started with shots of the town. Main Street, the school parking lot, shots out of my bedroom window, from the town bus that sometimes ran from the senior's home to the strip mall. Cars passing on the highway late at night. The bar on Mill Street, lit up in neon. The empty library. The park on the edge of town.

"But even if Durham is nothing, it's where I grew up. It's probably where a lot of you grew up, too. People live here and that's what makes it important." Sweep of the cafeteria. Shot of Huddy eating lunch. Parking lot of the strip mall on Main. Shot of cars filling up at the gas station. The sun rising over my street on the Sunday morning following the fight. I knew I was bordering on cliché. I hoped that it didn't matter. "It's where my brother grew up, too. For those of you who don't know, he died two springs ago. I'm not going to talk about that. I don't want to. I can't. Instead, I'm going to talk about an accident that he had when we were kids, which took place in the little forest on the edge of town, a forest that no longer exists." I'd climbed the jungle gym to get a pan of the recently razed land. "It doesn't look like much, but even in the middle of nowhere, in the most mundane places, stories happen that are worth being told."

I buried my head between my knees, staring at the carpet. I didn't want to watch the documentary and I was afraid of looking up at my classmates. I stayed that way until the end of the movie. It was eerily quiet and I worried that everyone was sitting in shocked silence, completely at a loss for what to say, united in their displeasure.

There was clapping once the credits ran. I didn't move. To my ears it felt forced, muted. I only looked up when Wright walked up to the VCR and ejected the tape.

"Well," he said, "that was certainly something."

My face fell. I was sure he hated it.

But he saw my reaction.

"No, Kent," he said. "I thought that was really good."

There were murmurs of assent from the rest of the class. Stunned, I walked back to where I had been sitting. Lauren punched me lightly in the shoulder. She was smiling.

"*Buddy*," she whispered. "Nice job."

"Thanks," I said.

"I'm glad I'm going tomorrow," she continued. "Can't compete with that."

"Jesus," I said, trying to hide my grin.

I was so relieved that I didn't even notice who was up next. It was Walid. For a minute I worried about what he had said outside class. What if he hadn't done his documentary on Watt? What if *I* was the subject of his movie? I cringed, expecting the worst, wondering if I should leave the room. It didn't seem fair that my relief could dissipate so fast.

But I didn't have to worry.

"As some of you know," he began, "my dad works at Head-waters." That's the hospital in Orangeville. "So I decided to do my video on him. As much as I could." He popped the tape in. The screen opened on a fluorescent-lit corridor. The word MRI appeared on the screen, then separated, reading MOST/RADICAL/IMAGES. There were some laughs.

The rest of the documentary was pretty much as advertised.

I guess I'd underestimated him.

*   *   *

I found out what Walid had been alluding to during a break after his video. I was talking with Lauren and this guy Mark from our class. I didn't know Mark very well because he mostly hung out with the skaters, but I liked him because he usually understood my jokes. He said that Walid had caught our fight on tape, and that he'd been showing it around earlier that day, playing it off his camcorder.

"The whole thing?" I asked.

Mark nodded.

My stomach dropped.

"But it looked like you kicked his ass," he said.

"Really?" asked Lauren, turning to me.

"No," said Mark. "It was pretty bad."

"Yeah," I said. "Walid destroyed me."

"Good try, though," said Mark.

"Thanks," I said.

"You're not much of a fighter, are you?" asked Lauren.

"No," I said. "Not at all."

"That's good," said Lauren. "Fighting is dumb."

My heart skipped.

"I, uh, also hate fighting," said Mark, looking at Lauren.

I briefly wondered whether something was happening between them.

"Do you want to not fight later?" I asked.

"Yeah," said Mark. "In the parking lot, after school."

"Perfect," I said.

Lauren laughed.

I decided that I didn't care that Walid was sharing the tape. I probably could have got him in trouble for that, but it wasn't worth it. I didn't care that people knew. I mean, maybe I would have cared if people made a big deal about it, but no one had, except Walid, I guess. Most people, I thought, wouldn't.

That turned out to be an accurate assessment. Maybe it would have been a bigger deal when I was younger. I remembered when Yanni Caucescu beat up Scott Michaels in grade ten, and how people had made fun of Scott for weeks afterward because he had taken a huge swing at Yanni and totally whiffed, landing on his face. Maybe I just hadn't embarrassed myself when I was getting beat up.

I felt a little bit proud of myself for that.

I was more concerned about Lauren and Mark, because it turned out they were actually dating. Or that they started dating pretty shortly afterward. I found out two weeks later, when I saw them holding hands in the cafeteria after school. One night I wrote her a long email, explaining that I had feelings for her, or thought I might have. I said that I felt hurt by the fact that she didn't feel the same way about me, that she'd jumped into a new relationship without exploring whatever was happening between us. Oh god, I wish I'd written that out as reasonably as I just did now. I was angry. But I didn't send it. I let it sit on the computer and then I watched some television and went for a walk and when I got back I deleted it. I didn't want to lose any more friends. It wasn't really any of my business.

I got an A-plus on the documentary, my first in almost four years of high school. It felt good. But also kind of hollow. It was nice to get the validation. But I also didn't think it mattered, not in the way I thought it would. I didn't even tell Mom.

Wright pulled me aside after handing our grades back.

"I want you to submit your documentary to the contest," he said.

"I don't know," I said, surprising myself.

He looked confused.

"I think it's really good," he said. "You have a real chance to win. Seriously."

"I'll think about it," I said.

"I don't see what there is to think about, but okay," he said, giving me a long look.

I left the classroom quickly, and took a few minutes in the hallway to compose myself before heading to my locker, pretending I was looking through my bag. I wasn't sure why I didn't want to share my video, even though I knew it was good, even though I might have been able to use it to get out of Durham, at least in a small way. I thought about that for a long time. Maybe I wasn't ready to go. Which was stupid, I thought. I needed to go. I had to leave. I told myself that I would submit the video.

But I never did.

Two

Sarah's Part

None of them were injured and at first they denied that anything unusual had happened at all. May said, "I thought it was just a dream, so I kept on going."

— Joy Williams, "The Blue Men"

I

I was trying to understand life and death, but everything was a tangled mess.

I was doodling on the edge of the notebook, writing my name in cursive, over and over: *Sarah, Sarah, Sarah*. Outside, rain pounded the drooping willow in our front yard, its limbs whips rattling in the wind. In the chapter of *Evie of the Deepthorn* I was currently writing, the water was coming down so hard that Evie thought she was blind. She was slipping through the mud and grabbing at trees to propel herself forward, digging huge black ruts in the earth with her boots. A long way back she'd become separated from her horse, Excalibur, and she could hear his mournful whinnying as he made his way through the brush. But she didn't know if he was right or left, ahead or behind her.

I needed to understand life and death because I was stuck on the book. I didn't know how to write anything that hadn't happened to me, and so the things I did write came out flat. Except the sections that were based on things that I had actually experienced. Like rain. Like confusion. Like slipping in the mud. But I couldn't have Evie wandering through the forest in inclement weather forever, forever alone — that would get boring.

For me, too.

There was lots of death in the book and I didn't know how my characters were supposed to react. That was a major issue. It all seemed so arbitrary to me — would they burst into tears? Go insane? Get angry? I had no idea.

The previous summer my mother and I had gathered the branches that had fallen from the willow during a similar storm. Mom had seen someone twist them into baskets on a TV show. The woman on TV wore a checkered blue shirt with a little red bandana tied sweetly 'round her neck. I remember passing the television and thinking, "That person is too twee to live." But I secretly envied them for how together they looked. I knew it was all on the surface, or at least that's what I hoped, but I was so far from being even together only on the surface that I felt like a member of a doomed second species, meant to live in caves and serve her kind on hand and foot.

I felt so ugly moving on the earth. I could never figure out the right kind of clothing to wear or the right way to style my hair. So instead I tried my best to be anonymous, to not stick out, to wear things that wouldn't mark me in one direction or another.

Sometimes sticking out is the worst decision you can make for yourself. Especially when you don't know what you are.

Especially when *everyone else* knows you don't know.

Anyway, we'd gathered the branches after the storm and put them in a big bucket in the laundry room. I remember looking up at the tree afterward with a kind of sadness. It had lost a lot of branches since we'd moved in. It had been majestic then, reaching from its full height of roughly thirty feet to the ground. My mother thought my dad wasn't watering it enough. My dad thought the change was due to the neighbours paving their driveway (it had been only gravel before). I guess it didn't matter what the issue was. Now it was thin and spindly and if you didn't know it was a willow you might think it was any other kind of tree, though nearer to the top the branches were still long enough to make rainstorms more dramatic from my window.

The willow seemed a kind of symbol, like it stood for the way a person is stripped and made emptier with the passage of time. Some days I had the ridiculous notion to take the fallen branches and stick them back on, like with a staple gun or something, as if that were enough to turn back the clock.

After watching the TV program about willow baskets, my mom went out to Home Hardware and picked up a book on crafts you could do at home. It had a picture of the same woman from TV, with her mouth open and a crescent of cool white teeth showing coyly between her lips. A little sticker, too, in case it wasn't obvious, reading: AS SEEN ON HOME & GARDEN TV.

When I saw the book downstairs, left in a prominent location in the kitchen, I got a bad feeling in my stomach. Somehow I knew that it had been left out for me. I tried to hide it underneath a stack of tablecloths, trying to make it disappear as casually as possible, like it was an accident, or like I was, but two days later Mom told me that she wanted me to help her with a special project. She said that we needed to spend more quality time together. She said I was getting weird, sitting upstairs alone in my room. That I would scare boys away if I cast too many spells by myself.

Getting weird?

I wondered, exactly, what boys I had scared off were going to come back once they heard that I was doing weekend wicker-basket projects with my mom.

But either way, I didn't cast spells. I had a couple of polished Tiger Eyes that I picked up at the alternative place on Main, little polished orange-and-brown stones, and I think that's what she was referring to. They don't have anything to do with magic or witches or anything like that. I just think they're pretty. And I like the idea that carrying around a pebble in your pocket can increase your blood flow and your self-awareness, which is what the little card at the store said that Tiger Eyes are supposed to do. They're supposed to calm you. I mean, I don't necessarily believe that, but maybe I also do, in a way. It couldn't hurt.

In any case I'm not a witch. And I don't pretend to be.

Maybe things would be better for me if I were.

I knew what she meant about getting out of my room, but it was the principle of the thing. She said I was being a brat and that she was trying to be nice to me. That if I didn't even hang out with my mother I was going to lose all of my social skills and then who would love me?

I got through about half a basket before it yawned open like that egg thing at the beginning of *Alien*. Except instead of spitting out a xenomorph it just fell apart. It was really frustrating. I didn't have the patience to fix it and everything I tried just made it worse. Mom told me to be quiet and stop complaining and start again — but with less attitude — and instead I threw the basket across the room. It broke into about a million pieces, the branches scattering in every direction. That felt really good. Even though I knew when I threw it that I was irrevocably bad. Like I was crossing a threshold that meant I was everything Mom said I was. But it also felt like I couldn't have done anything else — like I was always going to break the basket. Like I was forever trapped in that action. It's weird to feel fated to be ruined and to want to do better but also to enact that, over and over.

Then I stormed upstairs while Mom threatened to take away my TV privileges and my computer. What did I care?

"Sarah, I'm warning you!" she called up the stairs. "Sarah!"

"Fuck you!" I screamed, from the top of the stairs. *"Fuck you!"*

Not my proudest moment.

Then she grabbed me by the wrist and pulled me back to the kitchen and told me to clean up the mess and I said, "No, no, no, fuck you, fuck you!" and I squirmed away and ran out of the house. Just like that, without even shoes. I made it about a block or so before stopping to take off my socks, not that it mattered by then. They were grey and green from the grass and the asphalt. Then I wandered around barefoot, shy of seeing anyone, feeling stupid and deeply broken, until enough time had passed that I thought I could sneak back in.

I liked writing about Evie struggling through the rain, but I was scared of where she would go and what would happen to her there. Who she would talk to and how they would act.

When I wasn't actively writing, I was thinking about all of that and watching the grass shimmer in the rain. We hadn't cut it in a long time and it humped over, rustling and swaying in the wind. It was pretty. Or at least I thought so. Mom kept asking me to cut it, but I didn't want to do it because that was usually Dad's job. I thought she should do it if she cared so much.

I don't know why Dad had let it grow so long, but I thought that maybe he was depressed.

Maybe I felt a bit depressed, too. I hadn't wanted to do much but work on my story and look at my computer or out the window at whatever was going on out there. I had one hand on the windowpane and one hand on the lamp turned on over my notebook. The lamp gets hot, but not quite hot enough to burn. If I put my hand on it as soon as it turns on and wait for the heat to come it sort of cools down, or seems to. I mean, I can do it, somehow it's tolerable, as opposed to waiting until the light's been on for a while and burning my hand as soon as the hot metal touches my skin.

There's nothing I like better than sitting at my desk when it rains and looking out the window, except opening it a crack and getting into bed and pulling the covers up and listening to the water run down the house. I know that means I'm just like every other quiet teenager on the planet.

And I don't mind that, either. It's nice to feel at least in one small way that I belong.

Here's what's going to happen in my story, in case you're curious. Evie is going to save the whole kingdom. She's going to kill Llor, the ice queen, and cleanse the Deepthorn of her legions. I knew that before I started writing.

Evie of the Deepthorn is not going to be postmodern, or depressing, or whatever. It's going to be the opposite of that kind of book. It's going to make people feel better about their lives instead of worse. When readers get to the end of *Evie of the Deepthorn* they're going to feel like everything makes sense in their lives, like there is order in the universe, like cruelty can be reversed.

I'm going to feel that way, too.

*　　*　　*

But how do you learn about life and death when you're just a teenager sitting alone in your room? I'd never lived in a kingdom ravaged by an ice queen.

I'd never lost a parent, let alone two.

The only person I even remembered dying was Grandma Irene, when I was seven, but she lived in Alberta and I only remembered meeting her once, when I was too young to remember much about her.

She wasn't even my real grandma.

I was afraid that the emotional reactions in *Evie of the Deepthorn* made no sense at all. That they were totally fake and would seem made up. That their emptiness would reveal the limits of my experience. Which wasn't a problem just limited to my book. One of the things that Jess always said about me was that I was too quiet and never talked about anything important, like normal people do. That I never expressed anything without prompting. Once she even told me that she and Tiff felt like I was a kind of spy — though Tiff never said that to my face, I still had reason to believe it. Not a spy in the sense that I was going to betray their secrets, but like I was taking them for my own. Like I was a person made of clay, reaching into them and pulling out whatever I found. Sticking it onto me. Like I was a dark shadow roaming the countryside and gobbling people up.

It was true that I felt that hungry, sometimes, waking up from my dreams.

"You're like a couch cushion," Jess told me once. By which I think she meant, you are quiet, you gather up everything that is loose, sometimes you get sat on. I must have looked sad, because then she added, "I think that and then sometimes you make me laugh."

It didn't make me feel much better.

A kid from my school had died the year before, but I'd never even seen him around before. I can't remember how it happened — some kind of accident, I think. He was a few grades above mine. I'd seen his younger brother, though. He was in my year. A skinny kid who sometimes made jokes in class — witty little jokes that didn't hurt anybody. He was pretty well-liked, I think. For a few months he walked around the hallways with a dazed look in his eyes, and everyone got out of his way. Then the crowds closed in around him and everyone forgot what had happened. Or it didn't matter anymore.

I wanted to know some of what he did, except I didn't want to *actually* know what it was like to lose someone I cared that much about, because I didn't want that to happen to me. I didn't even want to go outside. I tried to imagine what it was like for the younger brother to walk those hallways alone, missing the one person he probably cared about most. Knowing that everyone else knew. Feeling exposed.

I think that would be the worst part, I don't know why. It's bad enough having everyone assume they know things about you just based on how you look. I hate it when people look at me and see how ugly I am and imagine that I don't have feelings, like I am without personality, like I am an empty husk, like nothing will ever happen of any value in my life just because I'm quiet and my face is covered in pimples, or the ghosts of them. It gets on my nerves being so overlooked, to see eyes pass over me like I am a fly or a distant lake. To assume that I have nothing to say, even when I'm saying it.

But then they sometimes stop and look at me, really look at me, up and down, like I'm behind one-way glass. Like they know the whole course of my life — beginning to end. Like all of my defects are theirs to discover. Like my body belongs to them. Like I'm not even there. And I don't like that either.

I would hate it if they knew something real. Or if they thought they did. I can't decide which is worse. For that reason I decided it was wrong to think so hard about what that kid might feel about his brother dying, that maybe it was a kind of exploitation, or violence, or *something* bad, and so I stopped.

* * *

Is there a way to access pain without getting hurt yourself? Should I be happier that the hurt I feel — dull, aching, confused — can't be connected to any one thing? Or is it worse that what I feel seems sort of never-ending? Inherent, endless, like how Evie's quest to defeat Llor feels to me right now? She's still in the forest, still being pummelled by the rain, because I can't figure out where I want to get her to go next. Because I haven't been able to sit down and concentrate since that last rainstorm. Whenever I take out the notebook and open it to the last page I was working on, I pick up the pen and press it to the paper, sit there staring down from my window, at the street where cars are slowly moving back and forth in front of the house, where the grass — still long and glittering — waves gently in the breeze, trying to think of what happens next. And nothing comes out.

Sometimes when I get stuck I go downstairs and bring one of my dad's *Renaissance* magazines up to my room, and leaf through it until I find something that gives me an idea. Once it was a detailed article on how to build an accurate thirteenth-century blacksmith's forge in your backyard. Another time it was a photo series of knights standing in front of tents set up in a green field, knights who were knights like my dad was a knight, actually middle managers or software engineers, balding men who sat in cubicles and drove Toyota Camrys and drank Diet Cokes. But for some reason I didn't think it would be enough to look through one of those magazines. I didn't think I'd learn anything. I thought leafing through pictures and articles featuring the sad men and women who spent their weekends and evenings sewing costumes and handcrafting weapons and imagining themselves galloping at top speed across a plain free of modern responsibility would be depressing. I mean, it was depressing most days, probably, to most people. But it also wouldn't teach me anything I actually wanted to learn. Those people in the magazines were just as stuck as Evie was, except for them there's no triumph on the other side, just the sad realization that must grow with every year, that no matter how close they get to the time they love, they will never quite reach what they are looking for.

I'd like to disappear with them, too, of course — or anywhere, a part of me wants that — but I know I can't. I've never been able to *fully* disappear, as much as I would like to. As much as I want to imagine myself walking through a forest alone, armed only with a knife or a spear and fending for myself, I know that is a hard and dangerous freedom to seek. And not really what I want, either. They never talk about that in my dad's magazines — what a pain it must have been to find food, shelter, places to go to the bathroom. How terrible everyone must have smelled. Ironically, it's a scrubbed-clean reality that they are escaping to, something from movies or books. Something without habit or routine, which is exactly what gets cut out of those narratives. That's why I think it's only in fiction where real triumph can be found.

When I was a little kid my dad would take me to the fairgrounds outside Saffronville, where maybe two or three times a summer they would stage a medieval fair. I'd dress up like a princess in an old Halloween costume and he would wear one of his chain-mail pieces and sometimes an open helmet, and he'd release the ponytail he normally wore, letting his hair fall to his shoulders, and we'd split a turkey leg and drink warm root beer and browse the shops staffed by too-affable men and women in period costume and watch men charge at one another on horseback and sword-fight with big, exaggerated blows. And I liked to do all of that, but I was always looking for something else, I think. I wanted both to believe it all and to catch them out, to escape into the fantasy, but also to destroy the illusion. That latter thing wasn't hard to do — there was always the odd thrumming generator, pair of Adidas sneakers, plastic ketchup bottle, truck parked behind a tent. They weren't trying to remake the entire world, just transform a little piece of it.

When I was really little I was always pointing this or that inaccuracy out to my dad. When I got older I wore a constant look of skepticism which I think convinced him that I had outgrown the fairs, and he stopped taking me and started going on his own. But it wasn't that I didn't enjoy them anymore, because I did; it was only that I couldn't let myself give in to them, because I knew somehow that I could have and I didn't want to turn into one of the men or women staffing the booths.

It was exactly like Jess said — I liked to take a look, but I didn't want to go any further. I was a tourist.

I didn't want it to be true, but it was true.

Sometimes, when Mom and Dad are asleep, I sneak downstairs and into the backyard, lie out on the back deck, close my eyes, and think about things with the breeze gently rolling over me and the sound of the trees and birds and bats rustling in the night, but never fall asleep, not even when I'm totally relaxed, or at least I think I don't. Or else instead of closing my eyes, I stare straight up into the night sky, where you can't see anything, really, but the moon and sometimes clouds and maybe a few twinkling stars or distant satellites — when I was little and Durham was smaller you could see a lot more, even the purply ribbons of the Milky Way — and think about what all of that darkness means and how it is up there but in me, too, and how I don't understand it at all and I feel deeply broken at every moment. Sometimes it seems like a shadow is chasing me, a shadow that I can't comprehend or understand, and I want to be good or to feel in control of myself, but that is always just out of my reach, or maybe not *just* out of my reach but actually on another planet, like I am on earth and it is on the moon, or it is on the moon and I am on the moon, too, but I am far away, like I am somewhere on the dark side and I'll never see the light.

Then I wish I could put on a costume or clutch a good facsimile of a sword and thrust my way through life and, just like my dad, find some solace or comfort in something small and meaningless, something that despite all of that I could nevertheless believe in. But I know that I could never believe in anything — not for very long, in any case.

In a little alcove by the washer and dryer downstairs, in what my dad called his "hobby corner" (even though I mostly tried to be sensitive with him I did sometimes make fun of him for calling it that), was where my dad kept his suits of armour. They were, of course, just reproductions, but impressive, even though you could tell just from a glance that they weren't authentic. When I was five or six he spent most of his evenings in front of the TV, on the couch, looping together a chain-mail chest protector that was one of his most treasured pieces, even though he rarely wore it out. That was due to a tear in the back, near the left shoulder, where some of the loops had started to come undone. He'd made it too heavy on that side, was how he explained it to me, and one of these days he'd find the time to fix it, but he hadn't yet. I think it was more work than he was ready for; probably when he thought back to how long it took him to assemble in the first place, the task seemed humongous and deflating. There was a lot that was like that around the house, a lot that went unnoticed or undone.

There was a tension working between our walls that I didn't quite understand.

Mom was always on his case about how he screwed up around the house, folding towels and sheets improperly, leaving marks on dishes and huge dust bunnies in rooms he was supposed to have swept. Neglecting the lawn, like he was doing now.

I guess that would be annoying if he were my husband, but I'd probably be like him, too. Confused and absent-minded. Feeling a little like a failure in my own house. Sometimes I wondered what accident had caused my mom and dad to get together, to stick it out, to have me, to build a home and last in it. I was grateful, I guess, for that. To be alive. But I didn't get it. Their tastes were the complete opposites of each other, and they both seemed to want different things from life and from a partner. For instance, Mom's dad died before I was born, but from the photos of him — even as an old man — I could see that he was tall and well-built, and that there was an edge or hardness to him. Something in his eyes that seemed veiled or angry. He had fought in the war and he was silent and authoritative and worked as a foreman at the Ford plant. None of which seemed like my dad, who was slim, just barely taller than my mom, quiet, nerdy, and soft. Who wore that ponytail that I knew my mom hated. (She sometimes walked up behind him wearing a mad grin and her hands miming scissors.)

The home that they had built was on shaky ground. They fought a lot and never seemed to resolve anything. I was frustrated with both of them. Mom always seemed like the more aggressive one, but she also seemed to have more of a *point*. I sometimes hated to admit it. Dad must have thought so, too, because he rarely fought back, though I wanted him to. He could say snippy little things back to Mom, or under his breath, but mostly he just took it. Tried to make it up to her even before she was finished. Made promises we all knew he wouldn't keep, but which sometimes placated Mom, anyway.

Later I'd find him lying almost comatose on the couch in the basement, or staring up at the ceiling in their bedroom. It was never pretty. It was like all of the untruth in the world that he had created was running through him, incapacitating him like it was the flu.

It was worse, though, when I found him doing something that he deemed productive — like polishing one of his replica swords, pretending like nothing was wrong. Maybe going to the vacuum and giving it a half-hearted spin around the house. I tried to keep out of his way when he was like that. I didn't want to see it. It felt wrong. Maybe it was exactly what Mom was complaining about (the vacuuming — never unpolished swords), but it still didn't sit right. It always felt like he was somewhere weird — like he was standing on the ceiling where everything was perfect and spotless and I was on the ground where the floor needed to be swept and the trash taken out.

He did sometimes get angry. But then he'd get on his motorcycle and roar out of the house. It was like it was the only way he knew how to focus his rage. Which was maybe weird, because his motorcycle was so rooted in the present time, in contrast to all of his other methods of distraction. Sometimes, uncharitably, I wondered if when he was doing turns on his Honda he referred to it as his "steed" in his head.

I wish I was more kind to him. Even just in my head.

Anyway, it made me worried when he went riding like that because I knew it was dangerous enough riding a motorcycle when you feel okay, and I didn't like the thought of him taking unnecessary risks just because he'd fucked up a load of Mom's shirts. Or dropped a bottle of fish sauce on the kitchen floor. Or whatever. I wished the consequences weren't as high as they were and I thought maybe there was a way in which they didn't have to be, but I couldn't see my way to there. No one could.

When Dad left during a fight, Mom would become wild with rage, practically nuclear, knocking things off tables, yelling at me to get back to my room or to shut the fuck up and leave her alone, even if I wasn't saying anything. Even if I was making a point of keeping quiet. Even if I was clearly already in my room, trying to concentrate on anything else. But she always calmed down before he got back. Usually she even managed to clean things up a little before then.

I think Mom wanted Dad to fight back, too. It doesn't really excuse her anger. But it sometimes felt to me like she was trying to raise him out of his grave. I don't think she was happy with things as they were, like she thought there was a way she could get them both back on even footing, but that the only way to do that was to stand him up in front of her and shake him until he broke out of it. Then, I don't know, I guess they'd trade blows in an empty room, like they were kung fu masters in *The Matrix*, go back and forth until they were blocking each other blow for blow and finally an even match. But that's not how it worked.

That's not how it worked, but it was the only thing she seemed to know how to do.

I don't know what Dad was thinking. I know he wanted to make things better for all of us. I know he tried hard to do that. I know he was frustrated. But I think the pattern, the back and forth, the rise and fall, made more of a kind of sense to him. Like one day he would figure it out and change it all, but until then he could sit in it, almost comfortable. Or maybe not — maybe the pattern itself was a kind of comfort, to feel mixed up, maybe even oppressed, by the one that you loved.

Sometimes I thought Mom was lonely. And that her anger came from loneliness. I understood that because I was lonely, too. Sometimes I thought that Llor was that feeling — of loneliness. But she was other things, as well, like the feeling you have when you've messed up, when you get angry and say something you don't mean, but you've gone too far to take it back. And there's no way to retrace your steps, or to pretend that it didn't happen. You're just broken, and in your heart you wish things were different and that you didn't have to be evil, but you can't see the way to change. So you're forced to work evil over and over, over and over, until something breaks, and you either find redemption or lose your power.

Llor was going to lose her power. Evie was going to find redemption. I was going to be like Evie, or I hoped so.

I didn't know what was going to happen to my parents.

*   *   *

It was more than just my relationship with my mom and dad that made me worry that like Evie I would need to be redeemed.

One day I stayed late after school, talking with my teacher about an English assignment that I had mysteriously bombed on. Like, really, really bombed. I'd put a lot of effort into it, and I think Ms. Browe could see that, but I hadn't really done much to satisfy the requirements of the assignment. I could see that in retrospect, looking at the evaluation criteria alongside the finished product. I didn't use the right number of paragraphs. I quoted from secondary sources, but not in the way that they wanted. I used primary sources, I don't know why I did that, because that's not what Ms. Browe had asked for. It wasn't what we were supposed to be focusing on and I didn't get any credit for it. My critical-analysis-to-explanatory-or-positioning-sentence ratio was way off. It wasn't a bad essay — Ms. Browe said that she'd enjoyed reading it, and after I went to see her and told her how confused I was she bumped the mark up to a seventy, which I still wasn't totally happy with, but which was better than nothing. Anyway, it wasn't the essay that had me worried about the state of my soul, but something that happened afterward.

As I was walking down the hallway to leave school, two guys came rushing past me, yelling back and forth for reasons I couldn't quite make out. The guy in front — Ross, from my grade — was laughing. It looked like he had something that belonged to the guy who was following behind. A hat or something equally stupid. I don't know who the other guy was, I'd seen him before and thought he might have been in my grade but I'd never learned his name. Maybe "Sean." Maybe "Steve." It all happened so fast. They brushed past me, close enough that they almost knocked me over. I'd had my headphones on and I was listening to my CD player and I was in my own little world, and so I was still spinning when I saw Ross make a turn to the front doors and put his arm right through the little pane of glass right by the metal panel you're supposed to push. There was a huge crashing sound and he staggered back from the door with the skin hanging off his arm like a tattered flag. His friend had somehow managed to stop himself before the puddle of dark red blood that was now forming at Ross's feet.

"Holy shit," Ross said, over and over, looking down at himself.

There was a hush and a silence that was deeper than any I'd ever experienced before.

Someone ran to get a teacher or a janitor or to maybe call an ambulance.

The glass had cut Ross deep. I thought I could see the white of bone peeking out from underneath the pile of mangled flesh hanging off of him. I am pretty sure it was bone because it was the whitest thing I'd ever seen. The whiteness of something normally wrapped in flesh.

It seemed strange to me that things could change so quickly.

Ross had his other hand cupped around his wrist, even though most of the damage was to his forearm, as if that could have stopped or slowed the flow of blood. But it was the only part of his arm down from the elbow that was coherent enough to touch. The only part that was still fully recognizable as an arm, even though the underlying structure held. Eventually a teacher came and took Ross with her somewhere — to the office, I guess, where there was a nurse's station but probably no nurse on duty. To wrap him up with something more substantial while they waited for the ambulance to arrive.

I was struck dumb by the slow puddle of blood spreading out on the floor.

Part of me felt sick to my stomach and wished I'd never seen the accident. Felt rude to stare. The other part wished I could have looked for longer. The vision was so strange and fleeting. That same part of me was happy even to have seen and taken pleasure from it.

That's what messed me up.

Ross was an asshole. There's no other way to put it. I had been in a couple classes with him and he had never been kind to me. Not even a little bit. The best he treated me was with ambivalence. I was an easy target, especially last year when my acne was really bad.

So, in one way, even though it's terrible to wish anyone harm, if what I had seen had to happen to anyone I was glad that it had happened to him.

But that wasn't it. That wasn't *just* it.

That same part of me that was not only happy to see his injury ... it wanted to see *him injured.* Because it wasn't just pleasure from the injury in the *abstract* — which I can't deny, that was it, too, to see harm, period — it was pleasure seeing the pain and shock and violence *done to him.*

I stood there in the front hallway, for a long time, by myself, until a janitor came and started mopping up the blood. Then I snapped myself out of it and put my headphones back on and adjusted the straps of my backpack and walked home.

On the walk home I kept thinking about the four or five seconds immediately after the accident, Ross looking down at his dripping arm, glass and blood puddling on the floor. I guess I wasn't really *thinking* about it. It just kept replaying in my head, over and over. His look of shock. The ripped flesh. I imagined I could see glass sticking out of his arm, and probably there had been some, but I'm not sure that was something I had time to notice.

Halfway home I realized that I was savouring the tableau. And that started to scare me. I thought I was a kind of monster. That only a monster could want to see another human being hurt in that way. I didn't even know then if he was going to be *okay*. All I knew was that he'd wrecked his arm and lost a lot of blood.

A lot of blood.

Really wrecked his arm.

That was more of a confirmation that something was wrecked in me than throwing a basket against a wall or fighting with my mom or dad. That was more than just feeling aloof from my friends.

I was pretty sure I was a monster.

That night I dreamed I was in school and that I had murdered someone. I couldn't remember doing it. I only knew that I had, and I knew that at any minute my crime was going to be discovered. There was a dead body somewhere and I tried frantically to remember where, so I could conceal my crime, but with a feeling of resignation, like I knew it didn't matter what I did, because I was going to be found out. I don't remember how I'd killed them. Maybe strangulation. Maybe a knife. Whatever it was, it was a deeply personal manner of violence. In other words it wasn't an accident, even though it might have happened accidentally. Or in an unguarded moment, I guess. When I woke up the next morning — a Saturday — it was only as I was eating breakfast that it gradually dawned on me that I was innocent.

A kind of innocent.

Then I sat out on the back porch with an old fantasy novel that my dad had given me when I was twelve. It was about eight hundred pages long and I'd tried to get through it multiple times, but something always stopped me before I even hit page one hundred. The characters seemed flat. Even at twelve I could see that. I wanted to read about their triumphs, I wanted to get involved in the world, but there was a perfection, a sheen to the male and female protagonists that made me feel almost sick to my stomach. You were meant to put yourself in their place and become them, I think. And live without flaws. An unearned perfection. It wasn't what I read fantasy for. I wanted to make my dad happy and read it one day and talk to him about it. But I couldn't. No matter how many times I tried.

Eventually I gave up on that and called Jess, under the pretext of telling her what had happened to Ross. I told her about how they'd raced past me and almost knocked me over and how everything had seemed normal — shitty, but normal — and then a second later Ross had put his arm through the window and time had stopped. I told her about seeing the bone and the blood and how I didn't know if he was okay or not but I didn't tell her about the pleasure that I felt when I saw him get hurt.

Then I took a bunch of deep breaths and crossed my eyes and stared into the sun.

"I bet you liked it," she said, when I had finished.

My heart beat faster, up into my throat.

"What?" I said.

"You didn't like it?"

"No," I said. Hesitant. "Why would I?"

"Don't you remember? In civics? Last year?"

I did remember but I didn't want to say it. Of course I remembered.

"When he said that — you know. About your face?"

"Oh, right," I said, trying to keep her from going any further. "Yeah, that sucked."

It was one of the first times anyone had ever said anything. I mean, directly. I mean, the way that he'd said it. In a mean way.

"So it must have felt good. To see him like that," she said.

I thought again about him standing there holding his wrist in shock. The pool of blood left after him. I thought about my dream and the murder I'd committed in it.

"I guess," I said. My eyes unfocused. Taking in the heat of the backyard. Staring into the sky or the sun.

I made an excuse and got off the phone.

* * *

Thanks to the medication I've been prescribed, my acne is getting slightly better now. But it's strange because it still seems like it's there, almost like it's sinking, like it's happening farther from the surface rather than disappearing altogether. Like it's being held closer to the bone rather than being totally expelled. My skin is smoother than it was before but there are red and pink continents lurking underneath. I'm told even these will go away with time.

That seems impossible to me. But even this improvement seemed impossible before I went on the medication.

I still get some on the surface, more than most people, but it's nothing like it was before. It was over the summer before last year when I really started to break out, when I went from one or two occasional pimples to glaciers, moving in slow unison across my skin. They were so sensitive that it hurt to touch my face. There were so many that it sometimes hurt to smile, all of them backed up and cracking together in the creak of my muscles. But the worst part was, of course, the way it changed the way others looked at me. That hurt, too, but in a different way. I hated to turn the corner at school, to show my face in the cafeteria, to re-introduce myself to Jess and Tiff at the lunch table in September. To see my new self in their eyes.

But even though over the summer I had received unsolicited advice or sympathy more than a few times, most people made a point of not acknowledging it, or at least referring to it in only the most oblique ways. They could tell I didn't want them to address it. I wished no one would. It wasn't like I hadn't noticed it myself. I'd tried every kind of anti-pimple cream on the market. I washed my face twice as hard, three times as often, as anyone else I knew. I tried to cut out fried foods and sugar, for long stretches of time. But it didn't matter. Nothing did.

Once when I was waiting in line at a convenience store a middle-aged stranger told me to immerse my face in nettle tea, to do this nightly. That they would go away thereafter. He said this, clear-faced, standing with his wife, who looked I think as horrified as I felt. He said it had worked for him. That it had been as bad as mine was when he was my age. I thanked him without getting a good look, nodding with my eyes on the ground, then after a few seconds I put back the chocolate bar or bag of chips or magazine or toilet paper or whatever it was that I was going to buy, pretending like I had changed my mind.

And ran home, as soon as I left the store. About as fast as I ever did.

That was about the only thing, the nettle tea, that I hadn't tried.

I doubted sincerely that it would work.

I didn't know you could see a doctor for acne until after the summer when it flared up. Civics class, maybe the first week. Mrs. Baker put us into groups. I was with Ross. Jess was in my group, too. A couple others I don't remember. I didn't know what to say. He asked me why I didn't go get it checked out, like it was the most obvious question in the world. I didn't know you *could*. I just looked at him, I think, or tried not to look at him, or tried to look at him, because after all we were all supposed to do the assignment together, as a group.

But it was hard because no one, up to that point, had ever called me disgusting.

Eventually I managed to detach myself and I asked for permission to go to the bathroom. There I didn't want to look in the mirror, because I knew I'd see what I'd gotten used to not seeing, even though I could never forget it was there. The blight and pain.

Every morning when I woke up I thought to myself, "This can't last until I'm twenty-five, can it?" But I knew that it would. That my whole life would be like that, oozing and painful, totally out of my control. I still feel that way, even though my acne's getting treated now. It's hard sometimes to realize that anything has changed. In the bathroom I felt angry, angry and embarrassed that no one had told me I could get help for it, that I had to find out from Ross.

Probably it was from about that point that I started hating him. But even so I'm not sure that means he deserved what happened to him, or that I should feel as good as I did when he got hurt. No one should get hurt. Why should I want anyone to get hurt?

What was wrong with me?

Why did I like it?

*   *   *

After my phone call with Jess I went back upstairs and got back in bed. I'd gotten sort of weird on the phone and said a quick goodbye. It was two or three o'clock in the afternoon. I closed the curtains and buried my head in the pillows. I thought it would be easier not to live than to be the kind of person I imagined that I was. A bad person. A violent person. A broken person. Someone who'd never figure anything out.

I wanted to die and I couldn't see any other future for myself. I mean, if I didn't die. I thought I would be fucked up and mean for the rest of my life, angry and unloved. Creaking into bitter and lonely adulthood. I imagined that my bones were corrupted, that they were filled with acid and poison, and that if I lay still long enough they would crack and consume my flesh. I imagined lying in a field, on the ground outside, lying down until the poison did its work and I was a shrivelled and blackened nothing.

And it felt sort of good to imagine all of that, to imagine a way out, I mean, even if that way out was about the worst one I could think of. I thought I shouldn't even imagine it, or that I should try not to, but it felt good and it was about the only thing I knew how to do.

3

Sometimes when I walk home from school it feels perfect. Timeless. Impossible. I don't know how else to explain it. The trees are green and tall, the air light and crisp, or pure and hazy, even the weeds choking the sidewalk have a sort of ethereal quality that makes it seem like they belong, like they're necessary, like they've always been there, like somehow I am part of them, reaching up from their cracks in the pavement and stilling themselves in eternity. Sometimes I stop and listen to the insects buzzing in the grass, listen for birds, or hear the wind blowing through the trees, and I feel like a part of something much, much larger than me. Like I don't exist and I don't need to. Like I'm just a minor detail in a painting — just a bystander standing far away on the acropolis, rendered in heavy oils by some top-hatted Romantic in the nineteenth century.

I like that feeling — a kind of annihilation.

Being emptied out, in the best way.

I feel closest to Evie when I'm in that mood. I imagine she is so much nearer to the earth, to its rhythms and mysteries. Her problems are larger than mine, but they feel easier to solve.

It's stupid. I *know* it's stupid.

But it helps me to imagine that I could solve everything that's wrong with me, feeling ugly and having parents who don't like each other and spending too much time alone and thinking too hard, through a single thrust of a dagger. And not even *my* dagger — Evie's. Evie's dagger.

It's easier for me to believe that I could fix things with a tool of Evie's than my own. Sometimes I let myself believe that everything would be better for me if I found the right guy. Like I could pour out my heart to him and he would fix me somehow. I'd feel whole, always. I know that's wrong, but a much larger part of me than I'd like to admit believes it. Maybe I'm not even sure I know it's wrong. Maybe it would be better — how could I know either way? I've never had a boyfriend. Not even close.

It seems pretty good.

But I'm also afraid that even if I did find the right person, I'd ruin it by being too honest with them. Like there's a limit to how much you can share before you betray your true self. And I know my true self isn't any good.

No one would love it.

That's why, right now, it's much easier to be interested in guys I never talk to. To watch them from afar. To imagine they are daggers, daggers I could use in my own hands, when the time is right, if that time ever comes. Mostly they are infatuations that I can comfortably nurse for months. Jess once told me that if I talked to them I wouldn't find them as interesting, and maybe that's true. She also said I should get a boyfriend and that it is easy to do that because guys are fucking stupid, and that's the reason they'd be less interesting to me if we talked. Maybe that's true, too.

But if so, what's the point?

* * *

In grade nine there was a boy in one of my classes whom I used to dream about regularly. I mean, all the time. I didn't even really want to, because I didn't think the happiness that I felt in my dreams would ever come true. Maybe sometime, vaguely, in a future that, to be honest, I still have difficulty imagining. Not with him, in any case. But I couldn't help it. Before I started dreaming about him, we'd spoken, really spoken, maybe one or two times. This was before my face broke out. In geography. He was in my gym class, too, but we never talked there.

I don't even remember our conversation — something about *pickles*. I'd said "pickles" was a funny word, I can't remember why — though, yeah, it's a funny word. Then, afterward, when he saw me in the hallway he'd say, "What's up, pickles?" In a kind way, though it made me nervous. I thought he was probably confused about me, like he thought I was someone that I wasn't. I *knew* I was going to disappoint him. I felt like I was disappointing him all the time, when I said my shy hello and disappeared into the crowded halls.

Richard. He had an unusual name, too grown-up, like he was already an accountant or something. I still don't know if he had a nickname or anything. Probably, though I'd never heard anyone call him "Rick" or "Dick" or "Ricky" or whatever. I might have even made fun of him for his first name, the way everyone I knew enunciated every syllable — eventually, if we ever got closer.

In my dreams he was always waiting for me — at the entrance to rooms, underneath tables, somewhere far away where my dream would never reach. It was like fireworks going off when we touched, if we ever got there, fireworks and like something in me was turning something in him, or vice versa. We never had sex in my dreams — not really, even if it was probably a sexual feeling that I woke up with. It felt like it. But just entering his aura alone was a feeling of completeness, of satisfaction. It was so euphoric that when I woke up in the morning I was almost afraid to face the day, knowing that I would be without that feeling that I knew I couldn't have on my own.

Knowing I might run into the unwitting object of my love. Or whatever it was.

Those dreams were confusing. Sometimes I would wake up and realize I was wet, ashamed because at some point in the dream Richard had turned into Jess, which felt weird and made me worry that I was gay. Not that there's anything wrong with being gay. I just didn't want to be. Not for any good reason. Now I don't know. Probably I'm not. Sometimes I woke up afraid — gasping for air, struggling against my sheets — because Richard had turned into something else. A kind of shadow — tall, gangly, with long hair, that would stalk me through my dreams. Familiar — something I knew but couldn't quite catch. It was a fear that felt big, and primal, like it had always been there, vibrating at my very core.

In the morning after each of the dreams I would sit with the two feelings — the euphoria I had felt with Richard, the fear that came in the other dream.

I didn't know which one to trust.

I couldn't trust either.

It felt rude to see Richard in the hallway and to know that he was going to talk to me, and that despite everything I told myself it was going to mean so much more to me, even if I startled and ran away. Even if I startled so much and so often that that's probably what he'd come to expect, forgetting his original object, instead content only to say a few words and watch me gasp for breath and turn my four knotty limbs against each other on the cheap tile.

In any case, before the end of grade nine Richard started seeing someone named Noreen. I saw their love blossom in the halls, and they became a serious couple, one of the few that have stuck, a union of two names that seem older, like they are fated to be, *Richard and Noreen*, and by the next year we were strangers again in the hallway. It was even worse seeing him then, with my face blemished — not only because it changed something he once might have liked, but because it felt like what had been in me the whole time, that he hadn't seen, but I'd known was there, what I'd been afraid of, had finally made its slow, oozing way to the surface for everyone to witness.

* * *

When my dermatologist prescribed the pills that began to tame my acne he asked me first whether anyone in my family had a history of depression. We were sitting in his second examination room on the third floor of a nondescript office tower just off of 89. It was September and felt like summer still or maybe it was early October and unusually hot. I remember my bare legs sticking to the plastic of the little bed they make you sit on, even though he'd also pulled a thin, paper cover over it. The window was open and the heat was oppressive and it smelled like car exhaust from the highway, and the fluorescent lights were burning my eyes. He had been both dismissive and efficient, authoritative, when looking me over: itemizing my condition, asking me whether I had any acne on my back or anywhere else. "Yes," I said, to all of his questions about the location of the outbreaks. "Yes, yes, yes."

A history of depression, he had said. It rang in my ears.

No one had been hospitalized or ever tried to kill themselves. At least not that I knew. His question had made me kind of scared — like to answer it I would be revealing myself in a way I wasn't prepared for, even though I'd given him everything else he asked. I said no.

"Good," he said. And he asked me my weight and then took out a pad and started to write out a prescription. "In certain cases, the pills I'm going to give you have been known to exacerbate depression. To make it a little more intense. Let me know if that happens to you and we'll switch you onto something else. But this is the most effective stuff."

I nodded. He kept writing, then turned back to his computer and fiddled with his charts.

"You should know, there have been some claims that that kid down in Florida was taking this, but it's not entirely true. He stopped treatment about a month before he killed himself."

"Oh," I said. I hadn't heard about him.

"In other words, don't worry about it," he said.

"Okay," I said.

"There's no significant evidence."

I nodded.

"It doesn't happen in a vacuum."

I didn't care. That was the price of a smooth face.

And *back*, which I hadn't even considered before, though of course.

He finished whatever he was doing on the computer and explained the dosing schedule. Then he sent me back out into the office, where my mother was waiting. When we got home I Googled the name of the medication, *Florida, teenager, suicide*, and I found an article about a kid who had stolen a Cessna and flown it into a Tampa office tower. A note found in his bedroom claimed that he was operating in concert with Al Qaeda (it wasn't true) and that he was trying to turn the upside down right side up. America was oriented in the wrong direction, according to his manifesto.

I looked at the photographs of the office tower and the sub-urbs that surrounded it and I thought that everything did look upside down. I printed out the photo and turned it upside down and hung it in my room, just above my bed. It stayed there for a couple months, as I kept taking my pills every morning and evening, as my acne started receding and my face started to get clearer, so much so that even Ross noticed and said it was a huge improvement, though I hated him for saying anything, until one day the poster disappeared when I was at school. Mom had taken it down, telling me when I got home that it was morbid and that she worried about me.

But it felt *true*.

My cousins on my mom's side used to live in Brampton, in a huge residential tower on a street of huge residential towers, high and wide and clear and bright, with ornate lobbies and concierges and underground parking lots. But in between them pavement, empty lawns, tiny trees and shrubs, and the howling of traffic going by on Highway 10. The rush of cars constant, ever-present, like the sound of blood rushing through veins. When we got out of the car sometimes I imagined the buildings being excavated a thousand years in the future and the assumptions the archaeologists would make, and how they would miss the one thing that was crucial to understanding what it was like to live there, the machine hum and throb, like the wings of fibreglass zephyrs swooping and diving, and I wondered what they missed now in the digs out in ancient Mesopotamia or in the Mexican desert that you could never even hope to reproduce, the dim, menacing rumble of a world hundreds of years removed.

It all seemed upside down to me, in the same way that the photo of the office tower in Tampa did. Now my cousins live in a little upscale subdivision in Waterloo, but when they were in Brampton we would sometimes walk over to the corner store to grab a can of soda, and I remember those walks being endless, us so far from the thing we wanted, even though that thing was nominally part of the complex from which we originated. The scale was not human — you were meant to drive. What was a blink in a car was a whole afternoon on foot. The avenues were wide and the distances between things large.

It was like we were walking on a treadmill, moving endlessly with only the slightest shift on the horizon. I think it took us something like forty minutes each way.

I remember in the car on the way home I paid more attention to the strip malls and suburbs that we passed on the road out, seeing the distances differently than I had before, when they had been innocuous blurs, quickly accessible via right or left turn signal.

I thought then that there was a menace to the distance that had been erected, the distance set up between everything. My cousins' home had always been its interior, intimate and warmly lit and engaging and varied, and I hadn't spent any time assessing its outside. I felt grateful to live in Durham, a place that was maybe nowhere, but was at least for human beings, with a main street off 89 with churches and restaurants and little stores and close houses and mature trees. But I could see Brampton on the horizon, or what it represented, in Durham. I could see it even though it was over an hour away, with the new developments on the north side of town and the new gas stations and the promised shopping centre that they were going to build south of the highway.

What will it be like to live through so much change? I wondered, at the same time that I was almost afraid to find out.

My dad had been upset about some of the new development and I hadn't until then been able to understand his anger or what it meant, only thought about the future fast-food chains and convenience that would come with them. But it felt after to me like an eradication heading straight for us, a nothing that was coming and going to turn us upside down. To concentrate us and pin us, smouldering, to the side of an office building in Tampa.

4

Ten years later, and I still feel like I'm living in the upside down.

I've been having this dream, lately. I'm walking in a deserted landscape. Everything's grey, twisted, destroyed. A layer of creepy fog brushes against my legs. Excalibur is with me and I'm holding the reins, leading her somewhere, although I'm not sure where. The ground is loose, uneven, and I keep stumbling, though I never fall. But my shoe catches on something and when I look down I see a woman's hand sticking out of the soil. I don't scream, because for some reason it makes sense. Like I should expect to see it. Instead I carefully brush the soil from what turns out to be Evie. Evie's lifeless body. Evie in her ragged leather armour. Looking peaceful, like a dove. I hear a voice.

"Ho! Hey! Mush!"

My father, dwarfed by Excalibur, is sitting astride the horse, trying to tell her where to go. He points to the horizon, where a city, silhouetted by a falling star, or a nuclear explosion, ominously waits for us.

I told this dream to my psychologist, who asked me what I thought it meant.

"That's *your* job," I said.

"But it was your dream."

"So?"

"So you know better than I do."

We sat there in the quiet for a little while. When this happens she usually asks me where I've "gone" when I finally bring my eyes back up to her.

As if I was anywhere *else*. I'd been intently examining the carpet pattern.

"I don't know," I said. "I guess I was thinking about my dad."

"You miss him."

"Of course."

"Where do you think he was pointing you?"

I hadn't considered that. It was only sitting on the GO Train later that I thought about her words again, and my dream. I was taking the train out to the suburbs, where I would board the bus that would take me to Durham.

From my apartment window in Toronto, facing east, you get a comparable cityscape to what I saw in my dream. Before the sun has risen, when the sky is just slightly coloured, the buildings that make up the downtown black obelisks in its light. But I was certain that it wasn't a sunrise in my dream. Closer to sunset, but not that either.

I wasn't sure what it was.

* * *

I keep choking on this weird feeling that caught me again as I was staring out the train window. A feeling I can't name but that's been bothering me ever since I agreed to come out here, and maybe even before that, too. It's the same feeling I get reading Kent Adler's book *Homesickness*, except when I'm reading Adler's poetry that feeling is somehow something I *want* to have. It's

a feeling of imminence. Like something is coming and I don't
know what.

But it's big and it's going to change a lot.

The poem that most affects me like this is "October 23,
2012":

> Heeding the birds
> As a car peels out
> I locked the garage
> An entire flock
> As a bear moves
> Shaggy with death
> And car horns
> Heard in delirium
> Waiting for the light
> Of a passing vehicle

I feel like I know exactly what he means. Like I'm with him,
waiting to be overcome. He was from Durham, too, so I think he
understands. Except for Adler the poem was set in the future, his
future, a future I think he knew would never arrive, and for me
it's my present, more or less.

Tom thinks it might help me to do meditation. He's always
putting on bells or chimes on his phone or on the computer or on
the stereo (his mom in Victoria sent him a Buddhist chimes CD
in a care package last April) and telling me to close my eyes and
breathe. Usually I resent it; it's none of his business, but I tried
doing some on the train. I did the one where you picture yourself
at the bottom of a pool of water, each exhale a stream of bubbles
carrying your troubles away and to the surface.

It was a little difficult getting settled. The train was crowded
and I'd been facing two middle-aged day traders or securities

executives or bank robbers or whatever, loudly gossiping about their colleagues or their rivals or both, talking tactlessly about moving crazy sums of money from one account to another. The numbers they used really were astounding, casually referring to amounts I never thought were possible outside of news reports, more money than I could ever dream of seeing.

Before a seat opened up and I was able to sit down I stood next to them and watched their stubbled chins move over this landscape, so foreign to me, with a confidence and lack of self-consciousness that I'd always wanted and never known.

And never *would* know.

Seated I tried to imagine myself under a great quantity of water, placing myself in the midst of an immense cool blueness, nourishing and safe, like a blanket of amniotic fluid. But no matter how hard I tried to imagine the toxins rising out of me with my exhalations, bubbles rising and bursting on the surface far above, I just couldn't concentrate on my breathing. I couldn't still my thoughts. I couldn't go where I needed to go.

Whenever I opened my eyes and caught a glimpse of my neighbours' tailored suits, trendy coffees, muted accessories, and expensive-looking phones — I got angry, angrier than I had any right being. The water I was trying so hard to peacefully bury myself under turned to a fierce boil. Instead I took a book out of my bag and stared hard at the men when they weren't looking, trying to will them into getting a nosebleed or a migraine. *Something* to make them feel fragile, or at least the possibility of fragile, even for a moment. As fragile as I felt nearly every day, whenever I stopped and caught myself.

It didn't work.

Which is just as well, because it wasn't their fault, even though it was. But it was only their fault in a way that was so much larger than them it felt useless to make them the target of my anger. I wanted a kind of security that just wasn't available to me, even though it might have been, maybe, a long time ago. But I had so much trouble letting it go. That was one of the reasons I was coming back to Durham, as much as I hated to admit it.

I'd stopped getting nosebleeds when I finally went off the acne medication in my undergrad, but I still felt like I was on the *verge* of getting them. There was still the *possibility*. I mean, spiritually.

In a way those businessmen would never understand.

When I was a little kid I remember that everything seemed so simple. Even if I wasn't particularly popular in my classes I always did well in school and was praised by my teachers. That changed by the time I got to high school, but I still believed in my underlying competence. I was still able to write *Evie* even though I'm not sure I believed in anything else. I still thought it would lead to something.

Even just in myself.

Now everything feels so hard. I've made so many sacrifices to keep working and writing and they haven't amounted to anything. I just feel drained and exhausted. I'm no closer than I was then, although I *have* made solid inroads into establishing a lifetime of feeling poor and trapped.

Really solid inroads.

Sometimes when I'm lying on the couch with a book open and abandoned on the ground beside me Tom will come and sit down gingerly in the armchair next to me, and say, in a saccharine voice that I once used to love because it felt like the mark of someone who cared about me, "*Sarah, I think we need to talk.*"

But what he means is: Sarah, *you* need to talk. It's never about *us*, though on that subject I have a lot I could say, but about how I could be doing more to centre myself, to take pleasure out of the everyday, to appreciate what I have, and to expand my support network. And I don't want to do any of that, although I think it might be nice to have more people to talk to so that I could occasionally complain about him.

Not that he's *so* bad.

But one of the reasons I was so excited about leaving our apartment for a week was to get away from us, for at least a little bit.

To still myself and take a breath and look around.

The truth is that sometimes I want to be depressed. Maybe I need to be, I don't know. It's not a problem that anyone needs to solve, especially not someone who doesn't really understand the cause. I mean, as much as I love Tom, or at least think I do, it seems difficult for him to see that my problems are larger than my immediate circumstances.

And maybe sometimes I need to acknowledge that, too. I don't know.

It's been a long time since I've been back to Durham. For a few months after I started school in Toronto I used to come down every week — nominally to see Tiff and Jess if they were in town, and Carl, who I'd gotten in the summer before my final year of high school (to add something light to the house, something for me). But I also came back home to feel attached or connected to something when everything else in my life felt so new and strange and different. I wanted the comfort of the house I grew up in, I wanted to hide in my room under the covers and look at the pathetic willow out the front window. I wanted to see my mom. Even if I didn't see her very often, because she was already dating Dan and didn't want me to know (I knew). Even if we fought a lot. There was still something comforting about spending time next to her, in eating her home-cooked meals, tastes familiar from childhood, in sitting on the couch together as we silently watched something dumb on television.

But then things got busy. I started to feel like I didn't have time enough to call home, let alone to spend my entire weekend travelling back and forth on a bus. And Mom and Dan got married, and after he moved in it didn't feel so much like my home anymore.

Looking out into the hills and the fields and the calm after the bus I transferred onto in Brampton escaped the suburbs and entered the empty highways on the way to Durham, surrounded by nothing but forests and fields and meadows, green turning yellow and gold, haze of life floating in the air, a clarity, homes dwarfed by the emptiness on either side, I realized how hungry I was to see it all again, to break out of the grey that I inhabited and into something that I was surprised to discover seemed alien and different to me now, but also deeply urgent and real, like it was somehow rising out of me even as it rushed past me on the other side of the window.

*   *   *

Carl was waiting for me when I unlocked the front door to the house, a little white-and-orange arrow streaking to the entrance. I pushed back with my foot, catching him off-balance, forcing him to sit back and blink slowly in the darkness. When I had the door closed behind me and put my stuff on the bench he brushed my leg and chirped meaningfully, which I knew meant *I want food*. Instead I picked him up, cradling him like a child, holding him close to my face, and I know he liked it because his whole body was soft and he was purring, but he also tried to bite me on the nose because he was hungry, so I pitched him forward and let him hit the ground and take a few steps forward.

He's not like most cats, because he chirps instead of meows, but also because he carries himself not at all like a cat but like a weird, insistent human baby, though also a sharp one, if you're not careful. He doesn't mean anything by his sudden moments of ferocity — sometimes I think he thinks that's what it means to show love: to bite down as hard as possible into the one you care about, to get your claws stuck in their hand as a means of demonstrating the depth of your feeling.

The house had changed a lot in the years since I'd left it. First Mom had re-shingled the roof and redone the floors, a dark, cool granite over the pale and fading hardwood that was there before. After Dan moved in they'd updated the living-room furniture and bought all-new appliances, taking down the far wall in the kitchen and bringing the room out fifteen feet to make room for a harvest table that stood in the sunshine pouring down through newly installed windows, large and angled and running pretty much from the floor to the ceiling of the new extension. To be honest, it looked pretty good. When I called home — which wasn't often — Mom would complain that Carl had taken an interest in the drawstrings for the new venetian blinds, plucking them with his claws when he was hungry and trying to get her attention. She said that some days she wanted to strangle him or throw him outside to fend for himself.

But I told her he was too soft and pliant to survive out there on his own. He'd never been outside in his whole life, except once when he was six months old — after hours of searching I found him covered in cobwebs and cowering out behind the shed.

"*I know*, honey," she would say, in a tone of voice that made me worry that she didn't know.

There was a note on the bureau in the foyer with some basic instructions, and that note explained there were more notes left around the house, wherever Mom and Dan thought they would be helpful. As if I didn't know the house at all or couldn't figure it out on my own. How hard was it to understand the thermostat, which I had adjusted up and down as soon as I was tall enough to reach the switch? The note in the kitchen explained that they hadn't had time to feed Carl that morning because they were running late for their flight. But they'd had time to write a note saying so? Also, it concluded, there were pork chops and mashed potatoes in the refrigerator. "*Bon appétit!*" she had written, with a little smiley face at the bottom.

After I got Carl his kibble, changed his water, and scooped out half a can of wet food, I opened the refrigerator door and stood in the light for a few minutes, totally dazzled by its contents. I have never been able to keep my fridge as well-stocked as my mother does, both due to economic and moral reasons. I took out some eggs, the mashed potatoes, the pork chop, some cooked peas, and the butter, and I fried the eggs, mashed potatoes, and the peas together and slid the pork chop into the compost.

I'm a vegetarian — I've been one for a while.

(It wouldn't have kept.)

(I know I'm still a brat.)

I sat at the table by the windows and watched myself eat in the reflection over the black, trying to make details out in the backyard. I thought there were a few trees that hadn't been there last time, and maybe the outline of a new barbecue. I could hear Carl by the cabinets, inhaling his food.

I knew my mom was much happier than she had been before, much happier, more comfortable, but I sometimes wished I didn't have to see it.

When I finished eating I poured myself a glass of orange juice — more for the novelty than anything, since I don't buy it myself — and went to sit out in the living room. I didn't want to go upstairs yet.

I don't know why, exactly.

I remembered my mother telling me that the couches had recently been professionally cleaned, but they were still plastered with Carl's little white hairs. Above the mantel there were new photos in bronze frames, many of people I didn't recognize. An older photo, with a label running along the bottom, caught my eye — my mother's grandfather and his brothers: Joseph, Edward, Robert, leaning against a worn-out wooden fence in front of a barn. The Stuart homestead was about forty minutes up the road, in a town I'd only known through the stories my grandfather had told me about his childhood. We visited it, once, but by that time it had long belonged to someone else — we'd only stood out by the car and peered down over the new white picket fences, trying to imagine the poverty and the wilderness of a time before, as it was in the stories, when they'd still had to clear and prepare the land, piece by piece, themselves.

All of the brothers looked to be about the same age I was in the photograph, in their midtwenties. I took a long, close look at Edward, whom I'd always been told I resembled, but I didn't look anything like him. Or at least I *hoped* I didn't — he was short and stout and his ears stuck out like a goblin's. And on the whole his features were much sharper than mine.

Or maybe that was just my imagination.

I liked to think in any case that my personal appearance had rebounded from the lows of high school. I'd learned how to dress myself in my early twenties, finding clothes that fit me and flattered my body, which had never really been so bad. I went running occasionally, too. Sometimes I did crunches or yoga with Tom. It had been a long time since I'd had any real trouble dating.

Beyond the trouble that everyone has and which always follows me around.

I noticed that there was a pile of Carl's barf hardening in the corner by the window. It was difficult to say how old it was. I went into the kitchen and got some paper towels and a rag and the bottle of vinegar and let the vinegar soak into it for a little while.

"Bad Carl," I said, while I was wiping up the last of the barf, much later. "You're very bad." But I think he could tell that I was happy to be saying something, anything, in that large and empty house. He raised his head from where he was lying on the couch and gave me what seemed like an odd kind of smile.

My phone buzzed on the coffee table. It was a text from Tom: "going out with Jerry. if i don't talk to you later have a goof night."

I decided to ignore the typo. I didn't want to be petty. When I texted him my "good night" he responded with a smiley face.

I hate it when he does that.

As promised, there was a cheque with the note in the foyer. I wondered briefly why it was so much smaller than I expected it to be. Watching the house wasn't a vacation for me. Not *really*. That's what I'd told her. I was missing a whole week of work. While I was thinking this over I did the dishes, slowly, letting my hands linger under the hot water. Carl went back and forth underneath me, rubbing first one leg and then the other. He was really a sweet cat. I gave him a bit more kibble, to make up for the morning, grabbed my stuff, and went upstairs.

At the far end of the hallway, across from the landing, was my parents' room. The door stood ajar, three or four inches, as if there were someone inside waiting for me.

I tried to ignore it.

There was a note on my bed. It was from my mother, explaining that it had just been made up.

"Don't worry," it said, "I've washed the sheets tons since the last time you were here. Over and over. And over again!" There was another smiley face by her name, but it didn't matter. The note was an arrow, flying at just the right height and speed. I threw it on the floor, next to the stacks of boxes that had been moved into my room during the basement renovation.

I tried to, but found I couldn't, cry myself to sleep.

5

My parents were always happiest in the mornings.

In the hour or so between waking and when my dad had to leave for work you could almost see why they got together in the first place, how my father softened my mother, how, in turn, she created hard limits for him, stimulating and spurring him forward — preventing him from becoming too soft.

At least in that moment. At least in their imaginations.

But just because they were happiest in the mornings didn't mean they were always happy in the mornings. Sometimes, especially after a fight the night before, I would pad downstairs only to find that they weren't speaking at all. Mom would be banging the pots around unnecessarily, or standing in the corner with her coffee, arms crossed, and Dad would be sitting silently, with a wounded expression on his face, pretending to read the paper. Or else he'd be gone already, not even touching the coffee Mom had poured out for him as soon as they woke up.

I'd ask whatever stupid question popped into my head first, just to disturb the silence. Something like "Where's the cereal?" or "Are we *reallllly* out of peanut butter?" Those questions always got the responses they deserved, indifference or anger.

But often the night worked its magic on them. My parents, kind to each other. My dad telling a corny joke and my mother laughing. Her bending down to kiss him on the forehead before he left for work. Sometimes even after a fight.

It was like utopia, just as unreal and hazy and far away.

It was like my parents chose to ignore all of the issues heaped up between them, like all that mattered of that history were their years of proximity, nothing else. Like closing your eyes and trusting the other person not to murder you in your sleep was all it took to reconcile. I couldn't imagine them actually talking about their problems, mainly because their fights were always the same thing, over and over, as regular as a metronome.

I thought they might have gone on like that forever, if they'd had a chance to.

It was kind of heartbreaking to see my dad come home after the good mornings, the really good mornings, already with a defeated look on his face from his hours at work. Or for me to come home from school and know, just from a sound Mom made upstairs, that she was in a bad mood.

Once I tried to cheer Dad up by asking about when he met Mom — maybe not the best question, in retrospect — and he told me the story of when I was born instead.

I'd heard it before.

"You were so little, Sarah. Like a loaf of bread. Just the tiniest little thing. I remember thinking — there's a whole human here. This person might grow up to be taller than me. There's a whole life here, a whole little life. It was the first time I'd ever held a baby. Your mother thought you had gas — she said you'd been cranky all morning. But when I picked you up, you got quiet. So quiet. It was like wind going through trees. I looked over at your mom, and she was smiling, and of course I was smiling, too, and in that instant I could see all of us, together, a little family ..."

We were sitting in the den. There was a TV show on but I don't remember what. Dad had the latest issue of *Renaissance* folded over in his lap.

"That's not what I asked you," I said.

He had a faraway look in his eye, which I knew meant the conversation was over.

"Hm?" he said.

"I asked you about meeting Mom."

Dad ruffled my hair, and it kind of seemed like he was looking right through me, so I didn't bother asking the question again.

* * *

The night I got in I had another dream. It was about the house, which in my dream was difficult to reconcile with the house that I was in: it was unfinished, unlit, dark, cracks in the wall seeping fog and light. Like in a standard horror movie, an abandoned house, raw camera footage heavily saturated with blue. I was lost, or maybe I wasn't lost, but paralyzed, even though I was moving constantly through the rooms.

Perhaps it was a kind of awe.

The house looked different, but I knew it, intimately.

Somewhere a phone was ringing and I managed to pick it up. It took me a long time to get to the receiver, and then a voice spoke clearly in my ear — a woman's voice — first a series of numbers, over and over, the same four numbers, 1313 or 3131, 3131 or 1313, or just three or just one, but somehow the same number, like it could be both at once, then it was speaking about the future or the past, the year in which everything happened or everything would converge, "like an arrow" — or like arrows? — the dream we were living or the life that we'd dreamed. None of it made any sense.

"What?" I said, but the line was quiet, not like it had gone dead, but like there was someone there who had decided to hold their breath. "What?" I said, with a feeling suddenly that there was no one on the other end but that I had been speaking to some*thing* else and that they were still there.

The house. A gust of wind. My dad.

Outside I saw a pair of headlights, far away, doing circles among the trees, trees that weren't there in reality, but were there in my dream, trees that I could only see thanks to the halo of light from the motorcycle's headlights, a motorcycle with an intent rider whose face I could not make out. Doing circles forever like it was the job of the motorcyclist to do circles. Like that was their purpose. It was like the motorcycle was being piloted by an intelligence that only understood circles — only circles, first one and then another, almost a figure eight, but not quite.

There was a bunch of other stuff in the dream, but all that I remember clearly is the phone call and the motorcyclist. And the house, of course, though it wasn't the house and I couldn't recall what it looked like, aside from the waste and the emptiness and the shifting light.

In the dream I watched the motorcycle, for a long time, until the limited intelligence of the rider (or maybe I should say *focused* intelligence) began to freak me out, like my vision was turning inside out, somehow moving slowly closer to a consciousness that I didn't want to touch.

Like if I touched it the headlights would turn toward me and ride down my throat. Like whoever was riding the motorcycle would open their mouth and swallow me in one gulp.

I wanted to stop looking out the window, but I was afraid to, frozen stuck. Everything in me was fighting this fear, kicking and striking out. Trying to scream, but hearing no sound.

That's how I woke up, struggling with my sheets, screaming — first choked off, sputtering, forcing out the sound, then full and high, long and terrified, over and over again. Like a warning klaxon sounding far away, outside my control. After I calmed down, panting and sitting up, I heard a chirp, hesitant and questioning, from the floor.

"I'm okay, Carl," I said.

Moments later he was up on the bed, nuzzling me, and I lay back down and pulled him close to my chest.

*   *   *

There was a huge fight the day Dad rode off for good.

I was fifteen. Mom decided she was fed up with the grass outside and went to cut it herself. It had grown little feathery heads full of seeds that twinkled with the morning dew. They were beautiful. I was working in my room and I watched her from my window. She overprimed the lawn mower — she was apoplectic with rage — and when she pulled the rip cord it blew out a huge black cloud of exhaust.

It was the weekend. Dad was out riding his motorcycle and I'd quietly shut the door to my room when I realized what she was going to do. I thought it was likely that at any moment she would storm inside and order me to take over. Even over the throaty call of the mower I could hear Mom curse and swear as she navigated over willow branches and other obstacles. For some reason she was wearing short-shorts and ballerina flats and her legs were coated in grass clippings.

I leaned back in bed and thought about Evie — Evie confident, galloping through the forest on the back of Excalibur. Focused and clear, marching through light flowing radiant in husky waves through breaks in the canopy.

Sometimes I think back to that moment, when I miss her, think back to how free and clear and definite she was once in my mind.

I didn't look out the window again until I heard Dad's motorcycle pull up in the driveway. When he realized what was happening he stood moping in the driveway with all of his riding gear on. Looking almost like a sad astronaut. Who had maybe just touched down on the wrong planet. A planet that had already been colonized. An astronaut embarrassed about having to radio control and explain what had happened. A moment later he came out again, without his helmet and gloves, and offered to take the lawn mower from Mom and finish the job.

"No," she shouted. "It's too late. It's getting done now. I'm doing it."

He told her that he was sorry. "Be reasonable," he said. "Let me do it." I was surprised I could hear him over the motor from the second floor. I guess he was shouting, too.

Mom just kept pushing. Dad went back inside. I could hear him moving around, slamming doors, rattling dishes. That was unlike him. He was restless and looking for something to do, but he was mad, too, and he wasn't afraid to be. I guess nothing seemed right. Finally he went outside again. Mom had moved to the backyard. I watched them from the office. He asked her again to let him finish, and she ignored him. It made sense to me — she was almost done. She'd done it so quickly. Why should he take credit for something that wasn't his at all? I wanted him to take out a rake or something and gather up all of the clippings, which were lined up like sown hay in little rows marking the path of the lawn mower. Instead he tried to take the machine away from Mom — stupid *and* dangerous — and managed only to shut it off as they were wrestling for control.

I couldn't understand him at all. Usually he just waited things out. Apologized later. Let her tell him how he was wrong.

Mom pushed the lawn mower away, knocking it on its side. The blade was still spinning, though slowly now. And slower.

"Fuck you!" she screamed.

"Let me finish it, Linz."

"I don't fucking think you will!"

"Just let me fucking do it!"

They left the lawn mower overturned in the backyard and continued fighting inside. I hurried out of the office and back into my bedroom, where I took out a textbook and lay down on the bed. Obviously I couldn't focus on the words on the pages in front of me.

Only it was better to be facing the door, should it open.

It was better to be reading something that was *unequivocally* for school.

After a while I heard a loud crash. Then Mom apologizing, in a tone of voice I'd never heard before. Maybe I'd never even heard her apologize, not really.

"I'm sorry," she said. "I'm sorry. I'm sorry."

Silence. I heard footsteps. Keys jangling. My mother, again.

"I'm sorry. I'm sorry."

The front door opened and closed. I heard an engine roar to life. The motorcycle. I ran to my window and looked outside. Mom was standing on the driveway.

"I'm sorry!" she said, more frantic now. "*I'm sorry!*"

Dad just kept revving the engine over and over again, drowning out her words. Looking out across the street. Not moving, but threatening to. I noticed he wasn't wearing his helmet. It must have been still inside. I opened my window and leaned out over the sill.

"Don't go, Dad," I called. "Please don't go."

I don't know why, but I had tears in my eyes.

Like I could see the future.

He looked back at me. For a minute — not even that — it looked like he wouldn't go. Then Mom tried to take the keys out of the ignition and he pushed her away. He revved the engine again.

"Fuck you!" he shouted.

Mom started crying.

"Fuck you!" my dad said again.

Then he put his bike in gear and roared out of the driveway.

*   *   *

When I was really little and my parents fought, I used to go down to the basement afterward, when my parents were exasperated or teary or spent, but mostly calm, and draw out cards for them on coloured papers with my battered and nubby Crayolas.

I always felt so sad descending the stairs, quiet and afraid and small, too, like at any moment I might get caught up in the web of another fight. Twisted and tangled and hung upside down from the ceiling while a hurricane ripped apart the house.

But there was something in the silence and the stillness following a fight that felt good, too, or almost good. Not good, exactly, because I was always too afraid for that. I was still recovering. I guess it was a kind of determination, or the feeling that I was going to knit them together with my goodwill.

I drew hearts all over the front of the cards and on the inside I wrote that I loved them. And I made sure to say that they loved each other, too, and that they should stop fighting.

Kind of heartbreaking.

I was thinking about that after my dad drove off. It had been a long time since a fight of theirs had made me feel so helpless. So long that I had forgotten what it was like. But instead of quietly writing out cards for them after he drove away I lay in my bed with my textbook open beside me and thought about nothing, even though I wanted to think about something, *anything*, lay like this for what must have been hours, panicked and unthinking, until the phone rang and Mom came into my room and told me what had happened.

6

I remember when I first got the idea to write Evie's story. We were all watching television downstairs. It was a nature documentary, the kind of thing that always used to be on TV. Something slowly narrated by a guy with a vaguely British accent. Mom and Dad were on the couch and I was lying on the carpet. I used to lie on the floor a lot because they were always on the couch when we were all watching something together and I didn't like to wedge myself between them sitting on either end. It was too much, somehow, to feel trapped between their bodies, too much to feel their individual heat.

I needed space from them.

Onscreen a camera watched a trap door spider crouched inside its burrow. There was that camera, dimly lit, and another one set up above the surface.

It was somewhere in Australia, I think, or maybe in the American Southwest. In any case, it was a chalky, yellow desert. The camera cut between the spider lying in wait and a little grey mouse that was sniffing its way around the hole. Then the mouse tripped one of the spider's leads and the hole went up, just a crack, just enough for the spider to get into position.

Then, in a flash, the spider's legs rose out of the hole and wrapped themselves tightly around the mouse, pulling it under. An instant only discernible because the documentary's cameras had caught it in slow motion.

But in the slow-motion replay, I could make out a little girl following them down before the lid closed. Not *little*, really — or at least that's not how I thought of her then, because she was the same age I had been. She was dressed simply, in neat but worn clothing, carrying a small, short dagger. She was going after the spider, but not to rescue the mouse. And it wasn't a mouse — it was a stag that had finally wandered too close, majestic and powerful and already dead by the great spider's venom.

The girl had been watching the trap for hours, her and the spider.

Obviously I was the only one who had seen her.

I picked myself off the living-room floor and walked up to my room, shutting the door and sitting at my desk. I felt like I was in a trance. Who was the girl entering the spider's lair? Why did she want so badly to kill the spider?

What was it going to bring her?

I wrote a couple pages out in my bloated and uneven script, pages following the girl as she pushed down the tunnel looking for the spider, hoping to catch it by surprise. I decided her name was Evie and that she needed to fight the spider because its venom was the only thing that could stop the ice queen, Llor. That Llor had killed her parents and was the most evil person in all of the Deepthorn. But that she was reclusive and dangerous and protected by an army of unimaginable size.

I said that Evie had seen Llor once, when she was old enough to remember. Long after her parents had been killed. Llor was wearing a blue dress, iridescent and shimmering, rising above the forest on a floating throne of ice.

I lost those pages a long time ago. I threw them out when I was in grade nine or ten, because I thought they were clumsy and embarrassing. And because Evie's story had changed a lot since then. But I still remember the feeling I had writing that scene with the spider out. I felt pristine, like I was perfecting myself, or perfecting *something*.

But I still don't know what that something would be.

* * *

After my father's funeral, I went up to my room and pulled out the eight spiral notebooks that represented all there was of *Evie of the Deepthorn* and threw them in the kitchen trash. Then I spent the next two hours or so picking lint from my stockings and staring out the window at the hot June sun.

Something about what I'd done didn't feel quite *final* enough, so I went downstairs again and waited around for my mom to leave the kitchen, waited until someone called — people were always calling then — and she answered in the living room, and then I pulled all eight of the notebooks out. I brushed them off with a paper towel and threw them in two grocery bags, then grabbed a can of lighter fluid and some matches from the garage.

There was a quiet place I knew in the nearby forest. A sudden and surprising clearing where the firs were tight. About eight feet in diameter. A place that was always empty, that I didn't think anyone else even knew existed.

The centre of the clearing was pristine, a smooth carpet of needles with only the barest trace of weeds. I have no idea why nothing ever grew there.

It was so private and quiet it was almost holy.

I dug a little hole and burned the notebooks, one by one, watching the fire carefully, making sure it didn't spread, until all that was left were ashes and a pile of twisted and charred metal spirals, like wrecked strands of DNA.

I kicked loose dirt over the ashes and stirred them up with a stick, the way that Dad had taught me, until I was satisfied there was nothing burning left. Then I pulled up a tarp of moss and laid it over the pit, saying a short prayer for Evie, Excalibur, and my dad.

Contrary to my expectations, I didn't feel upset.

I only felt solemn and serious from performing my little ritual.

There was a precision to my thinking on the walk home, a clarity, that I hadn't felt in the time since the accident. Maybe in months.

Though I wasn't thinking about anything in particular.

Instead I'd been vaporized, turned into clouds.

When I got back to my room and saw the drawers where I had hidden my notebooks still hanging half-open, I fell onto the carpet and began crying uncontrollably. Like I've cried few other times in my life. Crying like I hadn't been able to since I'd heard about the accident.

It was so *dumb*.

Mom called me down for dinner, but I ignored her and didn't go down, or move from my bed, and she didn't come up looking for me.

Many hours later, when I was certain she was asleep, I snuck downstairs to the refrigerator and ate a trayful of Saran-wrapped finger foods that we'd brought back from the wake. I meant to eat only one or two pieces, but I just kept going, one after another, until the whole thing was gone.

That's how I survived for the next two weeks, eating mostly leftovers or dishes that sympathetic friends and neighbours continued to bring us in the weeks following his death. Often late at night or early in the morning if I couldn't sleep, or as soon as I got home. Every day a little different. Mom spent much of that time on the phone, or lying in bed, or at my grandmother's house, and she was usually asleep by the time I got up for school. Some nights she came home late, waking me up off the couch with the sound of her keys, and other nights she didn't come home at all. Or didn't seem to.

It felt to me at the time like an encounter between us was indefinitely postponed, where either one of us might have been forced to account for our role in what had happened. I felt certain that we had each played a part in my dad's death and that we were each somehow responsible, but it wasn't clear to me, exactly, what our parts were. I think Mom felt the same way. We were circling each other like two draft horses chained to a wheel: never able to meet, only able to see the little that was in front of us, unable to address the death that had us twisting around and around.

One thing that we didn't have to worry about during that time was money. There was a little from insurance, though probably not as much as there would have been had he been wearing a helmet or not driving so fast. But there was enough. That, combined with my parents' savings, would probably have lasted us a while. Mom talked about it, if not to me, then over the phone. In my earshot. The house was paid off, too, or mostly paid off. I can't remember which.

What was a surprise to both of us was to learn that Grandma Irene had actually been incredibly wealthy, or that when they were alive together *both* of my dad's parents had been, and that after her death Dad had just been sitting on an account filled with their savings and liquidated assets (they'd long since moved into a nursing home) that no one else knew about, just sitting on it as if it never existed or it still belonged to his stepmom.

It was hard for me to understand how he could have kept a secret like that for so long, or why he didn't want to touch the money. Mom was understandably upset, saying that it might have come in handy, especially, for instance, to pay for Grandma Irene's funeral, which they had done out of pocket, but I think she also understood that there wasn't much use interrogating it. Something was going on in him that obviously was beyond our understanding.

Had gone on in him.

I think he probably had a plan, long-term, I think one day he knew he'd have to look at the money square in the face and decide what to do, but that until then he was afraid. Or sentimental. I don't know which. Maybe they're the same thing. In any case, he never made even a single withdrawal. He even left the account in the Alberta bank where his mother had kept it, just signing it over to his name at some time in the days following her death, when we'd all flown in for the funeral.

In any case it was that money that started the flood of renovations and repairs and redecorating in the house, that and the vacations that Mom took on her own and, later, with Dan. It was just a trickle, at first, until I think she became comfortable with the idea that the money really was hers and that it would be difficult to squander.

We went on vacation once together, when I was seventeen, to a resort in Mexico, where I spent most of my time reading in our hotel room or on the beach or doing laps in the pool, even though she wanted me to go with her to all of the mixers and events that the resort held during that week, in the evenings and during the day, and maybe it was for that reason that she didn't invite me to come with her again after I went off to school. I was too shy.

"I just need a break," she would say over the phone, whenever the subject of another vacation came up. Or "I've been realizing just how much I needed this time for myself." Or "It's really important for me and Dan to get out of our routines, to reconnect away from the hustle and bustle."

Honestly, it made sense to me in the beginning. We'd both been through so much. And I vaguely thought a part of it was coming to me, too. It started to become difficult to hear after I graduated, when I found myself working an endless series of crappy jobs, moving from terrible apartment to terrible apartment, each one worse than the last. I thought, if only I had a little of it — the money, I mean — I could have used it to go to the dentist, or to go on vacation, or to take time off and try to find something better.

And then I realized the money wasn't mine and it never had been.

*　　*　　*

I spent most of my time after the funeral watching television or staring up at the ceiling, waiting for a feeling to come to me that I hoped would help me make sense of things. I was angry at myself, angry for weakly calling to him from my window, for hiding away in my room during the fight, for not running down the stairs, getting in front of his motorcycle, and stopping him from leaving. Or for not trying harder to help him feel better when he was alive.

I thought there might be something for me to find, some memento or touchstone stored away with his medieval collection or in one of the many boxes they'd sent over from the office. Once school got out I spent every afternoon down in the basement, buried in his things. Haunted by my mother's voice ricocheting audibly down a vent from the living room, on the phone with high-school friends, relatives, government officials. As well as by the creepiness of wading through the particular and private possessions of my dead father, feeling vaguely like I was trespass-ing, even though Mom didn't care what I did and no one else had more of a right to his belongings than me.

I was comforted by the thought that I was somehow bringing myself closer to him, even if I was doing so in a way he might not have wanted or planned for me to.

I never found what I was looking for. Most of the boxes from the office contained tax files that we were meant to keep for at least seven years before their disposal. Among these were my father's meticulously kept day planners, each one filled with his neat and ordered script. Getting neater and more ordered as they progressed. Dating back to a couple years before I was born.

Apparently he was known around the office for this habit. "We are saddened to lose such a proficient and detailed record-keeper," they said, in the note that came with his belongings. His records only rarely — and always sparingly — touched on family or personal matters, so I was a little thrilled when I found the entry from August 15, 1988: he'd written "Sarah born," in a dif-ferent shade of pen. For that same day, though, he had *three* neat paragraphs of his business activities in an abbreviated and heavily jargoned English. ("Meet with Fr, Re, Ro, Pe: discuss int. fl. Too high? Ro for, rest against. Ja lat. prom., new div. Will sit in on hir. com.") Then, just under the note about my birth: "Sa has Li's eyes, Te's mouth. Will Sa take anything from me, I wonder?" I did have my mother's eyes. I assumed that "Te" was a reference to Grandpa Edward, the same one I had seen above the mantel, who died before I was born. I guess the comparison was okay if it was just to my mouth.

Or just when I was an infant.

The deeper I went into my dad's records, the less they seemed to evoke, as if he was becoming less particular, more abstract, as time went on. Or as if he was just less interested in taking notes intelligible to anyone but him. (Doubtless this was why his office sent the records back to us.)

Although he did note my parents' anniversary, and my (but never his or my mom's) birthday every year, something about his deliberate and emotionless record-keeping began to alarm me, especially in contrast to how floundering and random he could be at home. It was nothing I could pin down, just a feeling I had the more I read (or skimmed) through the planners, like I wasn't going forward in time but backward, being crushed — by something of my father I couldn't name or detect otherwise — under the weight of all the terrible *nothing* he had written while at work.

His swords and armour spoke even less, hanging inert, lifeless, from their brackets, offering only the distant smell, in their grips, of his hand sweat from years of fairs, and my distorted reflection in the clouded glass of their steel.

7

Sometimes I wish I could go back and read *Evie* again. To see what I made. To see if it corresponds to my memories. Enough time has passed that I think I'd be able to look past its faults, to the core of what I was doing, which I still think seems more vital than anything I have written since. And maybe it would be help-ful, too, to be able to *recognize* its faults (I'm sure there are many) and to remember that I have improved, that I am undoubtedly a better writer now. But it's still the longest and most comprehen-sive thing I've ever written.

When I woke up in my old room and saw the boxes full of my dad's old things, I briefly imagined that they contained all of my old notebooks, that I had written ten or twenty times what I remembered, that I could spend my week poring over them as if I was revisiting an old friend.

But of course, that was just a fantasy.

Outside the sun was high, casting long shadows, but there was still a slight chill in the air. Because it was so much warmer in the city I hadn't thought to bring a jacket with me. So I was forced to dig around in the closet for an old one from high school, the least offensive by modern standards, a puffy green jacket that had weathered the intervening years better than all the others. Outside there was a fragrance from the few leaves that had come down, and something about that smell combined with the cold to make the world feel scrubbed clean and new.

I grabbed a newspaper and a bag of chips from the place near the highway, closest to the subdivision. The woman who rung me up recognized me, even though I'd changed a lot. She asked me how long I was in town for, and then if I was still dating that guy she used to see me hang around with. Five or six years ago.

It took me a while to figure out who she was talking about.

"Paul?" I said. "No way."

"Oh, too bad," she said, "I liked him."

She gave me a wink, which I didn't understand at all. People in Durham think everything's their business and that they know better than everyone else. It got on my nerves.

What did it matter to her? Paul was a jerk. We'd dated for a year, and he'd come up with me to visit, once or twice, to meet Jess and once Tiff, and he acted like he was better than everyone I introduced him to, and tried to get me to give him a blow job in the main floor bathroom while Mom and Dan were watching TV, and then got sort of pouty when I wouldn't, which first made me confused — like, *should I?* — and then angry, and we'd gotten into a huge fight when we went back to my room and I'd kicked him out, which I don't think either of us realized was serious until after I had shut the door and locked it, and turned off my cellphone, and later I found out that he'd had to sleep in the train station while waiting for the early bus on Monday to take him home.

But he had a nice smile and he was tall and I guessed that was why the woman who ran the store liked him. Her name was Ann, I'd remembered, after I'd left.

I felt sort of angry after that and I'd wandered at random through the downtown, slowly eating chips out of the bag, sort of surreptitiously because I didn't want to feel judged, even though there were much worse things I could be doing downtown, out in the open, that no one would ever care if I did. I went down to the creek to see if the bike that got thrown in there sometime over my senior year was still there, and it was, caked in layers of mud and buried deep, or if it wasn't that bike it was a different one that looked pretty much the same as the old one had, part of an endless procession of bikes stolen and drowned and forgotten. I kicked dirt and rocks down at it.

"Fuck you," I muttered.

Then I checked to make sure that no one was watching me talk to myself or to the bicycle, alone and eating chips so close to the highway.

The way everyone made a point of noticing me, nodding, and making eye contact as I walked through town, made me feel like I was being watched. It felt so strange after years of living in Toronto, where no one ever looks at you unless they want something from you. I wasn't prepared for it, and it made me self-conscious, even though I knew that was just the way things were in Durham and it didn't really *mean* anything.

Anyway, it reminded me of the time I went to Tom's temple when he was away. I went to one of the night classes, which usu-ally included a meditation and a lecture and a question period following the lecture. The theme that night was "Removing Attachment."

I felt conspicuous the whole night. As if everyone there would realize that I wasn't really Buddhist. During the meditation all I could think about was whether my breathing was loud enough to disturb my neighbours. By the end of the night I actually felt more anxiety than I had when I had walked in. It made me angry.

I started wondering what the white person leading the group *really knew* about Buddhism, *real Buddhism*. I couldn't understand how any of the stuff she was saying could make me feel any better. It was just words.

And wishful thinking.

During the question period, I got angrier and angrier, until I felt like I was ready to burst out of my chair and denounce the whole room.

Then there was a loud and angry voice, clear and sharp as the tone of a bell.

"Fuck you, bitch! Fuck all of you!"

When I heard that come out of my mouth I was so horrified my entire body was shaking. My ears were ringing and I could taste blood in the back of my throat. I just sat there, with my vision blurring, wondering how I was going to get out of there. Or tell Tom what had happened the next time he asked me to go.

But then I saw the thin, middle-aged woman pointing at the teacher on the other side of the room, arm vibrating like a tuning fork, and I realized that she was the one who had spoken. Not me. There was a moment of silence as everyone recovered from shock and registered what had happened. Then the instructor calmly explained that the woman was obviously suffering. She'd said this in a way that was somehow devoid of pretence or condescension. She explained that we should spend the next few minutes silently relieving the woman of her suffering.

The woman just stood there, looking dumbfounded, as we all closed our eyes and entered into another meditation. I tried, but all I could think about was that I had missed my opportunity to be cared for by the rest of the group, that the attention could have and should have gone to *me*. I mean, thinking that, then thinking that was selfish. Then wanting attention again. When we finally opened our eyes, there were tears running down the woman's face, and she was smiling beatifically.

She wasn't the only one, either. A wave of goodwill and calm had spread throughout the room. Things were even more peaceful than they had been before. But I had been incapable of praying for her, and I felt more alienated in the awe that followed from that moment.

*   *   *

There was an even bigger television in the basement, leather couches, a glass coffee table (on its surface more remotes, a little basket of potpourri, and the box set of season three of *The Wire*). A new floor-to-ceiling mirror took up one wall, next to a set of weights and a new stationary bike and Stairmaster. But my dad's medieval gear was missing. The boxes from his office were up in my room now, but all of his armour and weapons were gone, not even in the closet or stashed in the garage, no traces even of where they used to stand — somehow they'd even taken out the marks in the carpet.

Had they sold it all? They might have been able to get a decent price for them if they'd had the industry to cart the stuff to one of the fairs. But probably they'd just put an ambivalent post up on Craigslist and sold the whole lot for thirty or forty dollars.

Or just left everything out on the curb.

It made my heart sick.

It was like he'd never even *existed*, like he'd been a mirage that only I could see. The last time I mentioned Dad, at the break-fast table, across Dan reaching for more pancakes, my mom only stared at me, then changed the subject.

I was too stunned to say anything. Later, when I asked her what had happened, she said she didn't know what I was talking about. That she would have talked about him if she knew what I was saying. "Sarah, you know I'm hard of hearing. You have to speak up."

That was the first I'd heard about it.

All I could think about was the look on Dan's face as he speared three more pancakes with his fork, like he was sneaking around the back of the house with an ice cream he'd stolen from the freezer, his ears red and burning, his face guilty but full of lust and glee.

*   *   *

What there *was*, in the basement, was a full-size fridge (the one that was in our kitchen when I was growing up), stocked completely full of beer. I knew they didn't entertain that much, so that seemed crazy to me, the idea that they could ever get through everything that was in there. Maybe that was the point. In the freezer there were also a couple litres of gin and vodka, with pristine layers of frost crisping the sides of the bottles. I brought those upstairs and set them on the counter, then poured two generous shots of each into a tumbler that I topped with ice and orange juice, so that it was a pale, glistening yellow.

I put a movie on TV and lay down on the floor, looking up at the ceiling, letting the soundtrack wash over me, wondering idly if I should burn the whole place to the ground.

Probably not, I thought.

I rolled over and took a couple deep pulls from my drink and after I had put it back down again and was still for a few minutes Carl briefly, tentatively, stepped on my back, the pressure of his two paws the most arresting physical sensation I had felt in — maybe — a month?

Which reminded me — where was Tom? I'd texted him after coming back in the house, short and needy ("I feel sad"), but so far there was no response. Which made no sense because he'd finished work hours ago and should have received it by now.

"Where the fuck is Tom?" I asked the empty room, over the volume of the television, startling Carl from where he'd settled by my head.

I sat up.

"WHERE THE FUCK IS TOM?" I shouted.

Carl ran to the other room, then peered at me from behind the doorway. It wasn't long before he was back again, rubbing his head against my knee. I closed my eyes and felt nothing, just a pinching emptiness that I was somehow expecting to feel. I lay back down and tried whispering to Carl in the hopes that he would get on my back again, but he just bowed his head and charged it into mine, collapsing awkwardly, so that his whiskers tickled my face, annoying.

Purring louder, somehow, than the movie.

"Go away, Carl," I said, without doing anything to move him.

I didn't really want him to go.

*   *   *

Lying down on the carpet, feeling the alcohol run through me, turning the sound up on the movie higher than I'd ever let it go in my apartment, higher and higher, until it started to feel like the pulse of my blood, something was beginning to dawn on me, something *large*, something that I thought if I lay down like that long enough might come into my brain and change my whole life.

But I was tired of lying down.

I let the movie continue playing and headed upstairs, taking pleasure in my slight delay, my lack of coordination. My drunkenness. Speaking of which, I was nearly finished my glass, and so I topped it up again before I mounted the stairs. I didn't put any more orange juice or ice in it, telling myself I probably wouldn't drink it all. In contrast to the pleasingly sick yellow it had been before, now it was almost clear.

I had a burst of inspiration. It took me a while to grab hold of the hook that brought the attic ladder down — I had to bring in a chair from my old bedroom, and then steady myself against the wall before I could grab at it with enough force to bring it down. Then, slowly, slowly mount the ladder as I made my way up, with one hand holding my drink. Stopping multiple times to catch myself and my breath. Once I got to the top I fished in the air for the light switch; it was hanging loose, so I searched in the darkness for the piece of ribbon that someone had attached to extend the old chain after it had broken.

When I finally found the ribbon and pulled it down, I had become so used to the darkness that I winced and blinked while I waited for my eyes to adjust.

Then I saw that I'd been right — there were all of my father's things. His chain-mail on the tailor's dummy, his clothes (in bags, his suits and costumes hanging up on one of those rolling hanger bars), the replica twelfth-century English standard that used to hang on the basement wall, pinned to the rafters, his weapons, even, leaning behind boxes and tucked behind shelves, framed posters from the fairs he'd gone to.

We'd gone to.

For a minute I felt relieved.

For a minute. Then I wanted everything to go away. They were just dead reminders, harkening back to a time that wasn't even my father's own. I would have thrown everything out the window if there was one to throw them out of. Even if I'd regret that later. Even if kids would have made off with the swords and armour before I thought to get it all back inside.

I understood why Mom had put them in the attic. I got it. And I felt insane for ever thinking that it should be otherwise.

I *was* insane.

I'd thought, mounting the attic stairs, that if I found his stuff I might select a souvenir for myself. Bring it home with me, hang it in my apartment. But what was I supposed to do with a sword, or a dagger, or a shield with his made-up heraldry on it, or a suit of busted chain-mail?

It would only weigh me down.

Instead I sat there, on the floor, and tried to imagine my father moving underneath his equipment, to attach him to it, to make it more personal, somehow. I'd seen him fully decked out more than a couple times when I was little, and despite his diminutive size he had struck an imposing (if a little unnerving) figure. I saw him there with me, sitting on a trunk opposite, his sword in his lap, his helmeted head looking hesitantly around him, as if waiting for something, maybe me.

* * *

I decided to stay in the attic, even though I felt so small, so unhappy, sitting up there. I don't know what it was about the attic especially that made me feel that way. I think it was that there was nowhere left to go, nothing left to see. I couldn't pretend any longer. I had to look back and realize the problem was in myself, as much as I'd rather hunt through my father's belongings looking for answers. I'd already found all of the answers I needed long ago, and they didn't change anything.

I liked sometimes to pretend it was Tom who was the real problem, just as I'd once thought it was Paul, or Joe, or Rick. Or Ross. Or Jess. And not that all of those guys weren't assholes — they all were. Including Jess, to be honest. But I was the only thing they had in common. I felt cramped and squished and claustrophobic, small and mean and breathless, and I was the one who had made my life that way.

It was such a terrible thing to realize, and it was the last thing I wanted to think about, maybe because I knew there wasn't an obvious solution. I felt trapped, and whatever it was that was going to fix me — and I thought probably nothing ever would — it wasn't going to come to me in a dream or in a meditation because I wasn't on *Oprah* and my life wasn't comfortable enough for that to work. I mean, for meditation you need a stable household, a consistent and generous income, a more or less stable social life. I couldn't afford to meditate. I was gasping for air, but more likely to choke to death than to find a handhold and pull myself up to some place where I could just breathe.

God, I wished I could just let it all go, forget about the money I thought my mother owed me, find another job and get on with my life, but I couldn't. I didn't know how. I'd tried and failed a hundred times. Just like I'd tried and failed at everything else.

It all seemed impossible.

I was twenty-six years old and I'd already completely wrecked my life.

It wasn't a great mood to be in, alone and half-drunk in a dusty attic among your dead father's things. With a full glass of vodka and gin and a couple shrivelled ice cubes and just the faintest taste of orange.

8

Whatever happened next, I must have been dreaming. That's about all I can figure out. I was lying on the floor of the attic, thinking about my future, like it was being projected on the screen: a long, empty highway scrolling endlessly, twisting and turning and with no one else on it, moving at a hundred miles an hour. The picture getting smaller and smaller, like I was rushing *into* something. Smaller and smaller, like my spirit was being compressed. But never so small that I couldn't see what was happening, making out the highway and the cracks in the road and the loose gravel spilling out into the ditch. I don't know how to explain it, but I knew the feeling was doom. A kind of pure doom that was crashing like a wave over and over again in my head. I knew with certainty that whatever was waiting for me at the end of the road would be bad, even if there was nothing there at all, even if the road *never* ended.

Then I heard a sound from the other side of the attic, loud and definite, like a block of wood falling from a great distance, and I looked up, expecting it to be Carl. Wanting it to be, so I could pull him closer to me and forget everything I was feeling.

So I could bury my face in his fur. But Carl never went up into the attic, even though he often tried. Sometimes he sat at the bottom and meowed urgently as if he had been left on his own at the end of the earth. The ladder was too steep for him. When I remembered that my heart seized up with fear.

"Carl?" I said. "Carl? Carl?"

I was unsteady and my head started swimming when I propped myself up on my elbows to look into the corner.

"Who's there?" I asked, catching myself, fighting the urge to throw up.

It was dark far down the attic, where the boxes were stacked high and the light from the single light bulb had difficulty reaching. But I thought I saw someone standing back there — a silhouette staring back at me from behind some junk.

"I know you're there," I said, my eyes watering. Unable to take them off the corner.

The figure — I could see now it was a man — had long hair, stretching down to its shoulders. It moved slightly, bending into itself. An acknowledgement, like it was bowing at court. When it moved its body shimmered, as if its teeth were caught in the moonlight. But it didn't have any teeth.

I wanted it to go away.

I shook my head and rubbed my eyes. It was still there, still watching me.

"Dad?" I asked.

It wasn't my dad, but I worried that it was.

"Who are you?"

I couldn't see its eyes, but I knew it was looking at me, or into me, like it was looking for an entrance. It didn't move, but it *was* moving, like an animal standing stock-still in the forest, or like a tree slowly shifting in the breeze. It felt alien, and alert, an intelligence that I couldn't understand. I knew it wasn't my dad, but it *looked* like my dad, or not like my dad, but familiar, in a way that I couldn't place.

I had always known it or it was related to me.

Or it *came* from me or was *coming* for me.

The silhouette stepped out from where it was standing, unfolding and folding its long limbs as it moved.

"What do you want?" I asked. It took me a long time to get that out. I was so scared I was pushing the sound out of my mouth one breathy syllable at a time. My whole body was quaking. I didn't know where the thing had come from, but it felt like I had invited it up there into the attic with me and I wasn't sure why or how. It was looking at me like it wanted to find a way in. Or like it knew the way in and it was just waiting for the right moment.

The silhouette didn't move. We both held still. Each holding our breath. Or I was holding my breath.

I don't know what the silhouette was doing, if it could breathe, or think, or have any intentions at all.

Then I noticed with horror that it was getting longer, that it was rising, inch by inch, rising and inclining its head toward me. I felt caught in the movement, a mouse watching a cobra rear up and slowly shake its head. And I *knew* it was exactly like that — that if I kept watching, it would get taller and taller and closer and closer, and then something would happen and whatever that was it wouldn't be good.

And I was almost ready for that.

I closed my eyes and felt it coming closer. I thought, It won't be long now. I thought, Just a little bit farther.

But something stirred in me that I didn't expect.

I forced myself to get up off the floor, though I tripped forward and caught myself roughly with my knees and the palms of my hands. I would find bruises there the next morning. I wasn't sure if it was the alcohol or the adrenalin or the fear that caused me to trip just at the moment of rearing up. But I got up again and launched myself at the creature, shouting at the top of my lungs.

Then it disappeared, pulling into itself like a puff of smoke. Scattering into the corner or down the trap door. Leaving me pitching forward, unsteady, violent, without a target. Momentum threw me through the gaping hole in the attic floor, where I glanced off the ladder and landed with a disturbing crunch on my arm.

*   *   *

Over the following week, I wondered whether I had chased the shadow away or made myself vulnerable to it. Where it had gone — if it was in me now or somewhere far away.

But then I thought, no, there hadn't been anything there, I was just wasted and half-asleep and deeply, deeply stupid.

This was after I threw up on the carpet. This was after I dragged myself to the railing and used my other hand to pull myself up. This was after I somehow hobbled downstairs and called for an ambulance. This was after waiting patiently outside for the paramedics with one arm clutching my shoulder, after struggling to stand up and sheepishly greeting them when they arrived. This was after they took me to the hospital and set my bones and put a cast on my arm.

The next morning I limped out of the hospital under my own power. It could have been much worse. I could have landed on my head, or twisted my neck, or broken a leg and had to crawl down the stairs or have the paramedics break down the front door. Carl was waiting for me by the front door when I came home, hungry and chirping in confused but relieved bursts.

I also discovered that there were three missed calls from Tom on my phone. He'd finally called me back, I think when I was lying in a heap underneath the ladder or outside waiting for the paramedics to arrive. He hadn't left any messages on my voicemail, but he'd sent me a few texts: "just calling to say hi," "baby are u there," "i wonder what you are up to tonight." I just stared at them, trying to decide how long I should wait to send him a response. I thought about telling him about my arm, or trying to talk to him about what I was feeling, maybe talking to him about my dad, but something made me think that he wouldn't understand.

I sat down on the couch and thought, vaguely, about crying. Probably I had every right to. But instead I realized how lucky I was, that I had lived through something so incredibly dumb. I felt a weird sense of calm. Something awful had happened to me and I was more or less fine. Things were a little worse, but it wasn't the end of the world.

It seemed impossible.

Then I looked around the living room, at the new furniture and the new floors and the new TV and the photographs from Mom and Dan's vacations on the mantel and I thought, fuck that, why do I feel calm, I shouldn't feel calm, my life is hard and there's no end in sight and I have nothing and I have been robbed. I lay back down on the couch with my broken arm tight against my chest and that feeling flashing in my head like hot lightning.

To take my mind off things I reached for my computer on the coffee table and drafted an email.

> Mom. Hope you are having a good time in Cuba. I know about Dad. (I don't mean Dan, of course.) (I mean the man who lived in your house before him and paid for all of your new stuff.) (Stephen, you remember.)
> How come you never told me?

But it didn't seem likely that my email would accomplish what I wanted it to, so I sent the following instead:

Mom. Hope you are having a good time in Cuba.
Carl is fine. I (Sarah) am fine. The house is fine.

The latter email was pretty much in keeping with the tone of
our recent correspondence.

Then I took a picture of my cast and bruises, intending,
maybe, to send it to Tom. But I didn't. I was suddenly sick of
myself. Instead, I put down the phone and put on my puffy green
jacket and went outside. My right arm hanging on the inside of
my coat, in a way that made me feel important, like a veteran of
the American Civil War.

Heading to the forest meant passing by Upper Canada
Secondary, so I found myself repeating my old walk to school.
The neighbourhood that way was older, with taller trees, each of
which had turned with the fall. I thought of a scene I'd written
long ago, when Evie looks out over a cliff and sees a city burning
from very far away.

Despite the horror that she sees, she is unable to look away,
transfixed by its beauty.

The path through the forest was a bit rougher than I remembered, and I got turned around more than once. It was only when
I pushed aside some brush to make space for myself entering the
clearing that I realized there was someone else there with me,
already inside the circle. He was tall, too thin, with hair to his
shoulders, and crooked glasses. For a minute I thought it was
the silhouette from the attic, waiting for me, but the longer I
looked at him the more I realized it was a real person, just another
human being, not a ghost or a dream.

He looked startled when he saw me, standing up and brushing dirt from his faded jeans, bowing his head under the branches
overhead. I dimly recognized him, I realized, from Upper Canada,
though if so he'd changed a lot.

He looked sad, in a quiet way. Like he no longer expected much from anything. He gestured to my cast, to the bruises on my neck.

"Are you okay?" he asked.

"I'm fine," I said.

That was apparently enough of an introduction. He sat down against a fir and I sat down next to him. Gingerly, though, using his shoulder as a support.

"Sorry," I said.

He shrugged.

"I thought I was the only one who knew about this place," he said, after a while.

"That's funny. Me, too," I said.

"But I never thought I'd come back here."

"You're not the only one," I said. Wincing. Or smiling. I was trying to do the latter, but it came out closer to the former.

He picked up a piece of rusty wire, twisted into a spiral, and held it up in front of him.

"What do you suppose this is? There's a bunch of them over there."

I shrugged. "I have no idea," I said.

He played with it for a bit in his hands and eventually threw it away.

"Didn't you go to UC?" I asked.

"Yes," he said. "A long time ago."

"When?"

"I graduated in 2006," he said.

"Really? Me, too!"

His eyes narrowed. "Why don't I know you?"

"Did you know everyone?"

"No," he said. "Definitely not."

It wasn't a big school, but it was big enough.

It was weird sitting with someone else in the place I'd always gone to be alone. There was a silence that kept descending, unheeded, but almost inherent to the place. It's not like me to be so calm when I'm meeting someone for the first time.

"Hey," I finally said, after I'd gotten a good look at him. "Are you sick or something?"

"What? Why would you ask that question?"

"Were you sick?"

"No. I was never sick."

"You seem like you were sick."

"I was never sick."

"But you're so thin now." I didn't remember him being anywhere near so thin, though I didn't remember him well.

He didn't say anything.

"What are you doing out here?" he asked. "I mean, assuming you left."

"I left."

"So what gives?"

"Isn't it obvious?"

"What? *You're* sick?"

"Do I look sick?"

He shrugged and looked me over. "Not really. Beat-up, maybe, but not sick."

"I just came back from the war. Afghanistan."

"Seriously?"

"No. Come on." I knew I didn't look like I'd been in any war.

"So — what happened? If it's okay to ask."

"It's okay."

"So …?"

"Traffic accident."

"What? Really?"

"Kind of."

"What happened?"

"Bicycle, car." I mimed the car hitting my broken arm. I don't know why I lied. It made more sense, I guess.

"Wow. Are you okay?" he asked.

"Yes. Are you?"

"I'm not sick," he said.

I didn't say anything. Instead I raised my eyebrows and looked off into the forest.

He sighed.

"Okay. I *was* kind of sick."

I turned to him, so fast that a muscle pinched in my back. I winced. "Really?"

He looked me in the eyes and tapped his fingers slowly against his temple.

I rolled my eyes.

"Oh, jeez, are you kidding? Everyone has that."

"Not like I did."

"Uh-huh."

"What's your name?"

"Sarah. And yours is Kent, right?"

"That's right. How did you know?"

I just shrugged.

We didn't say anything for a long time afterward. A cloud passed overhead.

"Okay. I *do* remember you now," he said.

"Really? From where?"

He thought for a minute. "I don't know."

* * *

When I got back home there was a voicemail waiting on my phone. It was Tom.

"Hey — are you okay? Listen, I'm sorry about the other day. I mean, I could tell that something was up and I should have gotten back to you sooner ... I got distracted. I'm sorry. But I really don't think it's fair for you to be punishing me like this for not being able to help you, even if you're hurting. Anyway ... call me back."

Now was the time to send him the photo of my cast:

As you can see, Im really hurtin, tom

Then I went upstairs and lay down in the bathroom's empty bathtub, with all of my clothes on. My phone started ringing. It was Tom, of course.

"Jesus, what happened to you? Are you okay?"

"What the hell are you taking responsibility for?"

"I just thought —"

"What the hell! Tom! Punishing you? What are you even talking about?"

He tried to respond, but I got up and turned the water on, holding the phone in front of the roaring faucet.

"I can't hear you," I shouted. "I'm taking a bath! Well, talk to you later!"

I threw the phone across the room, where it split into two pieces.

"I didn't mean to do that!" I shouted.

I turned the water off. All of my clothes were soaked.

"Now I'm all wet!"

Carl was standing just outside the room, one eye hidden behind the door frame.

"Who am I even talking to?" I asked. "Is it you?"

Carl didn't say anything.

* * *

At least I'd had the presence of mind to keep my cast elevated and out of the water. The phone was wrecked.

I am really dumb, I thought.

I toweled off and went to bed. In a fit of regret the next morning, I spent about thirty minutes trying to piece my cell together by re-attaching the wires at the hinge and holding everything in place with tape. My greatest success was about two seconds of the Rogers logo circling together before lapsing into distortion, black screen, and an ear-piercing whine. I jumped and dropped the phone, and that was the end of that.

I didn't know what else to do, so I went out again, back to the place in the forest where I'd met Kent, half hoping he would be there again. He wasn't. So I sat in the centre of the firs, unable to completely relax, thinking that I might see him at any moment. I wasn't sure what I had to say to him, but I had the feeling that I needed to say something, not to him in particular, but to anyone, and he seemed the most apt to listen.

But maybe I didn't have to say anything. I had the idea I could write him a letter, seal it in a Ziploc bag, put the bag in a jar, and bury it with a flag sticking up out of the ground in the centre of the clearing. Once Kent opened it — and if he'd unearthed those binding spirals, it seemed likely that he would — he could write me a response, leaving it where he'd found my letter.

I went home and drafted the first of these letters.

* * *

> Hey Kent. It's Sarah. It was nice meeting you yesterday. So nice that I decided to write you a letter. Hopefully you find it! Isn't it weird that

we came from the same town but never met before? I feel like I know you, I don't know why. Although I guess it's obvious why. Two people who go to the same school, at the same time, live in the same town, probably within blocks of each other (of course I don't actually know where you live), go to the same place to be alone, but never meet, until a chance encounter, eight years out of high school, in a town neither of them lives in anymore? That's got to mean something, right? That's the kind of coincidence they write novels about. I mean, maybe our friendship — am I getting ahead of myself? — could be really important, and if that were true then that importance might be reflected in the improbability of our beginning ...

I don't know. I folded the paper up as small as I could and jammed it in my pocket. I felt stupid for assuming so much about Kent, for thinking that anything I wrote could resonate on an emotional level with another person. As penance I cleaned out Carl's litter box, while he stood off to the side and made sure I did an okay job.

9

Whatever it was, it was right there in front of me.

The sky thundered ominously as I walked into town. I started worrying about my cast and I darted into the convenience store. Ann was behind the counter again, checking lottery tickets for an older customer. She said hello. I kept one eye on the street, waiting for the rain, while I browsed. Then I saw something I hadn't noticed before. Taped up on the side of the counter, facing the magazine rack, was a single sheet of paper, advertising a memorial service for Ann's husband, Henry. Who had apparently died the year before. He was pretty young — just sixty-four. I gaped at the paper while Ann finished with her customer. I grabbed an umbrella and put it on the counter.

"I'm sorry about Henry," I said, as she rang me up.

"Oh, thank you," she said, looking surprised.

"I'd like to come to the memorial."

"Well," she said. "I should take that down. It was a couple months ago now. But thank you all the same."

My cheeks flushed red as I fumbled for my cash.

"Oh," I said. "Well, I'm sorry ..."

I grabbed the change from her and hurried out, forgetting my umbrella on the counter. I didn't want to go back and face her again. Instead, I crossed the street at Oak and turned toward the river. I went back to the bicycle. The one in the river. I had this crazy idea that something might have changed. The bicycle gone, maybe, in the night. Or a cinder block compressing part of the frame. But everything was exactly where I'd left it, deeper in the silt by a minuscule increment, whatever had accrued in the time since I'd left.

How could such a gentle force do so much work? So quickly, but only when you weren't looking?

A car honked at me. I sat down on the riverbank. More cars honked. I wasn't sure why. It started to rain, just a little bit. I got up, turned toward the crosswalk, and ran home awkwardly, my cast beating against my chest.

* * *

"Greetings from Cuba!"

The rain really started coming down when I crossed the threshold into my mother's house. The door opened with a crash, propelled forward by the wind. Carl ran back and hid behind the stairs. There was a pile of postcards — all mailed separately — by the door, one longer message on the back of one (a picture of the café Hemingway used to frequent — my mother had also scrawled "great daiquiris!" beside the address) and just "Greetings from Cuba!" on all of the others, including a weird black-and-white card with a few lines of Spanish and some grainy corpses commemorating the successful foiling of the Bay of Pigs invasion.

Hi Sarah. How are u? The weather here is so
nice. Every night we eat by the ocean. Must be

no fun cooped up in the house! Has it snowed
yet? It's coming sooner than u think. We went
into Havana and it wasn't as nice as the resort
but Dan did enjoy looking at all of the old cars.
For my part I am getting a lot of use out of my
new bathing suits!

Be sure to remember to clean out Carl's litter
<u>thoroughly</u> before you go. I don't want any nasty
surprises when I get back. Dan says to remind
you to keep the thermostat down when you
are out of the house and at night when you are
sleeping. You can save us a lot of money this way.

Thanks again! Love u.

Mom & Dan.

I couldn't tell whether she'd written the message before or
after my email, or if they even had a way of checking their email
up there. I fired up my laptop, and nestled within a flurry of
advertisements and concerned messages from Tom (the last one
beginning, as I could see from my Gmail inbox, "I don't know
what I did to deserve this, but ...") was an email ("thougt you
migth want to see these sarha! love mom and dan xxo xox") of
photographs of their vacation: Dan posing in front of old cars on
Cuban streets; the two smiling together at dinner; Dan bleary-
eyed, waiting for their flight, still wearing his bomber jacket;
Mom on the beach acting coy for Dan behind the viewfinder
(why did she include that one?); the two taking turns posing in
front of a fibreglass swordfish that looked like it belonged to the
resort. Once I finished looking at all of the photographs I deleted
the email immediately.

I was angry that the email I'd sent, the one about Dad, had
been completely ignored.

I yelled "FUCK!" at the top of my lungs. But the computer had cost me a lot of money, and I needed it to write, and all of my work was on there. So instead of throwing it across the room like I wanted to, I gently closed the lid and slipped it into its protective case, and then I put my head on the table, then fell back into my chair, then rolled onto the floor, then crawled under the desk I had been sitting at, then pulled the rug over my face and felt my breath beating back against me in the darkness until, much later, a whiskered face tentatively pressed against mine.

* * *

It's helped me to write to you, to an extent you probably can't imagine.

I've noticed that there is something in the air in Durham, timeless and lazy, which maybe partially explains this weird funk I seem to be in. That feeling is also somehow menacing, for reasons I can't describe. It is the reason, I think, that everyone looks so old.

Do you remember Walid Khan? Weren't you two friends? I saw him, yesterday, still working in the pharmacy, although now it looks like he's the manager, or the owner, maybe. He's gained thirty or forty pounds, and he has all of these lines on his face, like he's a pack-a-day smoker, or something much worse than that. Anyway, he doesn't look like he's in his midtwenties anymore, even though he must be. I don't know for sure, but I bet he has children. It looks like he has children. And doesn't want them. Am I an asshole for thinking that?

Or are the lines on his face not from kids,
but from the changes that work makes to you?
I wonder if that's what I look like in Toronto.
Like a total lost cause. Sitting in front of my
console, moving my hands frantically while I
stare, dead-eyed, into the screen. I guess I have
ambitions — good as those have proved to be
— but I feel like I'm just scrambling from day
to day, working for no purpose. I can't see when
I'll get to rest — *if* I ever will. I don't really go
out, except to get drunk with Tom's friends. I
used to write more when I was a kid, and back
then I went to school, too, and spent a lot of
time worrying about my parents, and had at
least Tiff and Jess to confide in. At least, sort
of. More than I have anyone now. The truth is,
my life is smaller now, and I am smaller. And
exhausted. I don't know how it all got away
from me.

But I don't feel dead. Not completely. Not
yet. Something separates me from the people
up here. Is it just the lack of options? I don't
want it to be an accomplishment that I haven't
completely succumbed. I want to feel alive,
interested, excited. Genuinely. Like there's something waiting for me. Like I sometimes felt when
I was younger, despite all the problems in my
life then. That there was something waiting for
me on the horizon, that I just had to age into it,
that it would come to me, eventually, if I worked
hard, and applied myself, and was honest about
my limitations ...

I'm going home soon and I don't know what
to do.
    Sarah

That was the last letter I wrote to him, though I didn't deliver
a single one. I couldn't even be sure he was still *in* Durham, since
I hadn't seen him again even though I'd been heading up to the
spot in the forest every day.

I felt like I was on the precipice of something, and there was
something terrible behind me, and that the only way down was to
jump. But I didn't want to. I was afraid. I woke up in the morning and went to the bathroom and looked in the mirror and was
afraid of what I saw looking back. Who. A kind of challenge in
my eyes — but challenging whom? An unhappiness, an emptiness. Disappointment. But my disappointment was so general I
couldn't really tell what it was that disappointed me.

I was a type from an old novel: *the disappointed woman.*

Theoretically I should have been feeling better since I was at
least taking a break from work, but I only felt worse, somehow.
Everything just reminded me of how precarious I felt. How I was
sliding further and further back with nothing to show for it and
no idea what to do.

I'd responded to a few of Tom's emails, but not with anything
substantial. I didn't really want to talk to him. I told him I was trying to figure something out, that we would talk when I got back,
which, incidentally, would be soon. I didn't have a new phone yet.
Which was fine by me. I didn't have a clue what I was doing, so
how was I supposed to have anything to say about us? To him or
to anyone else?

But I would have to know within the next two days. That's
when I was heading back to our apartment, to work, to whatever it
was that I'd been doing before. In the meantime, more postcards.

A Cuban baseball team, one of Havana, an empty beach, fish in a market, and one of Dan and my mom with the resort's logo in the bottom left corner, a neon pink overlay. The same message on every one, never varied. *Greetings from Cuba!*

Didn't she have anything else to say?

*   *   *

Later I thought of my dream again, the one I'd had before coming up. My dad on the back of Excalibur, pointing toward the horizon.

I'd lost him, that second day.

Wasn't he worth more to me than that? Maybe the next time I came up there would be no trace of him left at all.

I went up to the attic and lay down amidst all of his old stuff, staring up at the ceiling. I tried to forgive him. For leaving me. For never telling me the truth. I said, "I forgive you, Dad." But my heart wasn't in it. I didn't mean it.

"Why?" I asked, of him, of myself, getting floaters in my eyes as I stared up at the rafters where the bare yellow bulb was hanging. I asked this question several more times, until I started creeping myself out. It was so empty in there.

And it feels creepy waiting for a response that you know isn't coming.

Since I had nothing else to do, I went down to my room and started going through the boxes from his office, hoping there might be something in them that might help to put everything in focus. I wasn't sure what I was looking for, exactly. I realized as I started leafing through the first box that I had gone through everything before.

I don't know what happened next. One minute I was reading through some obscure memo, the next I had pushed the box I was rooting through off the stack and was lying on the floor.

That part of my father was dead. A long time ago now. Nothing worth saving. Nothing ever living. After making sure that Carl was outside the room, I screamed and pushed all of the boxes down with a hip check and my good hand. They collapsed with a satisfying crash, folding in on each other. Then I closed the door and went outside.

I didn't really feel any better after that. I just wandered, at first reluctant to leave my mom's crescent. Doing a couple circles, then slowly expanding my orbit and circling the whole town, from the IGA to the Giant Tiger, to the LCBO, to Joe's in the plaza, to the river, to the gas station, to the pharmacy, and, finally, to the little park in the centre of town, where a decommissioned anti-aircraft gun stood, I guess from World War II, painted over with several coats of forest green. When I was a kid my dad used to sit me on it and point out targets: the barbershop, the town of Rouen, a dragon, your mother, the car.

I sat in the pilot's seat and tried to play the game again. But I'd forgotten that the gun itself didn't move, because all of the gears had been bolted to the frame. The wheel that was supposed to rotate the gun on the horizontal plane still worked, but they'd removed the gear attached to it, so it just turned without any resistance at all.

Why didn't he tell me?

Someone should have told me.

It was while sitting in the gun seat, making low shooting sounds under my breath like a total idiot, when I saw Kent again. He came up behind me.

"War's over, you know. Long time ago."

I almost jumped out of my seat.

"I know," I said. Pretending to be cool. "Just making sure."

He sat down on the rigging.

"I thought you might've left town," I said.

He shrugged. "No."

"What are you still doing here?"

He didn't say anything. Instead he put his hands on the wheel and gave it a few turns.

"Are you okay?" I asked.

"I'm fine. Why are you still here?"

"I'm leaving in two days," I said.

"Where to?"

"Toronto. Back to work."

"You're lucky you can still do that with just one arm."

It hit me suddenly. I sank down in my seat.

"What?" he asked.

"I can't. I can't do that. Oh, Jesus. Why didn't I think of that before?"

"Well, what do you do?"

"I work in a call centre."

"Why can't you do that with one arm?"

"It's not that kind of call centre. Most of it is automated, but I need to press a lot of buttons. Two workstations, four comput-ers, at once. I set up the calls. It's an awful job. I do ninety calls an hour. I have to. I need both of my hands for that."

He just looked at me. Vaguely concerned.

"Oh my god," I said, "what the fuck am I going to do?"

"I think there's a law or something ..."

I laughed. "If you can't make quota, you're out. They don't necessarily fire you, but they don't schedule you, either. I'm not really an employee. No one is. We're all contractors."

"Could you go on disability?"

"Maybe. Who knows."

I banged my good hand against the barrel of the gun.

"Hey, I'm sorry ..."

I stood up. "It's okay," I said. "Do you want to get a drink?"

10

Later that night, the night I met Sarah again and the night I decided to finally leave Durham for good, I dreamed of a torture chamber. Something out of the Middle Ages. Bare, splintering wood for walls, a door held together by cast iron bands. Nothing else. No instruments of torture, though somehow I knew what the room was used for, in the pain that resided in the walls (or perhaps a better word is *reverberated*, like a pealing bell). There was a crack in the plank nearest to me, and I thought I felt a draft on my face. I improbably hoped that the crack contained a secret passage — not behind the wood, but in the crack itself, somehow.

Someone or something was outside.

Whatever it was, it was making a lot of noise.

No, no, I thought, you can't come in yet, please no, no, I don't want you to, I just need a little more time. But I looked at the crack and realized that what I'd hoped for was useless, that there was no way I was getting through that. So instead I rushed up to the door and threw my weight against it, hoping that I could at least keep whatever was out there from coming inside.

I don't know what happened next, exactly. I know that the door opened, somehow. I have a close-up image of a bear's jaw opening and snapping shut, and the next thing I knew I was in the garage, except it wasn't really the garage because it was much larger than the garage. There were more doors leading outside. I was pushing past all of the junk in my way, frantically scrambling to lock all of the doors, because I knew something was coming later that night and I had to keep it out, but the locks kept coming undone, all by themselves, the doors rolling up a few feet, and I didn't know what to do except scramble around trying to keep everything closed. Somehow, far off, I saw a bear, a real bear, walking down a hill, through the trees, and I heard a loud ringing, which I knew was its sound, not the sound it made, but the sound that followed it. But the dream changed to something else, something I don't remember at all, and in a little while I woke up.

In the morning, when I came to take the breakfast dishes away, my mother was sitting up with the paper, her back propped up on pillows, and between a bout of coughing and a moment when I had to grab a paper towel to wipe up something red and brown that she had coughed up she pointed to an item in the paper and asked me if I knew that raccoon feces are deadly poisonous, that they could kill you or even make you insane, and I was momentarily arrested, thinking of my dream and wondering how she could know about it. In the end I thought it was better not to ask, because it was crazy to think that she could know, so instead I pretended not to have heard as I went around tidying up her room, and when I left I realized that I hadn't dreamed about raccoons but bears, which aren't even in the same family, I think.

Of course I couldn't leave Durham yet. Mom was beyond all hope, but she needed me there, and I was resigned to stay, even though I often imagined myself riding out on a bus, the first bus going anywhere, leaving everything behind me, passing into nothing, into freedom, even though I couldn't really imagine what that freedom looked like.

Everything prior to the dream had been awful. I had come home later than usual, only to discover that the woman who normally brought my mother her meals had not come. She'd had car trouble and hadn't bothered to find a replacement because she thought I would be there. If my mother waits too long past her regular meal-time to eat she loses her appetite, though she needs to eat to keep her medicine down. I finally got her to swallow her dinner, all of it, including the medicine, and I'd said good night. She grabbed my hand and squeezed it, and I went up to my room to read, but I was so exhausted I couldn't do much more than lay the book over my face, and soon after that I heard a cry from downstairs.

My mother had thrown up over the side of the bed, blood and vomit, some on the sheets, most on the floor. So I mopped and changed the bedding, and put the soiled laundry into the machine, and prepared my mother's medicine again, and another meal (just a smoothie, that powder, I didn't think she could handle much more than that), and gave it to her. After that I lay face down on the couch in the living room and waited forty minutes for her to throw up again, but she didn't, so I went to bed.

Yesterday, while the hospice nurse was visiting, I walked out to the park and tried to write. I felt weirdly homesick, for a feeling I used to have — for my poverty, for my independence, for my old apartment, even for the bedroom window that used to overlook the Dumpsters that would wake me up with their clanging every morning. I wanted to wander the streets at night, missing a romantic feeling I used to get — one where I felt certain I was heading somewhere, like my poetry could shape reality or at least alter it. Like it was real.

I thought there was something in that feeling I could maybe work into a poem, but nothing came out, and, frustrated and sick of myself, I wandered over to the centre of town, where I found Sarah playing make-believe on the old artillery piece sitting in front of the Legion. She seemed like she wasn't having a great time, but she couldn't imagine how much better shape her life was in, and I found it amusing to imagine her problems, which compared to mine seemed trivial and easy to resolve. Or at least possible to resolve.

We went to the lodge and grabbed a few beers, talked about nothing, playing catch-up even though we never really knew each other to begin with. I don't know if she was trying to come on to me or what, but I wasn't interested, mostly because I couldn't shake the feeling that every moment I was spending with her I was being erased, or rewritten, like my life was turning upside down, or it was already upside down and seeing her was what caused me to realize that — how I'd felt since I'd met her, as if now that she was in Durham I would cease to exist, or some part of me would. It was a crazy feeling, I know, and I'm not really sure where it came from, except maybe from the realization that the clearing in the forest wasn't mine alone, that someone else had spent their adolescence sitting exactly where I had, daydreaming of bigger things and meditating on their future prospects. I wanted to tell her that but I thought she might get offended, as I probably would if someone told me that my mere existence threatened their sense of well-being. The feeling became even worse when she asked me if I had written any poems lately.

"What? How do you know I'm a poet?"

She shrugged. "Facebook, I guess."

"I'm on your Facebook?"

"No," she said.

I leaned back in my seat.

"I don't even really use Facebook," I said.

"Neither do I," she said. "Not really."

"Are you stalking me?" I asked.

"What? Of course not," she said. I think she could sense that I didn't believe her, so she continued. "Someone must have mentioned it on my feed. I only remembered it now."

I told her that I hadn't written any poems in a while, that I couldn't write anything at the moment. That I was waiting for something to happen, and that it occupied all my thoughts. And that I didn't want it to happen, but that once it did I might be able to work again.

"But who knows," I said.

"Are you talking about your mother?"

There was silence.

"What do you mean? How did you know that?" I asked.

"Know what?"

I just stared at her.

"About my mother."

She gave me a look like I was crazy.

"I don't know what you're talking about," she said. "I don't know anything except that you used to write poetry."

"I've never posted anything on my wall about my mother."

"I'm sorry?"

I ignored her.

We finished our beers. Then we walked to the gas station, and the creek, where she showed me the bicycle she'd been riding when she broke her arm. It was half-buried in the silt and there was no way she had ever even touched it.

"I don't believe you," I told her.

She just shrugged.

"Believe whatever you want," she said.

Then to the park, lit intermittently, where we sat on one of the benches in the baseball diamond, just at the edge of a halo of light, until we realized that there was a man seated in the darkness of the opposite bleachers, staring at us, not moving.

"You give me the goddamn creeps," Sarah whispered to him, as we were leaving.

From there we walked over to Castillo's Pizza, which was of course closed, but we could see a light on in the back and we waited, hoping that someone might come out eventually and give us whatever was left over. Sarah said that had happened once, when she was a teenager, although she also said it was probably just because the kid who was working that night had a crush on her friend.

We walked along the tracks for a bit and went into the old train station, just a heated room with benches, because the train only picks up passengers every three days, and then only at weird times, which is probably why the station door was unlocked. It was creepy in there, so we went back outside and sat on a railing and I asked her what she thought about being in Durham again.

"I don't know, I can't really say. I'm going through a lot, I guess. The only thing I've really noticed is that I think people come out here because they feel entitled to something, and that the wide-open spaces reassure them about their lives."

"That's interesting, but not what I asked."

"Oh. What did you ask? What I feel about being up here, like, personally? I feel like a complete fuck-up, I guess."

"But you're leaving soon," I said.

"It doesn't feel like that. It feels like everything's coming apart at the seams. I almost can't remember ever leaving."

"There's no reason you should feel bad."

"I feel corrupted even being from here. I completely understand why you can't write."

"That's not why I can't write," I said.

"But even so, I understand it. I can't write, either."

"You write?"

It was a long time before she turned her head toward me.

"No," she said. "All I said was, 'I can't write, either.'"

"Why does it matter if you don't write?"

"I'd like to write, is what I mean. But I can't as long as I have this stain on my conscience."

"This town? A stain? What are you talking about?"

"Well, what else would it be? There's nothing good about this place or the people who come from here."

"What about you? What about me?"

"That's what I mean!" She got up and started walking in the other direction. I watched her for a while, but decided not to follow her. I felt strange, like I was watching a movie. "You're crazy," I said, but it was clear she couldn't hear me. I wished vaguely I had a cigarette, but I didn't have any on me. For Mom. Because of Mom. On my way home I thought it over. Sarah was basically right, but there was nothing about Durham that should have provoked such a passionate response. Durham is the opposite of passion. It's where you go when you don't want to feel anything more in your life, when you want to numb yourself and your pain. Durham is a figment of the imagination, more so than any other place I've ever been. It is an illusion and there's nothing real about it or the people who live here. But the same is true of anywhere.

That's what I had to realize in order to become a poet.

11

If I was honest with myself, I realized that I didn't want anything
more to do with Tom. Things hadn't been great between us for
a while. It was while sitting on the couch with an open notebook on my lap, trying to draft a list of things to say to him in a
response to all of the emails, when I realized that was true.

I mean. It made a lot of sense. Given my recent behaviour.

I was going back the next day. I didn't want to. I didn't want
to stay in Durham, but I didn't want to go back. I'd only just realized that. I thought about my mom and how obviously unhappy
she had seemed married to my dad. I didn't want to be like her,
needlessly pushing forward through something that only made
both parties more miserable. I guess that was my dad's fault, too.

I had thought that getting a place with Tom would make
things better somehow. That our relationship would deepen.
That we would understand each other more. And it was true
that some things had developed: I was now intimately familiar
with his morning stretches, his meditation routine. The way he
smacked his lips at the breakfast table. His shudder every night
before falling asleep. I knew what he looked like peeing in the

toilet. And how often he remembered to put the seat down again. But those things were all superficial. And in lots of other ways I felt totally exhausted by the idea of spending any more time with him, of seeing what *else* was waiting to be discovered.

Was I attracted to Kent? To his availability, or unavailability, or whatever it was? It wouldn't be the first time that I jumped out of one ill-conceived thing just to begin another.

But — Jesus! What did I even need *anyone* for?

One thing was clear. I didn't want to go back to Toronto. But I didn't want to stay in my mother's house either, or anywhere else in Durham, or in the country, or on the planet. I wanted to slip through a crack in the world and come out the other side.

I was tired of working, tired of money, tired of never having enough and always wanting more and feeling exhausted by everyone and everything. I wasn't even sure I wanted success, either, some deluded future of sitting in a corner office and checking on my meagre retirement every half-hour, coming home to a living room backlit with the acid glare from a constantly blaring television, bedroom as sterile as nuclear war.

I saw all of this from where I was perched on the couch, notebook and pencil tossed to the floor, looking out through the drawn curtains at the radium-blue neighbourhood. I saw my father, too, reflected in the attic window of the across-the-street neighbour's, hunched at his desk and trying desperately to recapture what was already fading away from him. What he thought he'd lost, but always had.

If only he had told me.

If I didn't do something — though what that would end up being I didn't know — I'd end up just like him. Like my mother, too.

I had to act.

But I couldn't think of anything to do.

Something slowly dawned on me.

I dropped my notebook and grabbed a flashlight and my coat and ran outside. I kept running until I reached the park, where I bent over and caught my breath, my broken arm throbbing with my quickened pulse. Then I stood up and surveyed the darkness of the empty field.

*   *   *

I'd never been alone in the forest at night. It wasn't a big place, and it's not like I was worried there were wolves, or bears, or killers, or whatever, since it was so quiet. But it was cramped and close and strange, and I could hear things moving — just squirrels, I told myself, or rabbits or raccoons hopping through the dry leaves.

I don't know what I was trying to prove. Or what I was look-ing for. But something told me I was on the right track.

I stayed close to the path, kept my eyes focused on the beam of the flashlight, and tried, most of all, not to imagine anything waiting for me. To regard my surroundings with a clear and cold objectivity. Maybe that's why I was so disturbed by what happened next.

As I was making the final ascent to the clearing, a deep, low sound stopped me dead. Not at all like a tree or the wind. After a moment of absolute terror I collected myself and calmly hunted for the sound with my flashlight. Telling myself it was nothing. A spooked animal, maybe. It sounded like something or someone was in trouble, but there was also a menace in its strangeness. In its pain. Like the moan of someone being eaten alive.

For a moment I imagined that the silhouette had lured me out into the forest and was only moments away from striking.

I decided that if I was going to die, I was going to die, but I wasn't going to run. I stayed put, surprised at myself.

Eventually I realized the sound was coming from inside the clearing. Every zombie movie I'd ever seen flashed before my eyes.

I knew it was a bad idea to go inside. I didn't really want to see what was happening, but I also had no choice but to look.

I took a few breaths and breached the trees, and my eyes struggled to make out a solitary figure writhing in the darkness. I could hear that, too: the dirt — or maybe the air — being pushed around, somehow I could hear that now that I was inside, louder even than the moaning. "Hello?" I said. There was no response. Silence, for what must have only been a few seconds, but felt like days or hours, the moaning and the writhing and my own breathing.

My nerves tensed up, the flashlight halted just to the left of the body, in the dirt, the body now still and quiet. Moving only slightly. But I could see it now. If I'd been capable of making noise, I would have screamed.

It was Evie.

What was she doing here? I couldn't believe my eyes. Why had she come back? Was she angry that I'd killed her? Had she haunted the clearing every night since the day I had burned her up?

Was it *Evie* I had met in the attic?

I slowed my breathing down and closed my eyes. Evie didn't exist. I didn't even really know what she looked like, though I could picture her in my mind. When I opened my eyes again the light was pointing at someone whose long hair lay tangled and dirty, his arms raised tentatively, delicately in the air. His eyes wincing in the beam.

It was Kent.

"Jesus Christ! What the hell are you doing here?"

He didn't say anything. I dropped the flashlight and ran to him.

"Are you okay?"

His shirt was wet, soaking wet, torn in several places, and my worst fears were realized when I brought the flashlight over and discovered he was covered in blood. His eyes were half-closed, cheeks pale and slick with sweat. His eyeballs twitched behind their lids in the halo of light, lashes fluttering, throat gulping down breath anxiously. Then I lifted the shirt where it was ragged and discovered a gaping red wound, dark and suppurating. I heaved and turned away.

I could taste acid at the back of my throat but nothing came out.

"Jesus, Kent — what happened?"

He didn't respond.

I didn't know what else to do — I put one hand over the shirt, right where the wound was, but that didn't seem to stop the bleeding and might have actually made things worse, because Kent moaned louder. But it encouraged me that he was still alive, I mean that he had enough breath and strength in him to complain.

"You asshole ..." I said.

I thought it was obvious that whatever had happened to him he had done it to himself.

I took off my coat and laid it over his stomach. Even though he'd cried out when I put my hand on him I thought it might be better if there was some pressure on his wound, anyway, since I'd be gone for so long, so I found a stick to lay over the coat, enough weight I hoped to staunch the bleeding at least until help arrived, but not enough to hurt him. Not that I could really tell one way or the other. He moaned but without as much intensity as before.

I slapped him. He cried out and his eyelids flickered.

"You bastard — stay awake! I'm coming back for you."

Then I grabbed the flashlight and ran out of the forest the same way I'd come, faster than I've ever run before. Not once pausing for breath. I kept running until I reached the first house with lights on inside, and I banged the door until a woman answered.

"Who is it?" she asked. "What could be so urgent?"

Her hallway smelled of meat roasting in the oven. An old man with a stiff pot-belly stepped into the hallway just as I was reaching the kitchen phone. "What's going on?" he asked, looking from me to his wife. I could hear the television in the background.

I dialed 911.

*   *   *

In one corner of the attic, underneath a little desk that I'd never seen before, was a box marked SARAH in my father's handwriting. I found it when I was drunk. Before I saw the shadow, before I fell out the trap door. Inside were a bunch of ratty old blankets and a couple princess dresses I must have worn at those Ren fairs at least twenty years earlier. At the bottom of the box was a journal. It was my dad's. He started it the year I was born. My father was twenty-three, my mom nineteen. Most of the entries were pretty mundane, an only slightly more intimate version of his journals at work. The entries came less and less frequently, until they stopped altogether. The last third or so was completely blank.

He seemed to be struggling with the idea of talking about his feelings, like he had started the journal for that reason but wasn't having much success. In the beginning of the journal he was dating my mom, and apparently that was the source of a lot of his frustration. Mom was my dad's first relationship and he took a lot of responsibility for the issues they were having. I read about twenty pages, skimming through them idly, before I found this:

> Some days I feel like Lindsay is only with me
> because she wants a father for her child. That
> if she didn't have Sarah she wouldn't have
> looked twice in my direction. I know that we're

mismatched. I know that. But even so, I also know that I'm lucky that Ted left her. I know that I will be able to prove myself in time. That she will one day love me with the same strength that I love her, that I love Sarah with, too.

When I first read that I was angry, and I'm still angry. But now I also think, "Dad, Dad, Dad."

*   *   *

By the time the paramedics made it up to the clearing, Kent was barely moving, but still alive. I'd led them through the woods, beam of light tracing wildly, racing ahead of them as fast as I could go, while they struggled through the underbrush, wrestling with the stretcher.

While they worked on him I stood off to the side and pointed the flashlight at his body. Far off, but maybe not as far off as I imagined, I could hear coyotes howling somewhere. I tried to tell myself that there couldn't be any in the forest around us, that we were too close to civilization. But I imagined them circling the clearing, smelling blood, waiting for Kent to die. I started shivering. It wasn't the cold, since the jacket I'd borrowed from the older couple was much warmer than any I'd ever owned.

12

At the hospital the doctor explained that Kent had been shot. The bullet had passed right through him and luckily hadn't done any serious damage. But he'd lost a lot of blood. His body, they told me, was in shock. An officer sat me down in a quiet corner of the waiting room. I told him that I thought Kent had done it himself. He agreed. We both wondered where the gun was.

When the officer let me go he went back to Kent's room to speak with the nurse on duty. A few minutes later he stepped back out into the hallway and finished his notes. Then he radioed his partner, who arrived with a tray of coffee for the cops and nurses in the ward.

Everyone stepped out of the room when I went in to see Kent. They all thought I was dating him.

I guess I had kind of told them that. Not explicitly, but I liked the misunderstanding.

It was more dramatic.

I went to the window first and looked out at the parking lot and the traffic roaring down 89. I could hear Kent breathing behind me. I turned and sat down next to him. His body was pale and dry. His lips chapped.

"How are you doing?" I asked.

Then laughed, because there was something wrong with me.

Maybe because there was nothing else moving, except his chest, and then only slightly, like he was an actor playing dead in the movies, the hair in his nostrils seemed to have an exaggerated animation as they quivered with his breath. I unconsciously addressed those little blond hairs, as if they were the only part of him alive.

"Why would you do that? You have a lot of promise, you know."

I touched his hand. It was much colder than mine.

"Get better, okay?"

It seemed like something was stirring in him. Something quiet, something not visible or that I could feel with my hand. Whatever it was, it was in the air, building, a release.

A release from what? I didn't know.

I stayed with him, though, until much later when the nurse came in and politely asked me to leave.

Three

Reza's Part

Someone was whispering far away in the fields. Purple and pink lights fell like flowers from the trees. I approached the little wall around the well. At the very bottom I could see the water reflecting me — the image I saw was strange. I felt afraid: the fear that children and dogs feel before a mirror.

— Silvina Ocampo, "The Imposter"

I

The night before I left for Durham I watched part of a movie on television. I came in about halfway through. It was about a desperate couple on a motorcycle being chased up and down forested roads by two obsequious cops. The cops seemed to be from another movie altogether. They kept deferring to each other with polite turns of phrase, travelling steadily, but in no real hurry — the lights were flashing on the cruiser, but they didn't appear to be speeding, their siren could only be heard in exterior shots, they even paused to allow animals and children walking with their parents to cross the road. But the man and the woman on the motorcycle raced away from the police officers at incomprehensible speeds, looking wild and afraid that they'd be overtaken at any moment.

Despite the fact that the motorcycle was faster and more agile than the police car, despite the fact that the two fugitives regularly took turns that the cops couldn't make, detouring over fields, weaving in and out of traffic, and shooting down dirt paths, they never seemed to widen the gap on their pursuers. I wasn't sure at first if I was watching a comedy, with the two cops its bumbling and clueless protagonists, or a horror movie. A horror movie about how terrifying and malicious politeness can be when it represents authority and conformity.

I thought the police were going to pull out rubber masks when they caught up with the couple, the kind that killers or bank robbers are always wearing in the movies, with presidential faces on them, like Reagan or Bush or Clinton or Jimmy Carter. That they would pull out gloves, aprons, tourniquets, saws. But continue to refer to each other and their victims with the same nauseating obsequiousness, even as they started to cut into them. I'm not sure why I thought that, and I wouldn't have wanted to be watching that movie because violence, especially that kind of violence, absolutely repulses me.

Instead, the two police officers somehow managed to back their car into the motorcycle as it emerged from a hidden forest trail: one officer, stepping out to trade insurance information, accidentally cuffed the man as he tried to take a swing at him; the other knocked the woman out as she was trying to make a break for it by opening his car door at just the right moment. As apologies flowed from the officers to their two waylaid victims, a backup car pulled up and congratulated the two cops for finally catching the conspirators.

Secret plots were revealed, good became bad, and the credits rolled not long afterward. In retrospect it was a stupid movie, of a kind that used to be fairly common.

* * *

Then I dreamed that I was standing on a cliff overlooking a valley, searching for a river flowing down below. I knew the river was there, but I couldn't see it. I paced back and forth, looking this way and that, occasionally consulting a guidebook that I was carrying (and which I couldn't read, but still seemed to understand).

Finally, just when I was giving up hope, I saw it, just the merest glint reflecting off a tiny strip of water snaking its way through a deep crevasse. I don't know why the river was so important, but I ran back to my truck (I have never owned a truck) to grab my binoculars and get a second look. But by the time I returned the river was gone. I searched up and down the valley, but couldn't find it again.

I woke up in the middle of the night and couldn't get back to sleep. I thought I must have been excited for my trip the next day. So I got out of bed and started rereading *Alert* on the couch, until I fell asleep again. Then the telephone rang and I answered it without thinking, still in the confused haze of sleep.

"Hi," said a voice on the other end of the line, a regular voice somehow echoing off of itself. A voice that was coming to me from the depth of something very far away, a place, I could tell, I didn't want to go.

I tried to ask who was on the other end, but found that I was too terrified to speak.

"I'm coming up," the voice said.

Without thinking I pressed the button that opened the door downstairs. For a moment or so I was frozen in terror, standing at the phone and wondering who it could have been. At first I thought it was Jeff, but of course it wasn't, because if it was Jeff I would have recognized him right away.

Then I knew who it was, like I was a dog picking up a scent. It was Adler.

He knew I was searching for him and he was coming for me.

There were two quick knocks on the door. Then another two, this time louder. I panicked, and the next thing I knew he was in my apartment and I was hiding in bed, tangled in my sheets, watching his legs and torso walk through the next room.

Something was obstructing my vision and I couldn't see his face. But I knew it was Adler and that his face would be horrible. Or completely blank.

Somehow he didn't see me. He just kept walking up and down the room, calling my name, until I woke up. In my bed. I'd just watched the movie after dinner and gone straight to my room — I'd even left *Alert* in the car.

I knew then that I'd have to leave for Durham immediately, either leave immediately or cancel my trip. But I still had some work to do which put off my departure until midday.

* * *

I stopped at a diner before making my entrance into the city, a place that a colleague had recommended when I told her where I was going and that I didn't know how I would pass the time and what to expect. "Make sure to get the deluxe," she had insisted, "and not the regular. You won't regret it." I ordered the deluxe hamburger combo, with a strawberry milkshake and fries, even though I never have sweet drinks and I don't eat fried food. I sat out by the window and ate my meal slowly, watching the people coming and going in the parking lot and the cars passing on the highway. The sky was bright but vacant, lonely, overwhelming the trees and cars below.

The food was about what I was expecting — salty and sweet and hot and messy. It was good, but good in a way that wasn't exceptional. The best part about the place was that it was on the side of the road, coming suddenly after a bend in the highway, after so much driving through empty roads.

I didn't know what I was looking for, exactly, why I had gone out of my way to come so far from myself, why I was hunting Adler in Durham and at the same time afraid of what would happen when I found him. I told friends that I was on a research trip (they all thought I was writing a book), that there was a cousin in town who had a box of Adler's personal effects that had been excluded from his papers, but this was a lie — the closest living relative of his I knew of was near death and living in Kingston, though of course there must have been others, though none that I had reason to suspect would know anything more than what was already available in university archives.

Though I was lying about writing one, there was a book in me, or at least that's how I described it to myself. There was another version of *Alert* — a private one — and I had come to read it, even though I was a little bit afraid of finding out what it said. Even though I was worried I wasn't coming to find anything, but merely *running*, getting as far away as I could imagine (out of reality, into a book).

Jeff and I had gotten into a huge fight the last night I stayed at his house. This was about six months earlier. I don't remember, exactly, if he was initially angry at me or his mother, who had called that evening and explained that she wasn't going to be visiting after all. It seems crazy that I could forget, since for at least a month it was all that I thought about. I still thought about it sometimes, as if I could resolve everything from that distance, as if I could turn it in a direction that caused it to make sense.

Jeff's mother didn't approve of me. It was the colour of my skin. My parents' religion. It was almost funny — her son was gay and she didn't seem to mind that in the slightest. As a result of her disapproval she often made plans with us and cancelled at the last minute, sometimes even expressing her surprise that I would be there. Even though she'd always known that well in advance. Even if I had met her a handful of times and was always polite to her, despite the fact that I had lots of opportunities to tell her off. Despite the fact that I wanted to more than anything else, found myself swallowing my rage, nodding my head mindlessly with glassy eyes as my insides burned and my consciousness rolled up into a corner of the room. So it wasn't that I ever wanted to see her — I hated her sniping comments, her gall, her false superiority. It wasn't that I particularly supported the relationship she had with Jeff, who would sometimes fly into a rage at something she said, screaming and yelling while she pretended not to notice, driving him into even deeper anger. But I hated when she cancelled because it put him in such a bad mood, and then it was just me and him, and more often than not I became his target. It was always my fault when I tried to talk about her with him, later — she was somehow beyond reproach, a topic that I was not allowed to broach because I could not pretend to understand their complicated history, the dynamics of control that she exercised over him and that he had to constantly navigate.

"What's to understand?" I had asked him, more than once.

"You wouldn't get it," he said.

But he was the one who didn't get it. I didn't understand why I wasn't allowed to talk about something that had everything to do with me.

We still hadn't made up later that night. I found it impossible to go to sleep: I thought I could feel him staring up at the ceiling through the darkness, his body stiff as a board. But when I turned around to look at him I saw that his eyes were closed.

It didn't matter. It was like they were open. Closed or open, Jeff was burrowing into himself, scraping away at a space inside him. Arming himself against me.

"Jeff?" I whispered, reasoning that if he was so upset we might as well try and talk things out. But he didn't answer me.

"Jeff?" I asked again.

There was still no answer. But I knew he was awake.

I felt like I didn't exist.

I opened my eyes and stared at the wall, thinking it was both completely debased and totally natural that my existence depended on his approval.

He's right, I thought. I'm weak, I'm a child, I'm utterly dependent. He has every reason to be upset with me. He might as well be dating a ghost or the wind.

Or a dream or a sunbeam.

* * *

It was a ten-minute drive from the diner to the cemetery. I parked in the lot before the cemetery's gates, in a ragged gravel strip marred with potholes. Behind the gates rose an asphalt path, about as wide as three people could walk comfortably abreast. The cemetery was built on a series of small, grassy hills dotted with graves — the path rose up one and weaved through a series of others that I could see behind it.

The day was so hot and dry and empty and airless that when I stepped out of the car a palpable feeling of doom and foreboding came over me, as if I wasn't walking to Adler's grave, but my own. As if the cracking heat would halt my footsteps and turn my bones brittle before I could make it up the path. I felt exposed standing on the parking lot so close to the highway, conscious of the fact that I was the only person in sight. Which made me a kind of target … but for what? Maybe the weeds peeking through the gravel at the side of the road, the cicadas leaking their infuriating August buzz.

But the day was also bright and clear and there were birds singing in the trees, too, singing and flitting from branch to branch. And I was on the verge of doing something that I had wanted to do for a long time.

I was stuck between these two moods when an orange truck pulled suddenly into the lot, one wheel hitting a deep pothole and kicking the suspension up and down with a loud "thunk." Punk music blared from the open windows and a spray of gravel and dust rose up as the truck made a hard turn into its parking spot, coming to rest immediately adjacent to my car. I stood in shock and horror as a burned and peeling shirtless man wearing red basketball shorts and what looked to be yellow Oakley sunglasses got out of the truck and began banging on the hood. He was either trying to get it open or to somehow turn the engine over through the metal and the cavity that separated the engine from his open hand. I wasn't sure which it was, but I noticed that there was steam rising from under the hood, I thought which meant that it was overheating. Another man leaned out of the passenger-side window and gestured wildly in the first man's direction, communicating nothing that I could see.

They had come very close to hitting me as I was crossing the lot, but I was so dazzled by the spectacle that I almost didn't notice. My veins had frozen in fear and shock and now they were running again, sending rivers of adrenalin up and down my body. I worried that if I stuck around the two strangers would start to work on me like they were working on their truck and so I shook it off and hurried through the gates before me.

*   *   *

Through the literary agency that represented Kent Adler's work, I was able to get in contact with the cousin whom I have already mentioned, his closest surviving relative, now in her seventh decade and living in a suburb outside Kingston. I sent her an email asking what she could remember of Adler's family, and she sent back a short note and a few scanned photographs.

"Of course I remember him," she wrote. "But not very well. The last time I saw him was a long time ago. We were just children. I was always a bit shy because we didn't really spend much time with that side of the family. And Kent and Jeff were both at least a few years older than me.

"But I do remember that Kent was the kinder one. Or at least he was always patient with me. Would let me beat him in checkers. That sort of thing. Jeff was more of a mystery. I remember he could be quite moody. Whereas when I think of Kent I see a little boy smiling amiably and reaching for my hand, Jeff is a hazy blur standing at the very edge of consciousness. One that I often wished to understand but could never quite make out. Some of that I'm sure was the age difference. The photographs do help, though.

"Of course it was still quite a shock when Jeff died. Very sad. And then to lose Kent and his mother, both so young. My own mother never quite recovered."

One of the photographs is an image of three children standing in front of a house. Two little boys and a girl. The smaller boy — this is Kent — has his arms around the girl. The photo is undated, but he looks like he would have been about six or seven. The older boy, Jeff, has his hands in his pockets. His posture suggests that he doesn't want to be photographed — but there's a reluctant smile on his face.

Perhaps even a glint in his eye. He is enjoying himself.

I don't understand why I'm less interested in Kent in the photo, why I find myself scanning over his image and passing on to Jeff. Perhaps, at that time, Kent didn't exist. Not in the way that he did later. Not in the way that he would in his poetry. He looks like anyone. Just a boy, unvisited by tragedy.

Maybe I'm looking for something that I should look for in myself. Maybe when I look at Jeff in that photograph I see something that I am missing.

On my last night in Jeff's apartment, when I couldn't sleep after our fight, I got out of bed and walked into the living room.

Then I stood next to the couch and looked out the window, into a courtyard between the three apartment buildings that made up the complex where he lived.

The moon was out. Nearly full. Waxing or waning. I wasn't sure which. I wanted to go for a walk, in the moonlight radiating through the side street that surrounded the buildings.

I wondered whether a person could radiate, dissipate and slip through the walls. I wanted to. But all of my things were in Jeff's room, on the floor or in my bag, and I didn't want to go back in there and disturb him. So instead I lay back on the couch and stared up at the ceiling. In the other room, too, was *Alert*, and I wished I had it with me.

Alert was published posthumously, and many critics panned it for its style: more expansive, less controlled, than Adler's other work. Less interested in creating sonic diversity or cultivating surprise on the line level. Perhaps they are right and it is not like the poetry that came before, but I wonder if it was meant to be. In any case, the poems call to one another in a way that echoes my own sadness.

I wanted to reach out to it that night, to live inside it, to become a word or phrase or one of its neatly composed stanzas. To inhabit the space beyond the real that I see in my mind when I read the book.

Maybe that's what it means to radiate, I thought.

I fell asleep on the couch and woke to the sound of the bathroom door slamming shut, the water running, Jeff's shower. I quickly went into the other room and gathered my things, throwing on pants and a sweater. I put my stuff by the front door and grabbed a few swigs from a half-empty two-litre of orange juice that I had purchased a few days before, then put on my shoes and walked out into the hallway.

At first I thought I might just go for a walk, or home to cool off, but after locking the door I turned and slipped my set of keys back into the apartment through the mail slot. Almost an instinct. Then I hurried to the elevator. I didn't want to know him anymore. And I didn't want to know anyone else.

I wasn't yet sure if that included me, too.

* * *

The cemetery was about a hundred and fifty years old. In the newer sections the plots were neat and orderly, regularly spaced, the grass clipped and the bushes trimmed. But there were areas densely packed with lines of tombstones, some leaning and so closely spaced that the ground between them was rough and overgrown.

In any case the grounds were much larger than I had anticipated. I thought — for a town the size of Durham — in the worst-case scenario I could just scan the markers one by one until I found it. I had no idea where in the cemetery he had been buried, but fortunately a sign alerted me to the fact that there was an office in town where I could get directions, a real estate office that was the home of the volunteer groundskeeper.

When I got back to the parking lot, the orange truck was gone. But someone had written the word *slut* in large letters in permanent marker over my white driver-side door. I checked to see if there was anyone else around, but the parking lot was just as deserted as when I had arrived. As I was about to open the door to get a rag or something from inside and try to wipe it off I noticed something else, smeared on the handle. I took off my glasses and leaned in for a closer inspection. The smell was overpowering.

It was shit.

Okay, I thought.

For a minute or two I stood without doing anything, unsure what I should do. Then I pulled a handful of long weeds from the side of the lot and stood in front of the door, trying to decide whether to use them to clean off the handle. Instead I climbed into my car from the passenger side. When I crossed the centre console I accidentally depressed the emergency brake and caused the vehicle to violently jerk two or three inches backward. I jumped up and banged my head on the ceiling as I scrambled to get behind the wheel and tried to prevent the car from rolling out into traffic.

Finally in the driver's seat, I thought about skipping the hotel, leaving the cemetery behind forever, and just driving back to Toronto. It seemed like a good idea. It wasn't very far and I could have been back by that evening. Well before. Instead I backed out of my space and turned back on the highway, toward town.

* * *

The office of Penelope Trin, realtor and volunteer groundskeeper, was in what counted for downtown in Durham, sandwiched between the dusty, abandoned shopfront of what had apparently been a bakery and a store that seemed to only sell figure-skating outfits for little girls.

The bell rang when the door opened and woman's voice, I assumed Trin's, called from somewhere in the back.

"Sarah?"

The office was otherwise empty. Inside it was cool, much darker than the street. Venetian blinds were half-lowered over the windows, and only a single lamp, behind the reception desk, was lit. A pile of papers sat on the reception desk, next to a computer with the Windows logo bouncing idly on the screen and a small cactus wearing a miniature sombrero. A thin wool cardigan was draped over the back of the chair. Another plant, much larger (I couldn't figure out whether or not it was plastic) stood in one corner, by the window, and real estate listings pinned up with thumbtacks lined the wall nearest to the door. At the far end of the room, where the voice had come from, was a door, half-ajar, probably Trin's office. There was the sound of someone back there, shuffling boxes, but no one came out.

After a minute I could hear someone mounting a staircase from somewhere below us. A woman, who I guessed was Sarah, emerged from a second doorway located between the desk and the office. She looked young, maybe in her late twenties or early thirties. She had straight brown hair that ended at her shoulders, glossy and well-kept. On her cheeks were the ghosts of acne scars. I thought I saw a sharpness in her eyes, momentary, that disappeared once she settled down behind the desk and flicked the mouse to dispel the screensaver.

"Sorry for the wait," she said.

"Don't worry about it," I said. "Actually I'm not even totally sure I'm in the right place. I needed to find a grave?"

Sarah looked up from the computer and stared blankly at me.

"This is a real estate office," she said, pointing to the wall of listings behind me. "We sell homes. For the living."

"Uh … okay, but at the cemetery —"

"I'm just messing with you," said Sarah, turning back to the computer. I thought I heard a short, low "*ha*" cough out from the office in the back.

"What was the name of the person you were looking for?"

"Kent Adler," I said.

She seemed to hesitate before typing his name in, so I repeated myself and then spelled out his last name.

"He was a poet," I said, almost defensively. For a minute she had looked like she'd known who I was talking about.

"Have you read him?" I asked.

She looked up from the computer and shook her head.

"No," she said. "I've never heard of him."

"He was pretty well-known," I said.

She shrugged and said something I didn't catch.

"I'm sorry?"

"A *pretty well-known poet*," she said.

"Okay, yeah," I said.

"He's right here," she said, pointing to the screen. "Plot E-22." She wrote the number down on a piece of scrap paper, folded it, and handed it to me. Then she looked back at the screen and scrolled the document up and down.

"Is that it?" she asked.

I wondered if I should tell her about my car and ask her where I could find a place to get it cleaned. But something stopped me. Somehow it felt too intimate a story to tell. Like I'd been marked. As if I would communicate something reprehensible about me, even though I had nothing to do with it and it wasn't my fault.

To be honest, I felt like asking her if Durham was a good place to live.

I didn't know why I wanted to live somewhere that obviously didn't want me, but I was suddenly curious about her, and curious about her life. I wondered if we had anything in common. But I didn't want to ask her that directly — it felt too violent and personal a question.

"Are you okay?" she said.

For a minute I felt like I might start crying. My eyes met Sarah's. I thought she looked horrified when she saw the emotion in my face.

She might have only been embarrassed.

"No," I mumbled.

"I'm sorry?"

"I mean — there's nothing more," I said. "*Thanks.*"

I stepped away from the desk and turned to the real estate listings. Feigning interest. I wanted to leave, but I thought it was necessary that I stay for just a few more minutes, to deny whatever had just transpired. Or to create plausible deniability. If I took my time with the listings she might start to doubt the reality of what had just occurred.

*   *   *

Before getting back in my car I purchased a pack of baby wipes and ran them several times over the car handle, over and over, until I'd used up the whole pack. In the driver's seat, I took out my notebook and set it on my lap. I wanted to write something about Adler but I couldn't concentrate on that. I kept thinking back to that last night in Jeff's apartment, the fight.

I tried to remember the colour of his eyes. "Green," I wrote. "No, hazel."

How could I forget?

There were days he was practically the only man I looked at, besides myself in the mirror, days we spent in bed while night turned to day and back again, slow weekends where we ate breakfast in the afternoons, his mannered breakfasts with so many moving parts: espresso and heavy rye toast with pumpkin-seed butter, fruit, a small piece of baklava or something sweet, a glass of water, sometimes muesli with cold almond milk. Those moments felt rarefied and I didn't want to be with anyone else. Even if our world was functionally as small as the little cups we drank the coffee out of.

I'd hoped coming up to Durham would help give me a little perspective, some distance, the ability to understand how I had let myself become so small. I thought that if I brought myself to the place where Adler had lived and died and written so much of his poetry that I could gain some small part of his ability to understand. Maybe his intuition, too. His genius.

I needed to submerge myself completely in his life.

I put my notebook away and drove at random through the town. Finally I found a car wash, where I bought a ticket from the fat guy at the register and drove into the line of cars waiting to enter. Once I'd gone through a kid came up to the driver-side mirror to give it a few token wipes. But after glancing briefly at the car he stopped what he was doing and gestured to another kid, who looked at the door and then up at me with obvious astonishment. At first I thought they were playing a prank, even though I knew very well what they were looking at.

I rolled down my window.

"It didn't come off?"

The kids shook their heads.

"Did you see who did this?" one of them asked. The first one again.

I shrugged.

"Not really," I said. "I can't be sure."

"You didn't see anything?"

"No. I mean, it might have been these guys I saw. Driving an orange truck. Out by the cemetery. But I don't know for sure."

The kids looked at each other significantly. "*Orange truck,*" they repeated. "*Out by the cemetery.*" The one who hadn't said anything to me reached into his pocket and pulled out a business card. It was for the owner of the car wash, identified as Walid Khan.

"What's this?" I asked.

"You should call him, as soon as you can. He'll explain everything."

"What do you mean? Explain what?"

But the kids had already turned to the next car pulling out of the wash. I didn't know what to do. I felt vaguely ridiculous sitting there with the window open and my car running, looking at the kids, waiting for something. I was hesitant to leave, maybe because it still felt like the most successful conversation I had had with strangers in months.

"What are you, CIA?" I called out, joking. They didn't seem to hear. I repeated myself, but louder. I thought I caught one of the kids glancing in my direction as he moved around the car he was wiping down.

*   *   *

According to the sign on the gates, the cemetery closed at five o'clock every day. It was still before five but the gates were firmly locked. I wasn't in the mood to try and hop them, even though it looked relatively easy and I doubted anyone would have cared. So instead I drove around until I found a restaurant that looked passable, a quiet Chinese place near the centre of town. After dinner I walked in circles around the downtown, veering off at random to explore the side streets. Much of the town's architecture consisted of quaint brick houses that had been built at the turn of the previous century, overgrown with the vines and weeds of late summer. Buried behind veils of verdure, everything, even the odd misfit house, ugly or ill-painted, seemed to have its place, as if the town had risen up out of the weeds on its own accord, as if it were a natural feature of the earth. I felt jealous. It was only where the grass was cut too close to the ground, so that it had burned out and left long, dark brown patches of mud, that Durham looked like something haphazard, planned.

The last time I'd seen Jeff was from the window of my apartment building. He had buzzed up but I didn't let him in, pretending I wasn't home. Instead I turned off the lights in my apartment and waited by the window, where I watched him walking back to his car. That night I dreamed the car was still there, its cabin lights on, noxious gas pouring from its exhaust. Jeff a distant silhouette, sitting perfectly still in the driver's seat. I woke with a start and went out on my balcony to get a better look at the parking lot, and stood there alone in the dark and chilly spring air.

I stood out walking the streets of Durham. I had only seen one other brown person in the whole town. From my car. And a general insecurity had long ago taken root inside me, telling me that I didn't belong. I didn't know who I was. I didn't know, quite literally, why I had come or where I was going.

After that guy came into the office, asking about Kent, or Adler, or whatever, I started to get the shivers. I put on my sweater, but I didn't warm up and I guess I was still shaking when Penny came out of her office, to see what he'd wanted and, probably, to get me to file something else downstairs. Instead she took one look at me and told me to go home.

"But I'm not sick," I said.

She wouldn't take no for an answer. Moments later I was outside in the August sun, still shivering even though I hadn't taken my sweater off and I was walking quickly in an attempt to get my blood flowing and my heart rate up.

It was true that I didn't feel sick. I felt disturbed, but I didn't know the source, as if a void had opened up before me or inside me and I could feel it yawning, but I didn't know where or what it was. Okay, I mean, I had some idea, but I didn't know why that guy asking about Kent would have freaked me out so much.

Instead of going home I walked to the cemetery and before long I was standing at Kent's grave. Looking down at the flowers I had laid the previous Thursday (just weeds, dried and mostly scattered now). My heart still beating, as if that guy might appear at any moment, jump out of the forest and start reciting verse, or reach for my hand, or break down on the ground in front of me. I picked up the flowers and peeled off the poem I had pasted to the stone.

Letter to a Poet

My father taught me
Nothing
A poet has died

Look up: the trees
Are singing
A poet has died

Everyone
Gets in their cars
A poet has died

I wish I had more
To tell you

I crumpled up the poem and took it with the flowers and threw them into the bushes. I didn't know where the guy was, but I assumed if he hadn't already come he would be on his way, so I thought it would be best to leave as soon as possible. Since I had the key with me I pulled the gates closed and locked them, and after I got home I called into the office a few minutes before five and let Penny know what I had done so she wouldn't go out herself.

When I got home I shut the door quickly behind me and glanced at it with trepidation every couple minutes. As if the guy was going to barge into my apartment at any moment, shaking and screaming about god knows what.

I think Carl guessed that I was nervous and kept climbing onto the counters — not for food, because there was nothing on them, but as if to confront me. To get at my height. I don't know why I thought that's what he was trying to do, he's just a stupid cat, maybe even stupider than most, but that's what I felt. He also kept staring up into a corner of the wall above my head that had absolutely nothing of interest there, a completely barren patch of perfectly white wall, as if from his vantage he was able to see past it into other dimensions, other dimensions where he was able to violate laws of time and space and see into my soul and all of my future actions and god knows what else.

Dumb animal.

I was still shivering so I sat down on the couch and pulled the blanket over me. I thought for a minute about calling someone, anyone — either Amanda, or Penny, or even (and this is how I know I was disturbed) Mom. But what would I say? This guy came into town and asked about this poet I liked and it completely freaked me out?

Eventually Carl settled down and climbed onto my lap and I put on a movie, something stupid that I wouldn't have to think about and which I don't even remember, and moments later I was asleep. When I woke up it was still dark out and the TV was still on and Carl was still beside me. I walked to the kitchen and from there to the balcony, where I stared out over the alley behind my apartment and watched as the night lifted, black to blue, watched until the sun rose up into the sky and I felt a kind of relief, although I couldn't say where that relief had come from or what it had meant, if it meant anything at all.

3

Eventually I got tired of walking around Durham and feeling out of place and found the hotel where I was staying, an old mansion — or maybe it had once been a hospital? — just a five-minute walk from the centre of town. Staggered vines clung to its surface, rust stained the stone foundations, and old wood lined the hallways and stairs, giving the building a sense of history and place. I felt like I could feel the many lives that had passed through. Or perhaps not the lives themselves, but the traces of them, of so many passing in succession, as if they all left behind a particular residue that could only be detected when gathered together.

I felt like I was where I belonged: small, forgotten, appropriately dwarfed.

*   *   *

The next morning I was in a better mood, even though I hadn't slept well. I'd left my windows open and the smell of perfume wafting indoors from the vines flowering outside had contributed to my bad sleep, waking me up throughout the night, as if it were the perfumed train of a long-dead relative come to give me a warning. Or just to haunt me. In my dream I saw Jeff lying with his back to me, but when I tried to rouse him or turn him over to see his face there was no response, not in him or from his body, just the back of his head no matter which way I looked, just the night and its stillness and a growing horror of his prone form.

As I was getting dressed I found the card the kids at the car wash had given me. I stared at it for a while, wondering if I should call, letting the absurdity of the previous day slowly percolate through me. It would be nice to have some answers. Or to have someone to talk to. I dialed the number and let it ring, over and over, but no one picked up and it didn't go to an answering machine. I put the card on my night table and went downstairs. After a bad breakfast in the hotel dining room — I wasn't that late, but the coffee was cold, the pastries picked over and forgotten — I went for another walk. The cemetery opened at nine, assuming the hours posted on the gates were correct, which I supposed I couldn't, given how early it had closed the day before. I found a florist, but it opened at ten, so I grabbed a coffee across the street, from a small deli that also sold pizza and submarine sandwiches. It was awful coffee, but at least it was hot, which is the most important thing.

While I had been eating my breakfast at the hotel I overheard one of the staff telling a guest about a woman who had complained about a ghost when she was staying there. The woman had woken up in the middle of the night to a high-pitched wailing which she thought must have been the radiator. But it was August, probably the hottest night of the year, and the woman was sweating through her sheets. She was on the point of calling down to the front desk to complain when she heard a man whispering in her ear: "That's not the radiator," he said. "It's my wife." Of course, she didn't sleep and the next morning she checked out as soon as she could. The man who was telling the story explained that they had checked the records afterward, and a woman had died during childbirth in that room, a long time ago.

I kept thinking about the story, about how strange it was that the two ghosts were sharing the same room. The woman who died giving birth and her husband, who might have lived to an old age, or at least probably didn't die at the same time as his wife, unless he killed himself. Maybe, I thought, there wasn't a man at all. Maybe the ghost of the woman who died had gone crazy from the solitude and was speaking to herself. Or the same thing had happened to the man. In any case I was glad I hadn't heard either of them the night before.

I had forgotten my notebook, but I had a pencil in my pocket and to kill the time I scrawled the words "early morning ... bad sleep ... dreams of ghosts ... fragrant night" on my receipt to remind myself of the breakfast and the night before. I didn't have much room, but I couldn't think of anything else to write. After sitting and drinking my coffee awhile, I saw Sarah, from the real estate office, crossing in front of the window.

I threw out my coffee and darted outside.

"Hi," I said. Probably a bit too eagerly.

"Jesus Christ!" she said, jumping back from me and nearly stepping into the street. "Where the hell did you come from?"

"I was getting a coffee," I explained, gesturing lamely to the deli behind me.

"Don't fucking do that," she said, catching her breath.

"Sorry," I said. "I wasn't thinking."

"It's okay. But I was going to work. I don't have time to talk."

"Can I walk you there?" I asked.

"Sure, okay. But it's just down the street."

"I know," I said.

We walked in silence until we reached the real estate office, where Sarah turned and said goodbye. I don't know why I was so eager to say hello to her, especially given the events of the day before. I felt like I was testing my limits. Like I could become someone else and it was just a matter of training or association.

But I didn't know who I wanted to become, who I was trying to be.

I walked alone for a while, then crossed the street and headed back to the florist across from the deli. I wasn't sure what to get — I knew that lilies were often at funerals but I never liked the way they looked when they were closed. They always seemed unpleasantly fleshy to me, like weird pustules. And open they just reminded me of what they looked like closed. So instead I bought a dozen red roses. Then I walked back to the hotel and got in my car and drove to the cemetery and found Adler's grave. With the plot number it wasn't very hard. Only after I laid the flowers down did I notice there was a poem affixed to the stone.

Letter to the Occupant

Please, turn your
lights off, I
can't breathe, it's like
an airplane, forever
rising. I fear
death, white of
electricity, height.
Please, please
you don't understand
my letters
the station master
whimpers
as we watch
lit house after lit house

recede into
the white
and only hope
keeps me at my desk
writing, please
writing.

I bent close to the poem. Lights? I thought. The paper was damp and it looked like it had been freshly pasted. I didn't recognize it and it was otherwise unsigned. I stood up and looked around, but the cemetery was empty.

Lights? I thought again, as I crouched down to the stone.

I felt like I was going to faint.

Who had done this? Where had they gone?

I considered pulling the paper down, but instead I ran my hands over the headstone, where it read: "Kent Adler/April 23, 1952–August 21, 1976."

The rest was blank.

*   *   *

I'd planned on reading aloud a poem from *Alert,* "Evie of the Deepthorn," a poem about a warrior making her way through the woods on her horse. And about the death that comes with or precedes venture. Or at least that's what I thought it was about. But for some reason seeing that someone had beaten me to him made that gesture seem redundant. As if my words were just echoes of another. As if I were just an echo of Adler. Insubstantial and incomplete. Whereas I was sure that the poem on the stone was original, perhaps even that it was addressed to me. As crazy as that seemed. I walked back to the hotel, leaving my car baking in front of the cemetery.

A few weeks before I'd left for Durham I'd received an email from Jeff, something about how I was disrespecting him by not returning his calls. That's all I could see from the preview in my inbox. I knew it would move into a discussion of how rarefied our relationship had been and how much I had meant to him. I deleted it immediately and was proud of myself for doing that, like I'd responded successfully to a challenge from God. But I knew that it would stay in my deleted files for thirty days before being completely eliminated from my account. It had occasionally been a source of temptation. As I was walking back to the hotel I thought about the email again and wished that I had read it, regretting that I hadn't brought my laptop or phone with me so that I could open up Gmail and pull it out. At least to start the clock again.

And then I was grateful because I didn't have to be tested.

In the weeks and months immediately following our breakup he sent me hundreds of texts, accusing me of everything from using him to being interested in women or of cheating on him. "I don't see how you could leave *us* unless there was someone else." It was insane. He was practically the only other person in my life, him and Adler, no one else. "Now you finally have the chance to fuck a girl," he wrote. I didn't think I wanted to fuck a girl. Finally I stopped responding and the texts petered out or at least slowed down. Then I blocked his number. It was a relief to not have to anticipate him, to not have my breath catch in my throat whenever I heard the familiar ping of my phone.

Though of course it still did.

I told myself I wasn't running from him, as if it mattered what I told myself about that. I am not running from him, I thought. It has been months since I have seen him and I am not running. And that was true. I was carrying him inside me. He went wherever I went. I still heard his voice telling me what he thought I was — too much, or nothing.

It would be a long time before I got his voice out of my head, a long time even after I left Durham. When I mounted the stairs to my hotel room I passed the ghosts of former occupants, owners, patients, doctors, photographs lining the stairs, men and women in their turn-of-the-century finery, standing in faded relief to a background foggy from time.

Time or silver.

Silver or aluminum. I don't know much about old photographs.

I thought I was going to kill myself.

I felt like I was being honest with myself for the first time in a long while.

I called the number on the business card again, over and over, with a kind of anger. There was no answer. I thought there was a good chance no one would ever pick up. It was getting harder and harder to care about what had happened to my car — that wasn't the reason I was calling.

I emptied my pockets and found the receipt from my coffee that morning. I was about to throw it out before I remembered the note that I had scrawled on it: "early morning ... bad sleep ... dreams of ghosts ... fragrant night." I didn't know what the words meant but they made a kind of sense to me. I thought of them as a kind of mantra. Or not a mantra, exactly, but a sort of oblique prayer. Maybe if I said it enough it would open into a kind of sense.

Anyway, I put it back in my pocket.

Bad sleep ... dreams of ghosts ... fragrant night, I thought.

Downstairs I asked if they had any recommendations for lunch. They directed me to a place nearby, a restaurant built into a grand old mansion, a dead and half-empty place with beige curtains and pastel-green seat cushions and light rose tablecloths. *Fragrant night*, I thought. The staff was attentive, but in a way that made me feel like I didn't belong — like they were making a point of accepting me. It was clear to me that I *didn't* belong, and I wished that I was anywhere else. *Dreams of ghosts.* I ate a boring meal of salmon and rice with asparagus on the side. Following the meal they served me a cup of flowery Earl Grey. It was fine, but afterward I felt like I had to cleanse myself. Like the muck had to be scraped from my body. Like I hadn't eaten food, but its opposite.

Early morning … bad sleep.

After my meal I started walking down the highway, but instead of turning down a side street I kept going in the direction I had come from: past town, beyond where the sidewalk ended, and where I had to walk on the shoulder next to cars that were going ninety kilometres an hour. There was a creek that ran alongside the highway, in a kind of ditch. Then it turned away from the road and into a small stand of trees. A forest, I guess. In the distance, far from town, at a major intersection, were two gas stations. Each seemed like they had materialized out of thin air. Like condensation had gathered into their orange-red neon and bright white fluorescence.

The creek wasn't deep and I forded it without difficulty. There was a thin, brown path, marred with roots and holes, that ascended steeply into the bush. I took it without hesitation, only beginning to worry about where it led as I proceeded deeper and deeper into the forest.

* * *

The path continued for at least a kilometre, the forest tight and here and there, strewn with bits of trash blown in from the highway, before terminating in a clearing about thirty metres wide.

It looked like it had been cleared a while ago, maybe for a house that had never been built, maybe by a hermit who had nothing better to do.

A rusted oil barrel stood in the far corner of the clearing, with a few tufts of heavier weeds growing at its base.

The clearing was calm and open, but the barrel felt almost menacing, a symbol of human industry in stark relief to the surrounding forest. It felt like stumbling on the ruins of a long-dead civilization, its iron heavy with ancient ghosts.

I knew that I would have to look inside the barrel, but for a long time I resisted, walking the edge of the clearing, peering up through the trees.

It was like it was staring back at me.

I knew what would be inside: branches, metal, perhaps garbage from the road. Ashes, if what I suspected was true and the barrel had been used to burn trash. Innocuous, but somehow the mere prospect of looking inside was terrifying.

I wanted to leave, to turn around and walk back down the path. Instead I moved to the edge of the barrel and craned my head over the lip, catching my breath at what I saw. It was something from outside this world. A severed head or a piece of rotten human flesh dripping from a branch propped up against the inside.

I took a couple of quick steps away, dizzy, my stomach heaving, trying to come to terms with what I had seen. Slowly I resolved to look again. It couldn't be real.

It wasn't.

Not flesh. Just a rubber mask. I pulled it out and held it in front of me: Jimmy Carter. Ronald Reagan was underneath and below that there was surgical tubing and what looked to be a hacksaw.

"What the fuck," I said, picking up the hacksaw and feeling its heft.

It was just like my dream, or not my dream, but the hallucination or premonition I had experienced when I was watching the movie.

I was walking backward through my own life.

Then I heard two voices coming from the trail: loud, threatening. "Little piggy, little piggy," they called. My heart stopped. Without thinking I dropped everything back into the barrel and darted into the woods.

"Come out, come out, wherever you are."

Everything told me to run, but instead I found a place to hide and watched from behind a tree as two young men reached the clearing and burst out laughing when they saw that it was empty. It was the two kids from the car wash, the ones who had given me the business card.

"We really creeped that fucker out, didn't we?" said the first one, who was reaching into the barrel and pulling out the masks. He put on the Carter mask and handed the other one to his friend. Reagan took out the plastic tubing and handed it to Carter. Then he pulled out the hacksaw.

"En garde!" said Reagan, to Carter, who held up the tubing in mock defence.

They quickly lost interest in that game.

"I bet that brown guy shit his pants," said Carter.

"Yeah," said Reagan, putting the hacksaw back into the barrel. Then he reached out for the tubing. "Give it to me," he said.

"No," said Carter.

"Jesus, hand it over."

"Fuck you."

Reagan sighed. "Fine. Whatever. Just don't fucking break it. We need it."

"What?" said Carter. "How fragile do you think this stuff is?"

"More like *how dumb* I think you are," mumbled Reagan.

"Oh, fuck you," said Carter, raising the tubing as if to strike Reagan, but evidently thinking better of it and dropping it absentmindedly instead.

There was a brief silence. I couldn't tell if they were saying anything to each other. But I could see the tension rising as Reagan continued to stand by the barrel and Carter wandered over to the far side of the woods.

I was wondering what they could possibly need the tubing, hacksaws, and masks for. I imagined the boys finding me, tying me down, wrapping the tubing around one of my arms and patiently hacking it off. As they expressed surprise that someone had vandalized my car. But even as I thought that it seemed impossible — they seemed incapable of violence: just boys, tall and skinny and awkward and weak.

But they were planning something.

"Hey, come back here," said Reagan, finally.

"What?" said Carter. "Why?"

"Just come here," said Reagan. Something in Reagan's tone seemed to pull Carter in, and he went, reluctantly.

"What," he said again, when he was closer.

In a much softer voice. Almost trembling.

Reagan grabbed Carter around the waist with one hand and with the other pulled up Carter's mask and put his mouth on his.

Carter resisted only momentarily.

I was starting to feel uncomfortable about spying on them, and I thought that if I tried to leave I would make it obvious that I was there. So instead I maintained my position, crouching behind a tree, watching them from a distance.

They began to thrust into each other as they kissed, grinding themselves up and down. After a while Reagan knelt down in front of Carter and undid his jeans. He pulled Carter's penis out and gave it a few strokes as it extended to its full length.

Then he put it in his mouth. By now both of their masks were off and Carter was running his hands through Reagan's hair. From a distance the act was so small and fragile that it was difficult to understand how so much importance could ever be put upon it.

After Carter came, jerking his body forward, and Reagan spit out his come, letting it slowly drip from his mouth to the grass, Reagan stood up and they continued kissing. Carter began fumbling with the fly of Reagan's jeans but they were interrupted by a noise coming from the path. I couldn't tell what it was, but they both quickly did up their belts and ran into the forest, thankfully cutting in a different direction from the one I had gone. In a hurry they left the masks and tubing and hacksaw behind, lying on the ground.

I wasn't going to stick around to find out what was coming next, and so I started to slowly work my way out of my hiding spot to try and skirt the clearing and get back to the road, where I figured I would be safe. It was as I was doing this that I heard a voice I knew. Then I looked to the path and saw Sarah emerge, singing softly to herself.

*   *   *

I asked her what she had been singing and she shrugged. "Nothing in particular," she said. "Sometimes I make up songs when I'm alone."

We were walking back along the highway.

"What was the name of that dead guy you wanted to see? The poet," she asked.

"Kent Adler," I said.

"I was thinking about it. I might have heard of him before."

"Yeah?"

"I think so," she said.

That was apparently all she had to say. I wondered if I should tell her about the kids and what they'd been doing. Ask her if she thought there was anything to worry about, regarding the contents of the barrel. But something told me not to. Maybe because I was afraid I would tell her what I saw and she would think I was perverted. Maybe because they seemed so small and scared and tentative and I couldn't imagine them committing real violence. Maybe because I remembered being a teenager and feeling upset and helpless, and how I had kept my own barrel filled with violent instruments I was never going to use, though it was only ever in my head.

"What's his poetry like?" she finally asked.

"That's a hard question," I said.

"I mean, how does it make you feel?"

I thought about it.

"I mean, I don't know," I said. "It makes me feel like there's this space. And I'm the only person who exists there. But someone else was there before me. And when I read his poetry I feel like we're there together. Even though I'm alone. And I feel alone when I'm reading it."

She sort of nodded.

"I don't know, it's difficult to describe," I said.

"No, I get it," she said.

"And like … maybe my life isn't tragic like his was. But I feel like when something bad happens to you, your life changes. And this thing opens up inside you that wasn't there before. And for some reason his poetry reaches me there."

"Hmm," she said.

I thought about it some more.

"That's the best I can do," I said.

She seemed preoccupied. I waited a long time for her to respond, but she didn't say anything.

"Do you read a lot of poetry?" I asked.

"No," she said. "I mean, sometimes. But I was thinking about what you said about your life not being tragic. Why would you say that?"

I thought that was a weird thing for her to ask, since she didn't know me at all.

"Well," I started, "his brother died when he was really young. He talked about how that changed him in interviews. Like he was suddenly aware of himself in a way that he wasn't before. There was the person from before his brother drowned, whom he knew, but he didn't understand. And then there was the person afterward. There's a photo of him from when he was a kid. You can see the difference. I mean between that and later photos. His brother looks more like him than he does. In the eyes. His mom died pretty early, too."

I could tell she was still skeptical. She didn't say anything.

"I don't know," I said, shrugging.

"Okay. But why does that mean *your* life isn't tragic? Do you think tragedy is something inherent to a person or to their experiences? And what's so great about it, anyway? If he was really so inaccessible to you do you think you'd like his poems at all?"

"No," I said. "That's not what I mean."

"Tragedy is just a device," she said. "It's not real. No one's life is *actually* tragic."

I thought that was wrong or that she was being pedantic, but I decided I didn't want to say anything. It felt like she'd made up her mind about that a long time ago.

"I think he was a coward," she said. "I think he was afraid. *That's* tragic. But I don't think his life was tragic. That doesn't make any sense."

"What do you know about it?" I said.

She didn't answer me.

"God," she said, after a while. "I'm sorry."

I shrugged.

"You don't have to apologize," I said.

By now we were back in town.

"I'm not like this all the time," she said.

I wanted to be friendly to her. It felt better having someone to talk to.

"I'm staying at the hotel just over there," I said.

* * *

"Why aren't you at work?" I asked her, when we were in my room. She was sitting in the chair by the window and I was sitting on the bed. She said she'd never been in the hotel before, but that when she was a kid she used to think it was an asylum for the criminally insane. Because of some movie she had watched with her mom. She used to fantasize that the guests she saw coming and going were patients given only temporary leaves. "I mean, I knew it was really a hotel," she had said. "Someone told me that. Maybe even right after I'd seen the movie."

"On the weekend I only go into the office for a couple hours," she explained. "Just Saturdays. I get Monday off, too. Penny is usually showing houses on the weekend and she doesn't work on Mondays if she can help it. On Saturdays I just check the messages and set up appointments, that sort of thing."

I nodded. "Sounds good."

"It's a good job," she said. "What do you do?"

"I'm a bookkeeper," I said.

"What kind of books?"

"You know, like accounts. Small businesses, mostly. Some estates. It's pretty basic. I work for a small firm."

"Do you like it?"

"Sure. I guess," I said. "It's pretty rote, but I don't have to think very hard."

"How come you're so interested in poetry?"

I shrugged. "I don't know. I just am. I studied it in school."

"What about movies? Or fishing? Or NASCAR?"

"I don't like any of those things," I said.

"Good. Neither do I."

"Okay," I said. What did it matter to her? I wanted to change the subject. "What were you doing in the forest?"

"Oh," she said. And shrugged. "Nothing, really. I like to go out there sometimes. No special reason. To be alone. It reminds me of someone I used to know."

"Who?"

"Just a friend," she said, standing up and looking out the window. "A very good friend."

"Someone you dated or something?"

"No," she said, turning to me. "Nothing like that."

The way she looked at me then made me nervous.

"You know, this place is supposed to be haunted," I said, to keep the conversation moving.

"Really?" she said. "By what, a ghost?"

"What? What else?"

"I'm haunted," she said.

"Huh?"

"You seem haunted, too."

"Okay," I said.

"I can tell you're running from something."

"How do you know that?" I asked.

After a long while.

"Because you won't look me in the eye," she said. "It's like you're afraid of your reflection."

"That doesn't make any sense," I said.

"What did you do?" she asked.

I shrugged. "I didn't do anything."

"I was running when I came out here, too," she said. "But it doesn't make you feel any better. Running, I mean. Being up here. It seems like it will be easier, but it isn't. Sometimes I think coming here was the worst decision I ever made in my life."

She was leaning against the wall, her eyes closed.

"So leave," I said.

"But I don't think that for any *practical* reason," she said, sitting down next to me on the bed. "I just don't know what to do."

I stood up and hovered uncomfortably by the door.

"Oh," I said.

"So leaving wouldn't make any difference," she explained. "I mean, I hate it here, but that's not why. Not because I'm stuck. I hate it for what it's taught me about myself. I hate it because it won't let me leave. Because I haven't learned anything."

"What were you hoping to learn?"

"The same thing you were," she said.

I hadn't told her anything about that.

"What?" I said.

"That place you were talking about earlier. I wanted it to exist. I wanted it to mean something. I wanted to escape there."

"You mean — when I was talking about poetry?"

"No one cares, Rissa. I don't even care."

"What?"

"There's ... nothing there."

"I don't understand what you're talking about," I said. "And it's *Reza*."

She laughed. "It doesn't matter," she said. "I mean, it does. I'm sorry."

I just looked at her.

"What the fuck is wrong with you?"

"I should go," she said.

"That would be great," I said, reaching for the door.

5

I was angry after Sarah left, but I wasn't sure why. I slammed the door behind her without meaning to, making me jump after I had turned away.

I felt like there was a lot she wasn't telling me, like she had been following me around and keeping tabs on me without my knowledge. I wondered, vaguely, if she knew Jeff somehow, if they were friends and if they had talked, but I realized how crazy that was, too. There was no way they had even heard of each other. And it wouldn't have mattered even if they had. There was a better chance she knew Jeff *Adler*, even though he'd died long before she was born. She was hiding something else.

I stared out the window until I was sure she was gone, watching cars pass through the trees and vines that blocked my view. I wanted to open the window and scream "Fuck you!" at the passing cars. But I didn't, of course.

I walked back to my car and drove through town, past the downtown, past the hotel, past the gas stations on the highway. I turned toward Toronto and gunned it, just a brown slut in a white car barrelling south at full speed. For a minute I thought about driving all the way back home and spending the night in my apartment, of leaving my clothes and bags and my copy of *Alert* behind in the hotel room and never coming back. Instead I turned off at the first interchange I saw and ate dinner at a fast-food place.

The place where I turned off was kind of like Durham, but much bigger, with more strip malls and chain stores. After eating I wandered absently through parking lots, watching awkward families unpack themselves from minivans and slowly saunter through the automatic doors of the nearest big-box retailer. It reminded me of growing up, of making that walk with my parents, feeling exposed and vulnerable and needy even in the hundred or so metres it took to get to the store. It never seemed to matter what I had been doing that day, I always felt a little bit worse when I was out with them, with their idiosyncrasies, their accents and bad clothes that matched my own.

The sun set as I drove back to Durham, and the light seemed to disappear faster than it did in the city, slipping behind a hill near the horizon and shrouding the countryside in an inky purple darkness that my headlights struggled to cut through. I regretted leaving my driving glasses in the hotel room as I watched the red and yellow lights from other cars smear and distort over my windshield. The sky was overcast and when I got out of the car I noticed that it was significantly cooler outside than when I had left. There was a breeze running through the trees, rustling the leaves above me in huge gusts of wind. A distracted spray of raindrops hit me from above as I walked back across the parking lot. I looked into the sky and thought I saw funnels reaching out of the clouds, black funnels straining to touch the earth, but it was too dark to make out the details.

That night I dreamed I was in the forest again.

Jeff was in the barrel. Just standing there. I wasn't sure if he could see me. First one and then the other boy climbed out from underneath him, like spiders pulling their long legs out of a pipe. Then I was in the barrel and I could hear the two boys, writhing somewhere in the grass. Their panting and exclamations. I was hard because I knew what they were doing, but it felt wrong to be aroused and I wanted to get away. But when I looked it wasn't the two boys at all — it was Sarah and Kent Adler.

"Hey, stop," I shouted. "Don't you know who that is?"

One of Sarah's hands was pressed against Adler's side, where he had a huge, gaping red wound. Not pressed up against: pushing inside. They moaned together as her hand gradually disappeared, digging deep into his flesh.

The next morning I discovered, to my embarrassment, that I had come in my underwear.

* * *

It had rained hard in the night, I heard it beating steadily against my window, and it was still overcast outside though the sky was considerably less threatening than it had been when I'd returned. There was now a giant puddle in front of the hotel, a swampy, dark mass that slanted across from an oak tree in the middle of the lawn and completely engulfed the walk. The hotel staff had laid down wooden skids from the hotel entrance to the sidewalk, and they had a desk clerk standing outside with extra umbrellas, directing patrons to the alternate route. I had to admit that I was impressed with the effort, or at least surprised that they had mustered it up so quickly, although the clerk looked like he was still in high school, pimply and awkward, and I didn't want to bother him for an umbrella because he was busy helping an old man cross the uneven skids, holding him by one arm.

On the main street there were little rivers running along both sides of the road, hugging the sidewalk and causing cars to drive slowly down the middle. Occasionally they would veer to the side

Evie of the Deepthorn

unexpectedly to avoid a collision, sending impossible sprays up into their carriages and over unsuspecting pedestrians. I overheard someone saying that it hadn't rained that hard in Durham in over thirty years, and I believed it.

My dream had disturbed me, and I wanted to talk about it with Sarah. Not to tell her any details, of course, but to ask her what she knew, really knew, about Adler. I had woken up with the same feeling I'd had when she'd left, that she had been lying to me, that she knew exactly who I was talking about and was intimately familiar with his work. That perhaps she was even a relative, a niece, or a distant cousin, who was protecting Adler through misdirection and evasion, like she was a knight or a nun guarding the location of the Holy Grail. I don't know how I knew that, or why it seemed like it was true. Or what she had to gain.

In any case it was obvious to me that she had been the one who had locked the cemetery two days earlier, her or the real estate agent that she worked for. But likely her. The more I thought about it the more I realized I was right. It couldn't have just been a coincidence.

I walked to the real estate office with the intention of saying some or all of that to her. But of course when I got there I realized it was Sunday and it was closed. I didn't know where else to find her, so I began walking out of town, back to the forest, across the gravelly mud on the highway's shoulder.

Overnight the little creek that flowed through the ditch had become a torrent of churning brown water, capped with swirling white eddies that rippled up against the sides of the ditch wall. I couldn't believe how quickly it had been transformed, and nervously I looked up at the sky, now darker than I remembered, regretting not having borrowed an umbrella from the kid in front of the hotel. I was a long way from town, a long way from shelter, and it looked like the clouds might erupt at any moment.

285

I came to the place where the path branched off from the highway, where I had forded the creek easily just the day before. Here the water was backed up higher than down the creek, like it had come to a dead end, though I could see that there was still a current running along the bottom, pulling dead leaves and silt through a gap in whatever was clogging its path ahead, as it cut through a hill before twisting deeper through the forest.

It made sense to turn around, to give up looking for Sarah, and head back to the hotel. Maybe spend my last day in the coffee shop in the centre of town, maybe go back to the cemetery for a final goodbye, maybe even pack up all of my things and check out early. I knew I wasn't going to find Sarah on the other side of the creek, especially not the way it looked then. But I jumped it, anyway, sloshing through the final two feet of water and soaking my shoes, slipping forward and scrambling up the path, tearing thick chunks out of the soil and getting mud all over my pants. After I stood up and got my bearings, I realized that if I'd thought about it for even a second I would have looked for signs of Sarah's footprints from the other side. But I kept going anyway, nursing a slim hope that I would find something that would clarify my experience and begin to make sense of myself.

The oil barrel had eighteen inches of stagnant water sitting at the bottom. That was it: stagnant water, plastic bags, rotten sticks. The tubing, the masks, and the hacksaw were gone. It gave me a sick feeling, like I had imagined everything that had happened the day before. I searched the clearing, wondering if I had missed them somehow. I looked back in the barrel, and almost jumped when I saw my reflection in the dark water, thinking it was either Reagan or Carter sneaking up on me from behind. I reached in and broke the surface with one hand, searching for signs, disturbing my reflection.

But I wasn't surprised when I came away with nothing, just ripples in the water. It was obvious that they were gone.

* I * *

I got caught in the rain five minutes from the hotel. It came down so fast and heavy that for a minute I just stood there, letting it wash over me. It was warm, or I imagined it was warm. Probably it wasn't. But in any case it changed quickly, mixing with hail that forced me to duck for cover underneath an awning, shivering and watching little specks of ice collect and melt on the ground. A car stopped a few feet away, its hazards flashing and windshield wipers furiously pumping. The cabin light was on and I could see the driver waiting out the storm.

When I got back to the hotel I stripped off my clothes and threw them into the bathtub with me to get out the mud. Then I ran a shower, as hot as I could make it. I hung up my clothes after I was done, rinsing them and wringing them out and draping them over the curtain rod. I grabbed the comforter from the bed and pulled it around my shoulders as I looked outside, watching the rain ripple the surface of the pool of water in front of the door. I felt protected in that moment, calm and clean and warm.

There was a knock on the door.

"Just a minute," I called, as I scrambled to put on dry clothes.

But there was no one there by the time I got it open. Instead, there was an envelope on the floor, slipped neatly under the crack. It was addressed with the letter *R* and inside there was a handwritten letter.

> Sorry, I don't know how to spell your name and I didn't want to risk embarrassing myself again. This is Sarah.
>
> I'm writing this letter to you because I want to apologize for yesterday. And for the day before. I'm not sure if you even noticed. Thanks

for putting up with me. I must admit that I took advantage of the fact that you're so passive. I do that sometimes without even realizing. It's a character flaw. The fact that you don't live in Durham just makes things worse.

Calling you passive isn't very nice, either, even though it's true.

Sorry.

It's exciting when I meet someone from out of town because I can say whatever I want to them, knowing that I probably won't ever see them again. When I was younger I wanted to talk about poetry with them, and art, and other things that I've mostly forgotten about now — things no one here cares much about. Now I seem to want to take something out on them, a kind of aggressiveness instead of fellowship. Compensation, I guess.

Again, I'm sorry.

It's possible you've guessed the truth, that I know who Kent Adler is and I've read his poems. Maybe not. I don't know why I decided to keep that a secret from you. In fact, you probably won't believe me when I tell you the extent of our relationship — it's difficult for me to understand, too. I knew Kent. We were friends. Or, actually, I'm not sure how he felt about me. I met him a few years ago, when I was like you, afraid and running. Maybe I was worried that you would find him, too, though I don't understand how that would work or why that would bother me.

I don't know how else to explain it, really.

I've liked his poetry for a long time. Sometimes I imagine that I went to school with him, that we grew up together, that I watched him die in a forest near my parents' house.

Other times I know that happened.

I used to visit him every day in the hospital, until the doctors explained that I couldn't come to see him anymore. My dad died in the same building, although I was just a teenager and I wasn't allowed in to wherever they were keeping him, even after he died.

I don't want you to get the wrong idea about me. I'm not telling you this because it's easy. In fact, it's quite hard. You're the first person I've met since moving here who knows about Kent at all and I feel like I have a duty to tell you.

He really shouldn't have killed himself.

It's not good for me to see you right now. I'm writing a novel. I need to focus on that. It's about a young girl and her horse. She's lost a lot in her life, but she's still going. In some ways it's the only thing that feels real to me.

I lied earlier. I love poetry. I love art. I love it here, too. I hope you have found whatever it is you're looking for. You seem like a nice person.

Though perhaps a little confused.

Take care.

Sarah.

I read the letter twice, then ripped it to pieces.

6

The next morning, as I was packing up, I dialed the number on the card again. For a few moments I waited on the bed with the receiver of the hotel telephone propped up against my ear, listening for the ring. I closed my eyes, expecting it to cut to a dial tone at any moment. I liked the idea of leaving Durham the same way I had come. But, to my surprise I heard the line pick up, the voice of a man on the other end.

"Hello?" it said. "Who is this? Why won't you leave me alone?"

"Oh," I said, suddenly confused. "I'm sorry, I —"

"Don't be sorry," he said. "Just don't waste my time."

"I mean — I'm looking for Walid Khan?"

There was a sigh on the other end. "That's me," said the voice. The tone of his response told me immediately that I had made a mistake. "What do you want?"

I wasn't sure what to say. I thought, somehow, it would be obvious.

Anyway, what I was about to describe felt like a million years ago.

"Um," I began. "I was referred to you at the car wash? Someone vandalized my car, and for some reason I thought you might be able to help me? Or that I could help you? I heard you were maybe investigating?"

I heard swearing.

"Those fucking kids."

"Excuse me?"

"Listen, I'm sorry about your car. But I have nothing to do with it. I don't even own that place anymore. Don't ever call me again," said the voice. The line went dead.

* * *

Maybe I'd come to Durham to run away from Jeff, but somehow I had run toward him, too. Was it an accident that in coming to Durham I'd also come closer to Jeff Adler, Kent's brother, the boy from the photograph whose eyes reminded me of my own? Or maybe it was Kent who reminded me of myself, Kent standing next to his brother in the photograph and looking back at photographs of them together years later. Sometimes I wished I could go back to a time before Jeff, a time before his anger and my pain, but I knew that was impossible. And maybe, confusing to me, not even something I really wanted.

Jeff Adler died in a freak accident when Kent was ten. Kent describes finding Jeff face down in a creek near their home in his long poem "Surfacing":

> eyes glossy
> like a cat
> drunk on milk
>
> I tried
> to say hello

In interviews he explains that he could remember who he was before the accident, but that that person didn't feel like the same person he was afterward. Like he was forced into a new awareness of himself at too young an age.

Sometimes interviewers would press him about these details, making connections to other texts as if he was merely attempting to resonate with the past instead of describing something traumatic that had happened to him. But he seemed hostile to demonstrations of erudition over intuition or empathy. In one of his poems, "Soundings," he explains that you "can't stretch/your past back/only press/forward, closing your eyes."

But that didn't mean that he avoided the past entirely. In later years some of his poems would openly ask whether the accident was intentional, whether Jeff had committed suicide because he had seen "something too soon/before him." He knew that to speculate on the accidental death of a thirteen-year-old boy so many years after he had passed was more about his own response than his brother's life, but he still couldn't help but imagine a world in which his brother was "allowed to/act," rather than be "acted upon."

After I checked out, I went back to the cemetery to say my final goodbye. I had planned the moment to be a grand farewell. I think I expected to be able to say goodbye to Jeff, too, my Jeff, like I could release him forever and go on without him. But I understood then that he would never leave me.

There wasn't a poem on the surface of Adler's stone. Maybe the rain had washed it away. Maybe Sarah had taken it down. Before I drove over I had purchased a small bag of flour and a bottle of water from a convenience store near the hotel. I mixed the two together and used them to paste up a page I had torn out of *Alert*, smearing the glue over both sides with my hands.

Evie of the Deepthorn

Evie pulls her horse Excalibur
both are very tired they are looking
for a place to settle underneath the grey
tines they want to slay
a dragon they have many enemies

Far away a field hand splits with his shovel
a white skull with a wormy rag
of flesh he digs a little finds vertebrae
ribs scapula humerus coccyx another white
skull missing its jaw shreds of cloth and a doll face
black from the earth Just the large two

skulls He has given up his other work curious
about who the doll belongs to That night he
barricades his door and puts a knife under
his pillow Still he is woken by sharp
voices calling from an emptiness

He dreamed of a woman moving
a forest so dark Just her eyes and the steam
rising from the horse's mouth She was looking for
something and when he woke he was angry
and went down to the river and bathed in the stream

Then he went back to the field
seeking the doll's owner Cut
the earth, the shovel through a girl
a young girl, splitting her
delicate spinal column

*   *   *

As I was driving back through town, I thought I saw Sarah on the other side of the road, walking in the same direction I had come from.

But instead of honking or waving I just kept moving, driving down the highway, out of Durham, turning right at the cross-roads to get back to Toronto.

Epilogue

Pain: A Manifesto

Out the window,
I saw how the planets gathered
Like the leaves themselves
Turning in the wind.

— Wallace Stevens

I

Two boys meet in high school. Nobody likes them (they don't even like each other or themselves). But through mutual circumstance they find themselves entangled, in the same way that planets with a shared orbit will eventually collide. One day one of the boys asks the other over to his house after school. The second boy agrees to this with some trepidation: it has been years since he has accepted an invitation to another student's home, fearing tricks or humiliation. The house is small and is crammed with things: old toys, boxes and broken electronics, tangled cords snaking over a grey-beige carpet. The second boy feels like an interloper, like an astronaut who has touched down on the face of an alien planet. The basement, where the first boy lives, smells like baloney and Cheez Whiz digesting in someone's stomach acid. The second boy doesn't know how he could possibly identify that smell, but that's what it is. A dog in a cage barks at the bottom of the stairs: a mean, terrified bark. A big brown dog with bloodshot eyes. "That's my uncle's dog," explains the first boy, when he sees the fear in his friend's eyes.

"What's he doing here?" asks the second, expecting to hear that the uncle is out of town or perhaps in the hospital. The first boy only shrugs, an indifferent shrug that is somehow infinitely worse than anything he might have said. The dog barks all evening and no one ever comes down to let him out of his cage. Eventually the second boy leaves, cutting through the forest — really just a few trees, a broken mattress, a collapsed tire, and a hubcap — on his way home. He reflects that he has never had a friend so poor, though he thinks that is because he hasn't had many friends. He tries not to feel alarmed. There's no reason that he should feel alarmed.

When he gets home he sends his friend a Facebook message, which he knows won't be seen until the next day: "The entire time I was walking home I imagined strapping that dog on a rocket to the moon."

It's not true.

2

They talk about filming a movie together, a movie about two aliens that look like U.S. presidents. Their spaceship touches down in the middle of the forest and the aliens wander aimlessly for a while, talking about how much the planet resembles their own. "The only problem is the sky," says one of the presidents — maybe Reagan or Carter, maybe Clinton or Nixon or Obama. "Yes," says the other, "too bad it's the colour of shit." Elaborate plans to produce real-life sky-blue shit, no CGI. The planet is of course Earth, but in the movie it's not Earth, but another planet, a third planet. Not the planet the aliens have come from and not Earth. Eventually they find a town and go to a movie theatre. At the theatre there's a movie playing about two aliens who touch down on an alien planet — a fourth planet. And et cetera. It's an intentionally stupid and impossible idea.

"Boy, the sky is really the colour of shit today," they will say to one another, without prompting, walking home after school.

3

Two boys meet in high school and they make everyone afraid, like they're going to pounce suddenly and rip out their throats. Not because of the two boys' size. Not because they are violent. Because they are sad and sullen and sometimes unstable in a way that reminds others, vaguely, of the Columbine shooters. Even though everyone, including the boys themselves, knows that they could never hurt anyone else.

The boys put up a brave front but sometimes they crack and let their terror through the mask. That's when they're most unstable and most liable to do something that will provoke real fear. But fear that maybe lasts for two or three seconds. Fear that is based more on seeing something you don't wish to become.

4

One of the boys says that he saw their history teacher, Mr. Demetri, lying on a stretcher on the side of the road. Twisted into himself, attended to by two frantic paramedics. His car crumpled into the front bumper of a black pickup truck swerved to the median. "Holy shit," says the second boy, in a Facebook message. That's all he can think to say.

While his friend is typing something else the second boy closes the browser and goes outside to lie in the sun. He imagines Mr. Demetri's consciousness escaping into the sky from out of his mangled corpse. The boy's phone — a cheap Samsung that he bought from his cousin — pings. It takes a moment for the phone to unlock so that he can read the next message.

"Yeah," is all it says.

"That's really fucked up," writes the second boy. A few minutes later his message is marked as "seen," but there's no response.

The next day the second boy expects an announcement over the morning PA, but there's nothing. And when he gets to history for third period, he is startled to see Mr. Demetri going over his lesson plan at his desk. The first boy bursts into laughter when the second sits down. Still, it's difficult for the second boy to shake the image of Mr. Demetri lying crumpled on the side of the road, even though he knows that nothing happened, that Mr. Demetri is okay and standing at the front of the class.

5

Two boys meet in high school and pass through the high school like ghosts. The boys believe in reincarnation. "After I die," the first one says, "I'd like to be a hockey player. A winger."

Oh, Jesus, thinks the second boy, not this again. "Why?" he asks, instead.

"To glide on the ice. To be limbs working. And maybe to fuck all the girls." The first boy is the right height to play hockey, but he's skinny and misshapen and all of his life he has been uncoordinated. He moves like someone who spends most of his time sitting down. The second boy is not much better: he's skinny, too, and sometimes he feels like a praying mantis blown about by the wind as he steps gawkily through the halls. He's sure that if someone put him on skates he would shake and stutter into his own team's goal.

"I'm going to be an atomic bomb," he says.

6

"Even in the coldest weather I can hear him coughing. Even when it's negative thirty degrees."

The second boy looks out and sees a white face with dark circles under his eyes leaning out of a window in a neighbour's house. Peeking out of the darkness. A resigned look.

"He looks like a sick dog," says the second boy.

"I think he has cancer."

The face retreats back into the house and a pale arm pulls the window closed.

Silence. They're pressed together, looking out the window above the kitchen sink. For a minute they hold that position. They've caught each other unexpectedly — neither can say what's going to happen next.

Sometimes the first boy looks at the second and wants to kiss him, a spontaneous outburst. Affection, love. He shakes the idea from his mind. Then he reaches into a cupboard and pulls down a large bag of barbecue chips.

7

Two boys meet in high school and play a game with each other.

"Who would you murder first?"

The first boy decides he wants to murder Mr. Wright. For exposing him in class. "I'd pop out his eyeballs and swallow them, one after the other." The second boy tries hard to think of who he would like to murder. He imagines a giant bulldozer randomly crushing one end of the school, everyone caught in the rubble turned to a bloody paste. Himself, standing over the wreckage and trying to feel its consequence. Even imagining specific faces. It might as well be an accident on the moon for all that it makes him feel. It's not real.

Am I a monster? he wonders.

"Principal Chalmers," he says. "He looked at me funny in the hallway today."

In a week the first boy will have saved enough money from his job at the grocery store to buy a used black motorcycle off Craigslist.

8

Riding on the motorcycle together is awkward at first and the second boy is sure that people are talking about them. But people have always talked about them. Maybe it doesn't matter. In any case they are careful not to ride together right after school.

They weave up and down gravel roads, the second boy leaning with the first boy to counterbalance the motorcycle. Leaning forward, too, afraid he will fall off. The second boy tries not to think about how when sometimes pressing into his friend on the motorcycle he feels a warmth flowing into him, a radiant warmth spreading out from his chest. They stop at the top of a hill and look out. The country is a sloping patchwork of forest and fields until the horizon, where a piece of the CN Tower stands like a compass rose.

Later they ride back to the first boy's house, where they will sit on the first boy's bed and play video games while clothes run in the washer and dryer in the room next door. The trip back is much faster than the trip out, the first boy gunning it on straightaways, taking corners quickly, pretending that they're being pursued. But no one catches them.

Today the cage is gone and the second boy asks what happened to the dog.

"My uncle took him," says the first boy. "And then he died."

9

Two boys meet in high school in a backward place where nobody understands them. They're under no illusions that there's anything particular or special that prevents their fitting in. All they know is that they don't belong. Probably they'll feel that way for most of their lives. They create a Google Doc called "Pain: A Manifesto" and it grows between them, filling with rants or ideas about ways to "disrupt the flow of contentment in the Town of Durham." The title of the document is only partly ironic. The same is true of the ideas themselves.

> idea: paint all white cars black and all black cars white
> idea: place hidden cameras in downtown intersections
> idea: tie off limbs with rubber tubing
> idea: (*following above*) hack off limbs during high-school graduation
> idea: slut-shame old men
> idea: slut-shame everyone
> idea: encourage littering in gas stations and parking lots
> idea: encourage littering (*universal*)

The document is like a brain growing between them. A *useless* or *festering* brain. An *unproductive* brain. A *stupid* or *lazy* brain. In the words of the second boy's father. Or at least that's what he imagines since he would never show it to him. Sometimes the first boy stays up until late at night typing ideas and complaints into their brain, coming into class the next day looking haggard and with deep circles under his eyes. "A List of All Best Possibe [*sic*] Universes," reads one section that the second boy spends his entire free period reading: part philosophy, part diary, part laundry list of complaints.

10

What would their lives look like under different restrictions or constraints? Born into different shades of privilege? An easy question to ask.

Both can imagine some part of themselves perfected and shimmering, moving with ease through the hallways of Upper Canada. With all of their *unproductive* detritus cast off. They both understand that their lives are accidents, that all lives are.

Neither includes the other in their fantasy.

11

Two boys meet in high school and one dreams about the other. Though the person in his dream is a girl, the boy is somehow certain it's his friend. The girl is wearing a letterman's jacket and a mid-length grey skirt, like some idea of the fifties incarnate. They're in the school library, but a different library than the one he knows, with higher shelves and stage lighting. A murky darkness surrounds them. He's inconceivably happy. They're working closely together, the girl leaning over his shoulder, occasionally grazing him with her breasts. His hand touches hers. Hers touches his. An electric shock. It's not the girl, it's his friend, and they're lying on the floor and kissing. It feels familiar. When he wakes up he is harder than he's ever been in his life.

On the way to school he decides that it's only that his friend makes him feel safe. It's that they spend so much time together. It's that he's never kissed anyone before. But he can't shake the feeling of the other boy's lips and when he sees him at school it is hard not to wonder what it would be like. He imagines that his friend is equally wary of him, like they shared or share the same dream.

At lunch their hands will graze each other's and he'll feel an electric shock. Jesus Christ, he will think, it's just like my dream. But his friend hasn't noticed and will continue talking about the idea that he had the night before: of a planet that is aware of itself and resents everything living on its surface. A planet that does everything in its power to eradicate the many species which depend on it for survival.

"Okay."

"I think it's a good idea."

"It's a good idea," the boy who had the dream will say, totally disinterested.

Then the bell will ring and the two will head to their respective classrooms. The boy who was describing his idea will walk to math slowly, almost cautiously, wondering whether something is wrong with his friend, wondering whether he has done something irrevocable that will mean the end of their friendship. It's a constant worry he has to push away: that he isn't even enough for this one friend he's not even sure he likes. In math he will imagine the parabolas on the surface of the chalkboard multiplied around a central point, like a spirograph twisting into infinity. Then he'll notice that the way the sunlight is hitting the neck of a ponytailed girl in front of him is like something out of a Renaissance painting. He tries to will her to tuck a loose strand of hair behind an ear. Tuck the hair, he thinks. Tuck the hair. The hair is frozen in mid-air, auburn turned radiant gold in the sun.

She never tucks it. The teacher interrupts her lecture and tells the class to break into groups. The boy looks left and right and isn't able to find a partner. In front of him someone sitting by the window is lowering the shade, and he watches the shadow descend in halting jumps along the far wall.

Acknowledgements

I did not write this book alone. Thank you to everyone who looked at early drafts of *Evie of the Deepthorn* — especially to Laura Dosky, who gave it so much attention, care, and counselling. There are many others I cannot name here, but not because I am not grateful for the help and the support you offered.

I was lucky to get the time and space to work on *Evie* through the M.A. in creative writing program at the University of Toronto — thank you to Bob McGill, Rick Greene, and everyone else there, and to the very generous family of Adam Penn Gilders, who helped me through a timely gift when I was starting on this book. But special thanks to Neil Surkan, Noor Naga, Ali Caufton, Joseph Thomas, Sam White, and Shannon Page, for so quickly building a community of extremely talented writers I did not want to leave.

Thank you also to Miriam Toews for such kind and careful guidance while I was making my first way through *Evie*. It was a joy and a privilege to talk about art and writing with you.

Thanks to my Saturday writing group — many of these pages were written, or rewritten, or at least probed, in your company. Thanks to the Holy Oak, which I still miss every week.

André Babyn

Thank you to my friends, and family, now and then.

And finally, thanks to Shannon Whibbs for paying such close attention, and Rachel Spence, Kathryn Lane, Jenny McWha, and everyone else at Dundurn.